SMOKESCREEN

A Novel of Medical Intrigue

Vernon Avila

Yvonne
7/29/03
Best wishes to
a lour 9 mystry.
I hope you
enjoy my novel

Penmarin Books
Granite Bay, California

Editorial Offices:
Penmarin Books
2011 Ashridge Way
Granite Bay, CA 95746

Penmarin Books are available at special discounts for bulk purchases for premiums, sales promotion, or education. For details, contact the publisher. On your letterhead, include information concerning the intended use of the books and how many you wish to purchase.

Visit our Website at www.penmarin.com for more information about this and other exciting titles.

Printed in Canada
1 2 3 4 5 6 7 8 9 10   04 03 02 01 00

Library of Congress Cataloging-in-Publication Data
Avila, Vernon L.
    Smokescreen : a novel of medical intrigue / by Vernon Avila.
        p. cm.
    ISBN: 1-883955-29-7
    1. Neuroscientists–Washington (D.C.)–Fiction.
    2. Presidents–United States–Fiction.
    I. Title.
    PS3551.V555 S66 1999
    813'.54—dc21
                                                            99-052462

The chants in the story are modified from *Wizard of the Amazon: The Story of Manuel Córdova-Rios*, 2d ed., by F. Bruce Lamb, Houghton Mifflin Company, 1975.

Disclaimer: This is a work of fiction. All of the characters, incidents and dialogue are fictional. References to public figures, events, products or places are used fictitiously and are not intended to refer to any living persons or to disparage any governmental agency or any company's product or services.

For my parents,

ELOY and ISABELLE AVILA,

And my family,

PATTY, PATRICK, RAQUEL, PAM and PAULA

ABOUT THE AUTHOR

 VERNON AVILA is a professor of biology, a former expert consultant at the National Institutes of Health, author of two successful introductory biology textbooks, and a former special assistant to the dean of the College of Sciences at the University of Puerto Rico, Rio Piedras. He uses his experiences and knowledge to deliver a gripping first novel of medical intrigue. Avila lives with his family in San Diego, where he is working on his second novel.

ACKNOWLEDGMENTS

There are many people I would like to thank for their guidance, support and encouragement during the development and production of this novel.

I would like to thank the many writers who gave me advice, suggestions and help as I evolved from a writer of biology textbooks into a writer of fiction. More specifically, Rudolfo Anaya, for his encouragement and suggestions; Larry Simmons for his "you can do it" support; Carolyn Wheat for her critique of the first draft; Judi Lind for her page-by-page critique of later drafts; Alan Russell, Ken Kuhlken, Carolina Garcia-Aguilera, César A. Gonzáles-T., Victor Villaseñor, Martinez Hewlett, Charles Knief, and Peter Gilboy for their willingness to answer my many questions about the writing of fiction.

Thanks to my editors, Laurie Gibson, Annette Cavender and Diane Barnes, whose advice and suggestions throughout the drafts of this manuscript helped strengthen the work.

Thanks also to my typists, Suzanne Lancaster and Diane

Barnes, who had the patience to read my handwritten manuscript and convert it into legible copy.

I would also like to thank those friends who love books as
I do and who were willing to read the earlier drafts of *Smoke-
screen*, including Dr. Alfredo De Alba, Kathy Felman, Ralph
Lavage, Edward Avila, Patti Lunsford, Gus Chavez and Chris
Dill, as well as the many others who provided me with their
honest critiques and encouragement to tell this story.

I am especially indebted to my publisher, Hal Lockwood
of Penmarin Books, who has the rare gift of insightful editing
and the ability to criticize yet encourage his authors to make
their work the best it can possibly be.

I would also like to thank Augusto Sandroni for the cover
design.

And last but not least, I owe my family special gratitude:
My wife, Patricia Avila, and my children, Patrick and Raquel,
patiently endured my many questions and read the various
drafts of this manuscript.

July 4, 1997

Not again, Clint Walker thought.

Pain consumed him. His head felt like it was going to explode louder than the fireworks flashing over the Mall and lighting up the Washington Monument. One moment he felt euphoric—stronger and smarter than ever—but then the euphoria vanished, like smoke from a flame, and was replaced by stupor. Thoughts evaporated, feelings bounced around in his mind, memory fled. Who was he?

Sounds called him, but from where? He looked around his office and saw no one, yet the screaming continued in his brain.

He tried to call out, but his voice was empty. His mouth and face were out of control. All he could manage was a twisted grimace, which then collapsed into a lifeless mask. He kept hearing the screaming inside of his head. His eyes searched the room again, but no one was there.

He stood up from behind his large oak desk. His gut was alive with fire and contractions. His skin burned, and sweat poured from his face. He began to shiver and staggered toward the bathroom, tearing at his clothes, ripping off his suit jacket. But where was the bathroom? He couldn't remember. He pulled at his tie and tore his shirt open, stripped off his pants.

Fear seized him. He needed air. His breathing was labored. His face was on fire. Stumbling and half falling, he reached for the door—but it was too late. His body shook and his legs buckled as he fell to the floor.

Am I going to die? he wondered. "Help," he tried to scream as he lay on the oval carpet. "Help," he tried again, only to hear a primal animal sound emerge from his throat.

"Clint!" Helen cried as she rushed to his aid. "Mark, come here! It's happening again!" Mark burst into the office.

"It's worse than before!" Helen exclaimed. She cried again, "Clint!" and dropped to the floor beside him to hug and comfort him. "What's happening to you?" she wailed. She held his head in her hands and wiped the sweat from his brow.

"Helen," he murmured. It looked like he was going to say more, but he just grunted. The grunts turned to spasms and his body convulsed, his eyes rolling back into his head.

"Mark, call an ambulance! We have to get him back to the hospital! Now!"

"Yes, ma'am," Mark responded.

Clint was barely breathing, and foam had gathered at the corners of his mouth.

All of a sudden he stood up and stared at her. She noticed that his pupils were dilated. What is happening? she thought. Is he going insane?

"Help!" she cried, as Clint started to swing his arms at her. He had found the source of the voices. He would destroy the demons.

Just as Clint started to strike his wife, two paramedics arrived. They grappled with Clint until they stabilized him, then placed him on a gurney, rushing him outside to the waiting ambulance. Helen jumped into the ambulance with Clint. Mark followed.

Fireworks filled the air, illuminating the Washington Monument at one end of the Mall and the Capitol at the other. Helen looked at her husband. Worry filled her face. Would he die? she wondered. Then she turned away and looked out the window as the ambulance rushed toward the hospital.

"Why is this happening? It's all so sudden," she said to Mark. He shook his head. She looked at her sedated husband lying quietly as the paramedics worked on him. She closed her eyes and tried to erase the vision of his anguish.

As they neared the hospital, one of the paramedics looked away from the patient and noticed a fire at the National Institutes of Health.

"Look, there's a fire."

"Forget the fire," his partner replied. That's not our concern. We need to keep our patient alive," and she continued writing down Clint's vital signs.

The first paramedic nodded and then stared at the bright orange flames shooting into the black night. "It looks like a bad one," he commented as he prepared to take the patient's blood pressure again.

"Yeah," the other paramedic responded. "And if he dies before we get to the hospital, *bad* doesn't begin to describe the amount of trouble *we're* in for."

The two paramedics glanced out the rear window of the ambulance at the line of black limousines following them. They both knew their patient's life could no longer be measured in days or hours. If they didn't reach the Naval Hospital within minutes, the president of the United States would be dead.

CHAPTER 1

Fall 1978

The skies over Lake Maracaibo were dotted with puffy cumulus clouds. As the afternoon progressed, the clouds turned black and then merged together, darkening the heavens. Scarlet ibis flocked to the trees along the shore, seeking shelter as the gentle breeze picked up and became wind. The heavy smell of a tropical rain storm filled the air.

Eloy and his brother Miguel were fishing from a tiny boat on one of the many small tributaries of the Santa Rosa River, which emptied into the lake. Eloy studied the swirling dark thunderheads. The wind surged into his face, causing his dark, almond-shaped eyes to tear. The ozone in the air tickled his nose and made the hair on the nape of his neck stand up. He glanced at Miguel, who struggled to control the oars as he rowed their boat through growing whitecaps.

"Hurry, hurry, we need to turn around," Eloy said, using a mixture of Spanish and Huni Kui, the language of their tribe.

Miguel shot a glance toward home, Santa Rosa de Agua, one of the small fishing villages that lined the shore.

"*Sí*, I'm trying, but I can't see," Miguel shouted as rain began to fall.

Drops of rain beat into his face, while lightning flashed ominously. Miguel rowed faster. The muscles in his youthful arms undulated with each stroke of the oars.

"Hurry, hurry," Eloy repeated. Wind-driven drops of rain began to splatter; thunder rumbled in the distance. Miguel rowed harder.

The wind gusted sporadically as marble-sized raindrops bombarded the brothers. Suddenly Eloy grabbed Miguel's arm.

"Wait. I promised Domingo I'd get the tobacco leaves for the purification ceremony. Turn around. We need to go back up the river, to the spot in the jungle where the sacred tobacco grows."

Miguel gave his brother a quizzical look. The rain was coming down so hard he could hardly see a meter in front of him, but Eloy was three years older—almost sixteen—and considered by their people to be a man. Miguel set his apprehension aside and did as Eloy said.

"*Apurate, apurate.*" Eloy's eyes showed the conflict between his promise to Domingo and his fear of the storm. A few minutes later, even as the waves formed larger whitecaps, the bow of the fishing boat touched the riverbank. Eloy ran down the muddy path through blinding sheets of rain. He stumbled on a root and pitched headfirst into the muck, but picked himself up and continued into the trees, determined to reach the tobacco. Lightning flashes illuminated the jungle and cast eerie shadows below the branches. The wind blew harder. Eloy slipped in the mud, crashing into the underbrush. Dazed, it took him a moment to regain his senses, but when he did he saw that he had stumbled into a patch of tobacco. He got to his hands and knees, feeling for the base of the tobacco plants growing there and plucked as many as he could. As he stood up to run back to the boat, thunder seemed to shake the ground beneath him. Miguel grabbed the oars and began to row the minute Eloy's feet splashed back into the boat.

The brothers arrived at the boat dock with the rain continuing to fall. They grabbed the tobacco leaves and the fish they had caught and ran to their *tambito*, the small palm-thatched hut built on stilts above the lake where they lived with their mother. She was waiting at the window. Even through the curtain of water, Eloy could see the worry in her dark eyes. Ever since the death of their father, Eloy and Miguel had been her sole support. They had matured far beyond their years.

Dr. Karen Williams stared wide-eyed out the window of the small plane as she twisted her long blonde hair between her fingers. Through breaks in the clouds, Karen spotted the Gulf of Venezuela. The small C-47, modified with pontoons for landing on water, bumped its way from Maracaibo's modern airport toward Lake Maracaibo some eighty miles away, where it would land. God, it looked bad out there, she thought. Lightning cracked and shock waves blasted the C-47, causing it to bounce up and down. She looked over at her research assistant, Dr. Don Romano, a stocky, balding man in his early thirties who was built more like a football player than a molecular biologist.

Don reached over and pulled her hand from her hair. "Relax. I'm sure it's fine."

"I know, but look at the team. All of them look terrified. God, I wish this storm would stop."

"Aw, try to relax. Here, put your head on my chest," Don said, pulling her to him.

For a moment Karen felt comforted, but she could hear

the quickened heartbeat in Don's chest. She pulled away. "Come on, I'm no baby."

"Hell, you are one of the last people in the world I would think of as a baby. You're one of the most stubborn, determined people I know, and you're only twenty-five. I can't forget the way that you told that old roommate of yours at NIMH that if they couldn't fund your research project, forget it. Then you just turned right around and called Gene Stein at the Woodie Guthrie Foundation. In less than six months you're funded, and here we are." He looked out the window as the aircraft continued to bounce.

Karen's blue eyes glistened in the light. "But what if I'm wrong? Maybe the high incidence of Huntington's disease in these villages is coincidence. Maybe Dr. Soto is wrong. Maybe it's all wrong. Why did I make that promise to my mother? Right now I wish I would have just stayed at the university and taught my courses."

"Oh, come on now. You expect me to believe that bullshit? You, of all people, would never be content to sit in a comfy classroom while Dr. Soto documented the incidence of disease. Hell, not even this horrible storm can stop you."

"I hope not." Lightning flashed briefly, filling the plane with pure white light. A clap of thunder rattled the window. The plane jerked up sharply about ten meters, then dropped down again, making the makeshift pontoons on the plane shudder. A series of lightning flashes sporadically flooded the interior of the old plane with bright light. Most of the ten members of the research team looked worried; several bit their nails and some wrung their hands. The furious storm grew stronger. The thunder was deafening, and the plane continued to bounce in the air like a toy on a string.

"Oh, God," Karen prayed, crossing herself. "I hope this

isn't a premonition. Please, God, let us land safely, and let our research be productive."

The pilot, Juan, even though experienced and used to flying in all kinds of weather, looked nervously out the cockpit window. Winds buffeted the plane as they descended. Juan looked like the Hollywood stereotype of a bush pilot: face unshaven and eyes bloodshot from lack of sleep and too much alcohol. He announced to his passengers, "*Señores y señoritas*, I can't tell you a lie. I am scared to crash. This weather is *muy malo*, and we have only limited *gasolina*. We have to land. It's going to be bumpy when we land on the *lago*. Be ready to hold on to everything. Get your seat belts on. *Vamonos con Dios*."

From the shore, in the small shelter near the pier where the plane was to dock, Dr. Soto looked up into the dark skies. Those *Norteamericanos*, he thought, they pick the worst part of the year to fly into *El Lago de Maracaibo*—October, the height of the rainy season. The smell of ozone generated from lightning filled the air. Dr. Soto shook his head in disbelief as he saw the small plane flying between lightning bolts.

In full view of the passengers, Juan gulped from a bottle of Polar beer, wiped his toothless mouth, took a puff of his Belmont cigarette, and yelled, "Hold on!"

The plane hit the water and skipped across the surface like a flat rock. It bounced, bounced again, and tilted from side to side. Frightened voices and panic filled the small plane. Karen and her colleagues were thrown around in their seats like crash test dummies, their bowels pinched with fear, and a couple of them began to pray aloud.

"Oh, God, please, not now," Don shouted. Even he couldn't hide his fear.

A blast of wind caught the plane from one side, lifting the left wing and tilting the plane to the right. The right wing ripped through the water, straining the makeshift pontoon struts until, with a deafening roar, they broke and the plane capsized.

"We're going to die," Karen shouted. "Please, God, no, no."

She was hanging upside down in her seat, looking at the ceiling of the plane, which was now the floor. The impact of the crash had thrown the doors open, and water rushed in. Debris was scattered throughout the plane. The smell of aviation fuel permeated the air.

Juan screamed, "Grab your bottoms. Use them to float!"

Karen began to giggle nervously. She envisioned herself and members of her team grabbing their bottoms. Why was she having these juvenile thoughts when the threat of death was so real? She was snapped back to reality as her colleagues frantically grabbed for their seat cushions.

Through the open doors, Karen could see that they were very near the shore. Villagers were screaming in Spanish, *"Cuidado con el caimán!"* Alligators? A new terror filled her. She tried to unbuckle her seat belt, pulling at it, but to no avail. Water continued to pour in. She needed to break free! Her panic rose with the water level.

"This damn belt. Why won't it open?" She tried again. "Open. Open, damn it!" The plane was sinking.

"Oh, God, I'm going to die," she screamed. "Don! Help me!" Looking through the cabin, she could see that it had taken only a few seconds for the rest of her party, including Don, to swim free. She slumped back as reality hit her: she was going to drown.

Her long blonde hair fell over her face and into the water as she hung upside down. The water rose and splashed on her face as the plane sank further into the shallow lake. So this was it. This is how she was going to die. She would never know if she had Huntington's. She would never find the cure. Karen prayed.

 "Eloy, come quick. *Ven acá.* Look, Juan's plane has crashed!" Miguel shouted through the thunder.

Eloy ran out of the hut and down the bamboo ramp and saw the plane upside down, sinking into the shallow waters a hundred meters offshore. The villagers were running through the rain and yelling back and forth. Dr. Soto was waving his arms, trying to direct would-be rescuers toward the plane. The passengers were fleeing the plane, swimming and wading in the shallow, murky waters toward shore. Bystanders hesitated to enter the water. The alligators' eyes glistened, and light-ning reflected off of their yellow reptilian irises as they gazed toward the plane.

"*Cuidado con los caimánes!*" someone in the crowd along the water's edge shouted out in warning. "*Ojalá que me entiendan,*" he added. Eloy ventured into the water to pull a large man onto the shore. His leg was bleeding and his face was cut. It was Don.

"Hurry, hurry! Get to the plane, damn it! Karen is still trapped," he exclaimed. The villagers, not understanding what he said, just looked at him. They murmured something to each other in Huni Kui.

Eloy then said in broken English, "I will help the lady." He clenched a knife between his teeth, ran into the murky water, and swam to the plane. Fuel coated the surface of the water, and smoke began to lift from the aircraft.

"Help, help!" Karen screamed from inside the plane. "Someone please help me." In the water just outside the cabin she saw the snout of an alligator, its eyes locked on her, regarding her predatorially. The smell of fuel and smoke was overwhelming, arousing her fear that an explosive fire might ignite.

"*Señorita, señorita*. Where are you? Where are you?" she heard a male voice call.

"Here. Here I am, over here!" Karen shouted in terror through the smoke. Eloy kicked at the alligator who was swimming toward the open doors of the plane, frightening it away. The teenager swam through the doors toward Karen. He grabbed hold of her seat, reached up and cut through her seat belt with his knife. Karen plunged into the water, but Eloy reached out and snagged her shirt, pulling her to the surface and then out of the plane.

"Hurry, hurry," she cried. "Please get me to shore!" With one arm Eloy clutched Karen around her neck and shoulder and with the other pulled them both through the water. Karen trembled uncontrollably. "Oh God, there's another one. Hurry, hurry!" she screamed, eyeing another alligator off to the right. Karen's legs flailed as Eloy swam through the water until her feet hit ground. When they reached the shore, Karen collapsed. Eloy lifted her up and pulled her away from the water's edge.

"Thank you so much. You saved my life," she cried. "Thank you, thank you. *Gracias*." Her thank yous quickly turned into sobs and tears. Panting and crying, Karen caught her breath and reached out to the young man. "Who are you?" she asked, still shaking.

Eloy straightened his shoulders and responded in English, "My name is Eloy Córdova Santiago."

"You are a hero! You saved my life. How can I ever repay you?"

"Thank you is enough." The corners of Eloy's mouth rose in a big, charismatic smile.

CHAPTER 2

s quickly as the storm hit, it rumbled away. Four hours
after the plane went down, the sky had turned blue,
and the only reminder of the storm was the salvage operation
being coordinated by Juan. He continued to drink small bottles
of Polar. Sweat dripping from his brow, he ordered the villagers to stack oil drums under one of the wings, then to use a
system of bamboo levers and ropes to upright the plane. After
repeated efforts, they turned the plane over, tethered it to an
old, rusty boat, and towed it to shore. The damage was primarily to the pontoon struts; with some welding, they could easily be repaired. Several young villagers helped gather the supplies and other belongings that had washed up on shore after
the storm and brought them to the research quarters set up in
the old school building next to the church.

In a hut near the cemetery the women in the village tended
to the minor injuries of Karen and her group of researchers,
while Dr. Marco Soto cared for Don's more seriously injured
leg.

After being treated, Karen walked over to the school building and pushed the door open. She gasped, overwhelmed by
the chaos. Supplies and equipment lay scattered across the large,
open space. Boxes ripped open by the crash lay on the floor,
their contents sadly broken or waterdamaged. As she scanned
the room, the enormity of the loss overwhelmed her. Karen
fell back against the wall behind her and slid to the floor, in
tears.

She thought, how will I ever be able to do my research?
Most of my equipment and supplies have been damaged or
destroyed, and God knows what's missing! "My papers, my
books . . ." She pressed the palms of her hands against her
eyes.

Karen wiped the tears from her face when she heard foot-
steps and voices coming closer to the building. Karen quickly
pulled herself up off the floor. The door swung open and Dr.
Soto walked in, followed by a villager carrying the last remnants of supplies from the plane.

"Oh my . . . what a disaster," Dr. Soto exclaimed, not
seeing Karen.

"Yes, it is," Karen grimly agreed.

Dr. Soto was startled. "Karen, I'm so sorry. First the plane
crash and now this. I can see you are very upset. . . ."

"I don't know what we're going to do, where to begin."

"Don't think about that now. You've experienced a terrible day. Try to get some rest tonight. Tomorrow we will
work together and save what we can of your equipment."

"Thank you, Dr. Soto. But I don't think I will sleep much
tonight."

"I understand. But leave this for now. Perhaps you would
like to rest for a few hours, then join me for dinner and a
ceremony of welcome by our people—around seven o'clock?"

"Well, . . . maybe. Dr. Soto, I hope our trip here hasn't been in vain."

"No, Karen. You and your team are alive. We will make it work. Go rest now, I will see you at seven."

Later that evening, after a few hours of fitful sleep, Karen made her way to the large, palm-thatched enclosure where the tribal community had gathered. She sat with Don and the other researchers at dinner. They sat on benches at a long table and were served a dinner of black beans, *caraotas*, fish and guava by some of the village women. Dr. Soto also sat with them. After everyone had been served, it grew quiet as they ate.

Dr. Soto suddenly looked up from his plate, swallowed, and said, "Karen, we are so happy that you are here, even though it has been a terrible day. One we'll never forget."

"I'm glad to be alive, thanks to Eloy."

"Yes, he did well. This is good." He sipped his beer. "You know, I am not good at small talk. My English . . . don't get me wrong, I am so pleased that you and your people are willing to work here. It will be hard after your terrible accident, but we will all work together to make your research possible. I know that it is almost not believable that there are so many cases of Huntington's in this village. I know with this effort we can establish the familial history of this bad gene, which has caused so much pain and death here."

Karen was struck by his words. For a few moments she was able to suppress the horror of the plane crash and recall the mission that brought her to this place.

"Not only in this village, but in the world," she said. "I don't know if you know it, but my reason for being here is not only scientific. My mother was a vivacious woman, full of life. Then, about ten years ago, when I was a senior in high

school, she began to show the symptoms of neurological problems. She became sloppy and uncoordinated. The muscles in
her neck began to tense spasmodically, and she would have
fits of violence.

My mother died five years ago of Huntington's chorea. I
made a vow to her to find the cure for this dreaded disease."
She slammed the table with her fist. "And by God, I will."

From the far end of the long table, Eloy heard the commotion and looked up. He saw the determination in Karen's
eyes. It was a look he had seen many times in the mirrored
reflection of his own dark eyes, the look of determination to
find the cure.

Eloy listened in awe to the conversation of Dr. Soto, Karen,
Don and the other members of the research team. The words
were so foreign, not only because they were in English, but
because they were so new. Suddenly he knew he could learn a
lot from this American woman, Karen.

But now it was time for him and Miguel to help Domingo
prepare for the ceremony of purification and welcome. The
brothers got up from the table, picked up the tobacco leaves,
and broke off some small bunches. They walked toward the
medicine man at the center of the room and handed him the
leaves, then proceeded to Dr. Soto's table.

Dr. Soto introduced the medicine man to the visitors.
"Domingo is the link between the villagers and the spirits. He
brings clarity to life, he heals the sick, consoles the dying, and
assures the gift of universal spirit. He knows the spirits of the
plants and he prepares the potions. He also blesses friends of
this village. He is here to bless you, and help you find the
cure."

Domingo was a small man in his late seventies, part Huni
Kui, part Spanish and part African. His oiled skin was dark

and leathery. He had a thin face, shallow cheeks and only one good eye; the other eye was lifeless. The villagers called him *El Ojo de Dios*, the eye of God. He wore a headband painted with red and black zigzag lines, to which brightly colored feathers were attached. Pink feathers adorned his earlobes, and one pierced his nasal septum. He wore a white ceremonial shirt and a loin cloth with brilliant feathers woven into the fabric. In his long, thin fingers he held a baton made of feathers and tufts of animal hair. He waved the baton and began a dance around the flickering flames of the small fire that burned in a pit dug in the earthen floor of the hut. He danced slowly around the fire pit, circling four times in each direction.

After he finished, Domingo welcomed the research team in his dialect of Indian and Spanish and began the ceremony. He sat on the ground, fanning a large bundle of smoldering tobacco leaves, swaying rhythmically. Periodically, he tossed lycopodium powder onto the smoldering leaves. Billowing clouds of aromatic smoke filled the night air—air that was ripe with hope and anticipation.

Domingo stood up, raised his hands to the sky and looked toward the heavens. With a majestic voice he began to chant:

Oh, most powerful spirit of the forest,
Of the plants of the forest,
Of the plant with the fragrant leaves,
We seek your wisdom.
Give us tranquility and guidance
To understand the mysteries of the lake,
The mysteries of the forest,
The mysteries of life,
And the mysteries of *El Mal*,
This dreaded *Mal de San Vito*.

Bring our friends your knowledge of this realm.
Reveal to all of us by our kindred spirits,
The knowledge to guide our way.

After Domingo finished the chant he strode over to Karen with a deliberate gait. His thin, leathery hands held smoldering tobacco leaves. He waved the smoking leaves over Karen and Don.

"Let the smoke find the cure," he intoned. "Let the smoke find the cure." With that, he approached Eloy and crossed the smoldering tobacco leaves over the boy.

"Eloy is the smoke. I have taught him the ways of the jungle. He can help you find the cure. His father taught him the ways of America. He can help you find the way."

Domingo sat down again and drank from a gourd filled with *honi xuma*, the drink of visions. Eloy remembered the first time Domingo gave him *honi xuma,* after the death of his father. He recalled his body becoming very still, and then almost without feeling or sensations. His spirit seemed to rise out of his ordinary self into another realm, and he experienced powerful visions . . . of strange women . . . of strange places . . . Looking down now at the medicine man, Eloy could see that Domingo had entered a transcendental state.

Dr. Soto remarked that the hour was late, that the visitors needed to rest and that Domingo would remain in his trance for the night. The villagers left and the Americans prepared for bed.

That night, as Eloy lay in his hammock, he envisioned again that fateful day five years ago when his father died. He remembered his mother shouting, "Eloy, Miguelito, *vengan,* come here! Your father is dying! Eloy had run up the bamboo ramp into their *tambito.* Inside, the hut smelled of sickness

and burning leaves, the smoke assaulting Eloy's nostrils like
the rancid odor of dead *caimánes* rotting on the shore.

Domingo was kneeling beside his father, who lay on the
thatched floor, and chanting prayers and incantations. A
strange light, reflected from the water of the lake, flickered
along the walls of the hut. Eloy's father thrashed and moaned,
his neck muscles tightening, his lips smacking, his whole body
twitching.

Finally, the twitching stopped and he lay still, as if in re-
pose. But his face took on a masklike appearance, a perma-
nent grimace, a mask of emptiness. Tears filled Eloy's mother's
eyes, and sorrow flowed over her face. Then she screamed.
Eloy rushed to his father, throwing himself across his inert
form and compressing his chest again and again, hoping that
his strength, his life, could breathe life back into his father's
body. Miguelito's eyes welled with tears and he whispered
reverently, "*Papá, te amo. Vete con Dios.*"

Even now, alone in his hammock, the thought of his
father's death made Eloy weep. Why did he have to die? Was
his father's death a sign to test him, to see if he had the gift of
the spirit, the spirit of understanding Mother Earth and her
mysteries? Domingo told Eloy he had the gift of being con-
nected to the spirit of the universe and that he was the smoke,
the spirit of the forest, and that he could become Domingo's
apprentice. But why him? Why was he the chosen one? Why
did his father make Eloy responsible for the family at such a
young age? Eloy fell asleep with these questions nagging his
mind.

The next morning Dr. Soto came to Eloy's hut and asked
if he could help the research team as a translator. Happy to
help, Eloy walked over to the schoolhouse that now served as
a research building.

"*Buenos dias, Doctora* Karen."

"*Buenos dias*," she responded, looking up from the boxes she was unpacking. "I understand you speak English."

"*Sí*, yes."

"Well, my Spanish is so-so, but with your help I think I can gather all the information I need. Coffee?" she asked, pointing toward the coffee pot.

"*Sí*," he said.

They sat on the folding chairs and drank coffee. Karen looked over the rim of the cup and said, "Dr. Soto told me that your father died of Huntington's five years ago. How strange . . . my mother also died of Huntington's five years ago."

"*Sí*, yes, I know. I heard you and Dr. Soto talking last night at dinner. Domingo says I am the smoke. I will find the cure."

"What does that mean?"

"Domingo has taught me the ways of the forest. He says that the cure for the curse is found in the plants. Domingo says that I am the smoke; the smoke is the spirit that will find the cure. He taught me the chant to wake the spirits of the forest. Do you want to hear it?"

Karen nodded.

The young man closed his eyes and recited the ancient chant. Although the language was foreign, she gave herself to the spell and sensed the powerful words.

"Could you tell me the chant in English?"

"*Sí, doctora*, I will translate."

Spirits of the forest,
Reveal yourselves to us by *honi xuma*,
The drink of the spirit quest.

Bring us the knowledge of our people,
Bring us the wisdom of the jungle,
Give us the stealth of the boa,
The acute hearing of the deer,
The brute endurance of the tapir,
The grace and strength of the jaguar,
The knowledge and tranquility of the moon.

"Thank you for sharing your magic."

"There's more," Eloy said, reaching into the small leather pouch tied around his waist to remove some tobacco leaves. He lit the aromatic tobacco and waved it in front of his eyes as if summoning the spirits. As the forest spirits emerged from among the wisps of smoke, Eloy began to pray:

Watchful spirits, guide our way,
Smoke find the cure,
A cure for *El Mal de San Vito.*

Karen saw determination in his eyes, and heard strength and passion in his voice. She sensed in Eloy a soul of innocence, filled with a desire to find the cure and a belief that the cure was to be found in the magic of the jungle. She knew that she had to help this young man with his quest. She felt that in this way she could repay him.

"More coffee?"

"*Sí, por favor.* The coffee is very good.

"How did you learn the ways of the jungle?"

"Domingo has taught me many things. He taught me that good things come to those who wait and have faith and that the secrets of the jungle can be revealed by *honi xuma.*"

"Is that what Domingo drank last night from the gourd?"

"*Sí*, this is the way of the medicine man."

"Domingo showed this to you?"

"*Sí*. One day he said to me, 'My son, follow me into the forest and I will teach you the ways of a medicine man."

"Why did Domingo pick you to be his student?"

"I don't know, *doctora*, but whenever he came to chant and give medicine to Papá, I would ask him questions about the wisdom of the forest, the spirits that cure, and he would say that I had the gift, the soul of a medicine man, and he would show me the way. So when my father died, I told him I was ready to be the smoke, the spirit of the forest. I followed the old man into the jungle. He walked with a strong gait that showed reverence for Mother Earth. His feet tread softly on the earth from which all life springs."

"Where did you go?"

"A place where the trees were so tall they touched the sky and blocked the sun. I was afraid, but Domingo said not to worry."

"What did you do?"

"We arrived at a clearing, where there was a fire burning, with sweet, fragrant smoke. Ayahuasca vines hung from the trees and Domingo, *El Ojo de Dios*, told me to sit on the ground. He gave me a gourd filled with *honi xuma*. While I drank, Domingo chanted to summon the spirits to reveal the secrets that we need to find the cure. Then I went into a trance."

Karen sat motionless, captivated by Eloy's words.

"Visions came into my head. I could see the future. I could see the past. I could float above myself. I saw a white woman, a strange place and a strange house and our village churchyard. Then I knew that the vision meant that the cure was not only in the jungle, but in places far away, the strange houses.

I told Domingo my vision, and I have become his apprentice. He says I learn fast. I will learn the ways of the jungle and find the place far away, the place to learn."

"Do you want to go to school to learn the ways to find the cure?" Karen questioned.

"*Sí*, I went to school here in this room for six years. I can read and write and do numbers. I love to learn. I want to know everything."

"Do you remember when you first learned your dad might be sick?"

"Ever since I can remember, something was wrong with Papá. He acted strange. Sometimes he was happy, sometimes sad. Sometimes he would yell and become mean. I thought he was drunk. The other men in the village drank. But Papá would dance like he was possessed by the devil. His body would shake and he would get very sad. The sickness got worse and worse, and finally killed him.

How was your father buried?" she asked hesitantly.

"He was buried in a Catholic ceremony here in Santa Rosa, in the cemetery next to the school, but not in the ways of the Huni Kui."

"Why? How do they bury their dead?" Karen questioned, wondering why the family had abandoned its traditional ways.

Eloy set down his coffee cup. "When my grandfather died, we buried him according to ancient custom."

"How's that?"

"The old women used smoke to purify him and to turn him into a mummy, then folded his body into a large clay urn and buried him deep in the earth."

"Why didn't you bury your father the same way?"

"When he died, I was afraid that my *abuela* would want Papá mummified like my grandpa. But Mamá said, '*No, mi hijito*, we are civilized. We are Catholic; we will bury your Papá in the churchyard in the way of God. There is no good in the old ways.' I remember telling Mamá that Papá used to say that there is good in the old ways and good in the new."

"My mother used to say the same thing before she died."

"How did you bury your mother?" Eloy asked.

"We didn't bury her. We cremated her."

"What is *cremated*?"

"We burned the body."

"In a fire? Why? How do you remember her? How can you plant flowers on her grave? I thought you were Catholic. I saw you cross yourself. In the church we learned that our souls will all return to our bodies, but how will your mother's? Her body is gone, burned to ashes." Eloy could see the sadness in Karen's eyes. A sadness he knew. "Sorry," he said, realizing his outburst had shocked her. He paused.

"*Doctora* Karen, do you want to see my Papá's grave? It is here in the churchyard," Eloy said, trying to change the subject.

"Yes, I'd like that."

At the grave, Eloy crossed himself and began to pray. Karen could see the depth of his love for his father. She put her arm on his shoulder and with her other hand crossed herself.

When Eloy finished praying, he said to Karen, "The people of the village said Papá died because *El Mal* was caused by greed for money, which came from the black gold that the oil companies pumped from the lake. They say that the men who left the village to work in the oil fields here in our country and in the refineries in Puerto Rico brought back the disease. Papá worked in the oil. He learned English in Puerto Rico. He rode the oil tankers and learned the ways of the *Norteamericanos*."

"Oh, so that's how you know English," Karen interjected.

"*Sí.*"

"Do you remember where you were when you knew for sure that your dad had Huntington's?"

"*Sí.* We were fishing, and Papá, Miguel and I were talking as the sun was setting. The surface of the lake looked as if it was on fire, burning with the flames of hell. I asked Papá about hell and about death and if he had *El Mal* because people said that he did. 'Yes,' Papá said. I asked if he was going to die of *El Mal,* like *mi abuelo.* 'Will you go to hell like the villagers say?' I asked Papá."

"What did he say?" Karen asked.

"He said, 'No, *mi hijito.* Hell is only in the minds of the evil, and we are not evil.' But the people in the village said he was evil because he was teaching us English. They told Papá not to cast out our language for English. To do that was to embrace the devil's tongue. I asked Papá if he was afraid of dying, and I remember that his voice was not clear even though he tried very hard to say his words. He said 'No, *mi hijito,* I am not afraid of dying. To fear death is to insult life. Death is a part of the cycle of life. You will continue my life through your children and your children's children and your children's children's children.' Then Papá's eyes filled with tears, and he started to cry. '*Dios mio,* please don't let my Eloy or my Miguel have the curse. Please don't let me give it to them,' he said." Eloy then looked directly into Karen's eyes and asked, "*Doctora* Karen, do I have the curse?"

Karen wished she could give the boy the answer he wanted to hear. She looked away from his father's grave. She hesitated. "I don't know . . . maybe . . . let's go back to the schoolhouse. We have a lot of work to do."

CHAPTER 3

Fall 1978

Who does that Amish teetotaler think he is? Saying that smoking is addictive, that smoking is a health hazard? What in the hell does Cooper think he's doing?" the Republican senator from Kentucky demanded of the president. "You said the surgeon general was in your pocket. He's a pediatrician, for God's sake. You said he would do our bidding. Now the hard-nosed S.O.B. declares smoking is a health hazard. What does he know? We should kick his ass all the way back to Pennsylvania."

"Come on, Orville. Settle down," the president said. "There's no need for all this excitement. You know this administration is a friend of the tobacco industry." The president sat calmly behind his desk, hands folded in front of him, with only a small patch of sweat on each temple betraying his apparent serenity.

"If you're our friend, why did you appoint this Dr. Cooper as surgeon general? You should shut him up." Orville's ruddy face turned even redder, his polka dot bow tie bobbing angrily against his prominent Adam's apple.

The president, also a Southerner with agricultural interests, knew the economic impact the antismoking campaign
would have on tobacco farmers. He remembered the peanut
pesticide scare of the '70s that almost broke his business. "Relax. Have a smoke and a shot of good-sipping bourbon."

Orville sat down, lit a Lucky Strike, took a deep drag,
hacked on some phlegm, and sipped his drink. Then, just as
quickly as he calmed down, he got worked up and his face
reddened again. He stood up, threw the cigarette pack on the
floor of the Oval Office, and crushed it with his foot.

"The tobacco industry is invincible in this country. This
is not the beginning of the end—I won't allow the tobacco
industry to crumble. Those damned health warnings on cigarette packs—what a crock of crap!" Orville stomped on the
blue carpet, deliberately wiping his shoes on the seal of the
president of the United States.

"You won't hear the last of this!" he bellowed and stormed
out of the office.

The president's Secret Service agent looked over. "Do you
want us to do anything, sir?"

"Oh, no. It's okay. He's just posturing."

One week after their traumatic arrival in Venezuela,
the researchers had settled into a routine of gathering
the family histories of people from the village.

One afternoon Eloy walked into Karen's office in the old
schoolhouse and found her carefully drawing a pedigree on
the chalkboard. Although sparsely furnished, her office was very
tidy and organized. On her desk was a picture of her family.

"*Doctora,*" Eloy inquired, "why do you use these circles
and squares? What do these all mean? Why the lines connecting them?"

Karen explained the construction of pedigrees: the circles stood for females and the squares represented males, and the lines drawn between them were genetic connections.

"How can circles and squares cure the curse?"

Karen explained the importance of establishing a pattern of inheritance and how Huntington's disease was due to an autosomal dominant gene, which meant that the chance of a person acquiring the gene from an affected parent was 50 percent. Eloy grasped the implication immediately.

"That means I might have it?" Eloy wanted to know. Waiting for her to respond seemed to take an eternity. He thought about his father's death and those of other friends and family.

She quietly replied, "Yes, Eloy, there is a 50 percent chance that you have the disease. As you enter your thirties and forties, the gene may begin to show itself."

"*Dios mio,*" Eloy cried.

Karen understood. "I also have a 50 percent chance of having the gene." Their eyes locked in shared dread.

As the research work progressed, Eloy undertook more responsibilities. He was not content just doing the routine translation of family histories. Eloy wanted to know more about genetics—especially molecular genetics. He would ask question after question. How could a molecule serve as the "blueprint for life"? How could a gene be transmitted from parent to offspring? Many times Karen would have to refer his questions to Don. When Don explained the various biological and genetic concepts to Eloy, he grasped them with astounding intelligence.

Karen remembered how her mother used to say, "You can earn a degree in science, but curiosity and the true creative insight common to all great scientists is a gift more of the genes than education."

Eloy had the genes.

It took much longer than expected to gather the data. Many of the villagers were reluctant to discuss their family histories for fear of upsetting the spirits. But Eloy's presence was invaluable. Because of his apprenticeship with Domingo, Eloy convinced the villagers not to worry, that he was the connection to the spirits and that no harm would come to them.

Over time Karen became more appreciative of Eloy's scientific aptitude. Almost a year later, while they were working in the laboratory, Karen said, "Eloy, I've been talking to Dr. Soto about you. He has a friend at the university in Caracas who would be willing to train you in research. You can also take some classes. Would you like to go?"

"*Sí, sí,*" Eloy smiled, his face filled with happiness. But then his expression grew sad. "No, I can't go. I promised Papá that I would take care of Mamá. I am the man of the family now."

"I thought you might say that, so I talked to your mother. She said she has always wanted you to learn the new ways, and if you want to go, she'll be okay. Your Aunt Isabel can look after her and Miguel. Besides, Miguel is going to be a man soon."

His hopes raised, Eloy ran home. His mother was lying in her hammock smoking a cigarette. Through half-opened eyes she regarded him through a haze of smoke and said, "Eloy, *mi hijito*, is that you?"

Looking at his mother, Eloy thought: No, I had better not go. I must stay here with Mamá. He walked over and held her hand. She looked so small and old. No, he should stay. Then he looked toward the hammock where his father had died, and he remembered his vow.

"Eloy, why so sad? Are you sick, *mi hijito*? Tell me. It's about the university, no?"

"*Sí, Mamá.* I want to go to the university, but I can't. Who will take care of you?"

"Don't worry. I'll be okay. Go. I know that you will find the cure. Don't worry about an old lady. I'll be okay. Tia Isabel will take care of me, and I have *mi Miguelito.*"

"*Sí, Mamá, sí.* Thank you for your understanding. Your support means so much to me. I'll send you money often. . . ."

"*Sí, mi hijito.* I know your dreams. I trust God has put you here to find the cure." She crossed herself and with her other hand gave Eloy a loving pat on the shoulder.

Miguel was staring at Eloy from the table. Quietly he said, "Don't worry, *hermano.* I can take care of Mamá. You find the cure for *El Mal.*"

A week later all of the arrangements had been made. Eloy felt sad as he said goodbye to his family, but he tried not to show it. His mother was strong and told him again not to worry. Eloy gave Miguel and his mother a long *abrazo*, then got into the old river boat that would take him and Dr. Soto to the *Golfo*, the first part of their trip to Caracas.

CHAPTER 4

Fall 1979

D r. Soto's family greeted them at the dock. During the hour's drive back to Caracas, Eloy couldn't help thinking about his future. Doubts clouded his mind. Was he really as bright and talented as Karen, Don and Dr. Soto told him? Could he, a *maicero* from a poor fishing village with only a sixth-grade education, compete with the other students at the university? Karen and Dr. Soto had expressed confidence that Eloy could succeed, but now it was left to him to prove them right. He was determined to do so.

Dr. Soto navigated a turn on the winding road in the mountains above the city. "Eloy!" Dr. Soto said, pointing down to the bustling city of Caracas. "Look over there on the other side of those skyscrapers, next to that big glass building. There's the campus. And up in those hills about twenty kilometers from the campus is the *colonia* where Dr. Rodríguez and I live. I'll just drop off my family at home and then take you to his house. He's anxious to meet you."

"*Gracias*," Eloy said. He sat in the back seat looking out of the window in silence.

"Eloy, why so quiet? Things will be okay. I know you'll do well."

Dr. Rodríguez lived in a modern, two-story house. With Dr. Soto beside him, Eloy knocked on the door. Soon an average-sized man, who appeared more Spanish than Indian, opened the door.

"*Hola*," he said. "Welcome to our *quinta*." Dr. Rodríguez had a round face, large dark eyes and receding black hair that looked tonsured like a monk's. Eloy thought he seemed more like a man of the cloth than a scientist.

"Let me help you," Dr. Rodríguez said as he reached over to carry Eloy's small tattered suitcase.

"Thank you, but I don't have anything else."

"*Entra, entra.*"

Eloy and Dr. Soto walked into the living room. The walls were painted pastel pink and blue, and the floor was covered with beige tile. The aroma of cooking filled the air.

"Let me introduce you to my family." A short, attractive woman in her mid-thirties came into the living room, wiping her hands on her apron. She gave Eloy a hug.

"*Mi nombre es Alejandra*, and these are our two boys," she said, turning her head toward the kitchen table, "*José y Blas*."

"*Hola*," the brothers said.

"Iris is making *pavellon*, white rice, black beans and fried eggs for dinner," she said, looking over at a light-skinned woman in her late twenties. "This is Iris, our housekeeper. She lives in the room next to yours upstairs. Iris, show Eloy his room while I get the table ready. Freshen up and then come down, *mi hijito*."

Iris led Eloy up the stairs to his bedroom. "This is your room. The bathroom is here," she said, opening the door. "My room is on the other side." She ran her hands down the side of her curvaceous body, resting her hands on her hips just long enough to see if Eloy was looking at her. She glanced at him and wiped a strand of auburn hair away from the side of her oval face. Eloy returned the look.

"Unpack your things. This is your bed," she said, "and here is your closet. I have to go help the *señora*. Come down in half an hour for dinner. And don't be late. Dr. Rodríguez doesn't like it."

Eloy surveyed the small, partially furnished room. He sat on the bed and wondered if he would be comfortable. He hadn't slept on a bed at home. He was used to his hammock. Eloy bounced on the bed to test its firmness, which reminded him of a time when he was six and he and his father visited the oil tankers on the docks in Maracaibo. He had met his father's friend, Manuel, one of the officers on the oil tanker. They took the bus from the coast to Caracas so that he and his Papá could visit the city. It was that night in their small hotel room that he slept on a bed for the first time. He remembered his father sleeping by his side, the comforting sound of his snoring and the sweet smell of tobacco smoke in his hair.

Eloy walked to the window, which overlooked the city. Through a light haze of smoke that veiled the hills, he could make out the edifices of the university. Staring fixedly, he doubled his fist and gently but firmly struck the window sill. "I will, Papá. I will," he murmured.

 After dinner, Eloy and Dr. Rodríguez went into the living room and sat on the couch as the women cleaned the table and kitchen. Eloy could overhear Alejandra and Iris talking; occasionally Iris would giggle.

Dr. Rodríguez reached into his pocket and pulled out a pack of Belmonts. He offered one to Eloy.

"No thanks."

Dr. Rodríguez lit one and then blew the smoke into the air away from Eloy. "Let me tell you about our research. We're looking at natural products as sources of pharmaceuticals— you know, plant compounds, and especially chemicals produced by poison frogs."

"Yes," Eloy said. "Dr. Soto told me you were interested in frog neurotoxins. Especially batrachotoxins secreted by the genus *Phylobates*."

Dr. Rodríguez put out his cigarette and regarded Eloy admiringly. "How did you know that? I couldn't have said it better myself."

"I've discussed the subject with Don and Karen, and Dr. Soto gave me some papers that you wrote. I read them because I want to learn as much as I can about nerve cells and especially the way that nerve cells communicate. I'm going to find a cure for *El Mal*," Eloy said, his voice filled with innocent conviction.

Dr. Rodríguez nodded his head. "Don and Karen were right. You *are* bright and determined. Look, I have to prepare a lecture for tomorrow, and you are probably tired from your trip. Get some rest, because we get up early here. See you at six for breakfast. If you need anything, ask Iris," he said as he got up from the sofa. He reached into the liquor cabinet and poured himself some rum. "Drink?" he asked.

"No thanks. But I would like to thank you for letting me live in your home. I appreciate your hospitality very much."

"You're always welcome here, Eloy," Dr. Rodríguez answered, laying his hand on Eloy's shoulder in a friendly gesture.

"Thank you again. Well, *hasta mañana*," Eloy said, walking upstairs to his room.

The next morning, Eloy and Dr. Rodríguez took the subway to the university. Eloy was in awe. He had heard about the Metro, of course, but this was the first time he had ever ridden it. The thrill of rushing at high speed through the dark tunnels, the lights flashing quickly as they sped past, and the clanging bells and rhythm of the wheels on the rails bombarded his senses. The sight of so many people all talking and scurrying about, their days filled with important business, overwhelmed his sense of proportion. It was so different from Santa Rosa de Agua.

Eloy's heart beat fast with anticipation as he walked across the campus. He knew he would like it here. So many young people anxious to learn . . . he already felt at home.

"My office and lab are here," Dr. Rodríguez said, pointing across the lawn to a two-story building. Once they entered, Eloy was amazed at the number of books and journals that lined the bookshelves.

"Eloy, sit down," he said, pointing to a wooden chair. "Francisca, bring us some coffee, please," he called to his secretary. "Cigarette?" Dr. Rodríguez asked as he lit one for himself. Rubbing his head, he said, "Here's what we plan to do. I've talked to the dean of sciences, and he agreed that we could enroll you in some courses to strengthen your background. I know you're young. Seventeen, right?"

"Yes, I just turned seventeen."

"Hmm. That's young, but not too young. We do have a special course for *los cien*, the hundred brightest students in the city, and from what I hear, you fit into that category.

Here, I want you to read this," he said, picking up a scientific journal from his bookshelf and flipping through the pages. "Here, read this article. It's about the most recent research we're doing with frogs. We have discovered a new, natural product that has neurochemical properties. I have to teach a class right now, but I'll be back in an hour. We'll talk about the article when I get back."

Eloy read the article. It explained how the newly discovered chemicals in the frogs upset nerve cell transmission, which causes the paralysis and eventual death of their prey. An hour later, Dr. Rodríguez returned.

"Here, sit down. What did you think of the article?" Dr. Rodríguez asked.

"I think it was very interesting, but what I really question is why and how the frogs synthesize the toxin. Obviously it has survival advantages for the species, but what is the source?"

"That's a very good question, Eloy. What do you think is the source?"

"Well, the source of the toxin either has to be related to the diet or the maturity of the frog, or possibly there is even a difference in the amount of the toxin between the sexes, but I would hypothesize that the source is probably related to the diet."

Dr. Rodríguez stood up, reached over and put his arm on Eloy's shoulder, and gave him a look of approval. "Dr. Soto was right. You are the smoke. Now, let me show you the lab."

At first it was difficult to get used to the routine of going to classes in the morning and working in the laboratory in the afternoon. The other students seemed so much smarter than he, but within a couple of weeks Eloy's fears of not being able to handle the course work disappeared.

His professors commented on the excellent exams that he wrote. Based upon the recommendations of his professors, and especially that of Dr. Rodríguez, the dean allowed Eloy to matriculate for his bachelor's degree.

His work at the university was not Eloy's only pleasure. He also enjoyed Iris. Iris had shown an interest in Eloy since he first arrived. She was unlike any girl in his village. She flirted shamelessly with Eloy, enticing him with her body language and looking seductively into his eyes when they spoke. For several weeks they exchanged glances, and Iris found every excuse to be near him. Eloy enjoyed this game. Eloy found Iris incredibly attractive and wanted her desperately. He wondered if their flirtations would ever evolve into what he really longed for.

One Friday evening, Eloy returned to the Rodríguez home after working in the lab. When he arrived, he expected to find everyone seated at the dinner table. But as he walked toward the front door, he noticed that no lights were on inside the house, except the one in his bedroom. He passed through the foyer and entered the kitchen. There was a note on the table: *Eloy, we've gone to dinner at El Campo. If you get home before too late, please come meet us.*

Eloy set down his books and papers and went upstairs to shower and change before taking the Metro downtown. He ran the water for his shower, took off his clothes, showered and dried off. He wrapped the towel around his waist and walked into his room.

The light by his bed glowed, and a gentle breeze blew through the open window, lifting the gauzy curtain. There was Iris, sitting in a chair in the corner, her legs propped up on a stool. She had wrapped herself in one of Eloy's shirts. Iris looked at Eloy, stood up slowly, and let the shirt fall open.

"I've been waiting for you, Eloy."

He smiled and went to her. Eloy was nervous. He had never been with a woman before, yet Iris was so self-assured and so seductive that she made him feel at ease. Iris moved close to Eloy, lifted her head, and kissed him. A gentle kiss became passionate, and soon all Eloy's fears were gone.

After that, Eloy and Iris spent many nights together, delirious with the pleasures of youthful desire. She took him to the height of physical satisfaction. The secrecy of their relationship ignited their desire even more. Their passion not only satisfied a need for physical affection but served as a diversion from the homesickness that weighed heavily on both their hearts.

For Eloy, however, it was his work rather than Iris that filled the emptiness of not being with his family. In the laboratory, Eloy learned the methods of modern science. Among other things, Dr. Rodríguez taught him how to extract potent neurotoxins from plants and animals. In exchange, Eloy provided Dr. Rodríguez with his knowledge of the jungle and the Indians' techniques of preparing and hunting with poison darts.

It was a hot, humid day in the Colombian jungle, and Eloy was collecting specimens for Dr. Rodríguez. Hueso, one of the Emberá Chocó people, lifted a long blow gun to his lips and gave it a quick puff. The dart, made from the rib of a palm leaf and fletched with fluffs from the Kapok plant, had been tipped in neurotoxic secretions from *Phylobates terribilis*. A monkey fell from the trees convulsing, then went rigid with a grimace on its face that reminded Eloy of his father's death mask.

"You got him!" Eloy shouted.

Phylobates terribilis lived in the lowland area of eastern

Colombia. It was brightly colored, usually a bright yellow to gold. Eloy knew that to touch the frog would be foolish and fatal. But Hueso showed Eloy how to catch the frogs by grabbing their feet with a tobacco leaf as protection from the toxins. Hueso also taught Eloy how to gauge the toxicity of the frog's secretion without harm by holding the frog in a tobacco leaf and tasting the skin with his tongue. Eloy was always impressed with the practical knowledge of the Indians. They didn't know that saliva contained chemicals that broke down the toxin; they only knew that they could gauge the amount of toxin by the degree of numbness of the tongue.

Once Eloy transported the frogs back to the laboratory in Caracas, he bred them in a terrarium. But the batrachotoxin levels of the frogs decreased in the laboratory. Eloy noticed that in the lab the frogs were fed mealworm larvae, crickets and other foods that were not part of the frogs' natural diet. He suggested to Dr. Rodríguez that if he fed the frogs what they ate in their natural habitat, then the batrachotoxins might return to levels found in the wild. Dr. Rodríguez thought his hypothesis was sound, so Eloy collected tropical ants and springtails and varied the amount of natural foods and laboratory food to test it. After several weeks of monitoring the results, he determined that the frogs' natural diet was necessary for maximal batrachotoxin production.

Eloy couldn't believe that his discovery had scientific significance. He had actually made a contribution. He was filled with silent pride, knowing in his heart that this research finding was the first of many he would make.

Because of his research skills and talent, Dr. Rodríguez gave Eloy even more responsibility in the laboratory. Over the next three years he increased his expertise in identifying neurotoxic alkaloids in plants and animals. Eloy continued to focus on these alkaloids because, as a class of compounds very similar to morphine, cocaine and curare, they worked at the junction between brain cells, nerve cells and muscle cells at the neurotransmitter level. Many symptoms of neurological disorders like Huntington's, Alzheimer's and others could be induced by using neurotoxins to upset normal nerve-to-nerve, nerve-to-gland or nerve-to-muscle communication. This inability of the nerves and muscles to communicate was the molecular basis of many of the symptoms of Huntington's.

But one day, after working there for four years, Eloy regarded Dr. Rodríguez's lab with different eyes. There was enough equipment for this level of research, but the lab was sparsely furnished, and he knew that if he was ever going to learn the neurochemistry required to understand *El Mal*, he would have to move on to a more sophisticated laboratory and a more ingenious mentor.

Eloy looked in the terrarium at his yellow tree frogs. "Oh, *mis Ranitas*, I too feel trapped," he said. "We must go to the United States if I am ever going to find the cure. I don't have the papers to work and live there. I don't have the *doctorado*. I will only have a bachelor's degree. I am just the son of a poor fisherman and oil refinery worker, the son of a man who had the curse."

Then an idea struck him. "Papá—he had papers! He worked in Puerto Rico, and Puerto Rico is a commonwealth of the United States!"

"*Vámonos, mis Ranitas amigos.* We're going on a journey." He saw himself travelling toward the white woman, the strange places, and the great house painted all in white.

CHAPTER 5

December 1983

Eloy was so happy to be home that he jumped off of the old boat and ran up the ramp to their *tambito*. It had been almost two years since the last time he was there. "Mamá!" he shouted, running through the door.

"*Mi hijito, mi hijito*, you're home!" his mother cried, hugging him tightly. Her arms were thin but strong. "Let me look at you. . . . You're an *hombre*. You look like your father. I am so happy . . . Miguel, Eloy's home," his mother said through her tears.

Miguel ran to his brother. "I'm so happy to see you." He gave Eloy a big hug. "*Mi hermano*," he said with a big grin. "*Gracias a Dios.*"

"Sit down, my son. Tell us of your life, your dreams. All we've had is your letters." She ushered him to the table, which she had ready and laden with a dinner of mashed bananas, beans, fish and rice.

As they ate, Eloy showed them his diploma with pride and recounted his experiences. He talked about his frogs, his research with the alkaloids, the friendship of Dr. Rodríguez and the excitement of research in Caracas.

Miguel asked, "How can working with poison frogs help find the cure?"

Eloy explained as best he could the ways of science: logic based upon data, information not based on faith in God but on the faith and endeavors of man.

"Maybe one day I can work at the university and help you," Miguel said.

"Yes, maybe one day, maybe very soon," Eloy answered, putting his arm around Miguel.

That night Eloy lay awake in his hammock, gazing at the stars through slits in the palm-thatched roof. The sounds of the tree frogs' *cur-awk, cur-awk* blended with the melody of the tropical whippoorwills, easing him to sleep. The calling of a trumpeter bird floated in the night air. The peaceful sounds of the jungle, so familiar to Eloy, were only broken by the piping of nocturnal monkeys, repeating their one-note call in an ever quickening sequence, only to be followed by silence. During the stillness he could hear the quiet rhythmic breathing of his mother and brother. He inhaled the lingering aroma of the delicious meal his mother had cooked. All this made him remember how much he loved this place. How could he tell them that he must leave again?

The next day, as he and Miguel fished from their boat, Eloy reminisced about his life in the village, and Miguel brought him up to date on changes and events that had occurred since his last visit. Eloy could hardly believe that four years had passed since Karen Williams's research team had returned to the United States and he had gone to the university. Yet Eloy felt increasingly focused on the future, and after telling Miguel a little more about his research projects at the laboratory, he decided it was time to divulge his plan.

"Miguel, I have been talking to Dr. Rodríguez about leaving Venezuela and working in his brother's lab in Puerto Rico. He agrees that if I am going to be effective in curing *El Mal*, I have to learn more modern techniques."

"But what about the work you are doing? You are the smoke—you know, the jungle?" Miguel asked, turning his head to look into the water.

"*Sí*, I know," he said, reaching into his pocket to hand Miguel a letter. "This letter is for Mamá from Dr. Rodríguez. He is asking her if you can work for him, and help him collect specimens."

"But who will care for Mamá?"

"Don't worry. You will collect the specimens here most of the time. Caracas is not that far away, and you will be close to Mamá."

They spent the rest of the morning fishing and talking, then rowed home. Eloy explained his intentions to his mother. She agreed that Miguel could help Dr. Rodríguez. Eloy asked about his father's work papers. She carefully lifted the floorboards under her hammock to reveal the secret hiding place where she had hidden all of her treasures in a large clay urn. As she sorted the contents—slowly and with reverence, as if turning the pages of a prayer missal—she found the work papers.

She encountered them underneath a worn black-and-white photograph of her husband. How handsome he looked, short and stocky with the proud stance that made him appear larger than five feet three inches. Those muscular arms that embraced her so well, that smiling face and those dancing eyes, his laughter, his love of life. Her eyes caressed his face: the olive skin slightly flawed with acne scars, the thin mustache, those perfect white teeth and the magnetic smile that made him loved by all. Tears came to her eyes. How much she cherished this photo, the only one she had of him as a young man, before the curse.

She turned to give the papers to Eloy, and in that moment, looking at her son, she felt as if the past had returned. Eloy had grown into the image of his father. It was as if God had created Eloy to replace him. "How similar," she thought, "but are they the same on the inside too? Will my son get *El Mal?*" And with this she started to cry, sobbing with the sorrow and anguish of a woman who knew she might not ever see her son again.

"Miguel," Eloy said, "be sure you and Tia Isabel take care of Mamá. I will send you money when I get to Puerto Rico and the United States. I will write. Remember to take the letter to Dr. Rodríguez. He is expecting you," Eloy said. He gave Miguel a big *abrazo.*

His voice breaking, Miguel said, "I will always think of you . . . I will take care of Mamá."

"Miguel, this is just the beginning. I'll be back. Maybe one day we'll work together to find the cure, *los hermanos Santiago.*"

"*Sí,*" Miguel laughed, waved to his brother, and said, "*Va con Dios.*"

Eloy boarded the rusty old boat that would putter its way back to the *Golfo de Venezuela,* where he could catch a ship to take him across *El Caribe* to Puerto Rico. As the familiar landscape passed by, he revisited in his mind the recent sequence of events leading up to his present journey: how he had discussed his plans with Dr. Rodríguez and how he had lied and said that he had legal documents to work in Puerto Rico. Yes, he had lied; but now, with his father's papers in hand, he could work in the laboratory of Dr. Nestor Rodríguez at the University of Puerto Rico. Maybe he could eventually work with Don or Karen in New York or Boston or Washington. "Such big-sounding names, so far away," he whispered, eyes fixed on his little pets in their containers, the yellow tree frogs, his Ranitas. "Come on, my friends, let's go to Puerto Rico."

The oil tanker *Santa Theresa* steamed out of port like it had so many times before, except that this time she had a stowaway. Manuel Cruz, the old friend of Eloy's father, still worked on the oil tanker, except now he was the first mate, so for a few *bolívares* and a little whiskey, it had been easy for Eloy to convince Manuel to smuggle him aboard and to hide him in the engine room.

Once they reached the open sea, Eloy was free to explore the tanker, think about his future, smell the ocean air, feel the salt spray on his face, and gaze out over the beautiful blue Caribbean.

"This part is easy. It was easy to slip out past the port authorities in Venezuela, but what about when I get to Puerto Rico? How will I get off the ship? Won't *la Migra* want to see my passport and my work visa?" Eloy asked Manuel.

"*Amigo, no te preocupes.* I always carry a little persuader with me." Manuel rubbed his thumb and forefinger together.

"Do I have to pay off the immigration officers?"

"*No, joven.* Don't you know the ways of the world? I slip the customs official some cocaine, and he looks the other way. He will stamp your father's papers as if they were yours." How ironic, Eloy thought. The jungle plants can do so much good, producing medicines to relieve pain and cure diseases. But they also provided the devil's powder and other drugs that were the source of suffering and death.

Four days later, on a moonless night, the *Santa Theresa* neared the southwestern tip of Puerto Rico. As the tanker approached the coastline, the water was aglow from the chemical reactions of microscopic algae that made up the famous *Bahia Fosforescente* in the area of La Pargueara. The old tanker turned east, motoring another ten miles to dock in the *Bahia de Guánica.*

"Eloy," Manuel shouted, interrupting his thoughts, "go below and wait until I come for you so that we can pass through immigration. *Recuerda*, I will buy your papers with the devil's powder. *Para trabajar en los Estados Unidos.* Go, *amigo*, and wait."

Eloy went to his hiding place and sat in the dark, alone with his tree frogs and his thoughts. He remembered waiting alone in the dark before, in his room at the Rodríguez's house, waiting for Iris to come to him. He thought about Iris and how she introduced him to sex, the nights she had spent with him in his bedroom. She had made him a man, but he still didn't know love like the love his parents had for each other. He also thought of the kindness of the Rodríguez family.

Eloy could hear voices on the deck above. It began as formal conversation but soon changed into laughter and the conversation of friends. The hatch covering the small compartment opened, and Manuel's voice rang out.

"*Mi amigo*, welcome to Puerto Rico. Welcome to the United States!" Manuel gave the stamped, official papers to Eloy.

"*Gracias*, Manuel," Eloy said. "What do I owe you?"

"Nothing," Manuel said, but Eloy suspected that "nothing" might come to mean "something" in the future because Manuel struck him as the type of man who didn't forget favors.

Eloy gathered his few possessions—his clothes, his books, his journals and his Ranitas—and stepped off the tanker into the humid air of Puerto Rico. The coqui tree frogs, indigenous to Puerto Rico, sang their nightly serenade—*coqui, coqui.*

"Listen, my frogs. You are not alone," he said to his pets. "We are welcomed."

CHAPTER 6

January 1984

Animated conversation filled the *públicos* that transported Eloy from Guánica east to Ponce and then north to Caguas and finally to San Juan on the coast. He was quiet and tired but listened raptly throughout the three-hour trip to the melody of voices talking about the New Year's parties they had recently attended.

As dawn bathed the city in morning light, they arrived in the Rio Piedras section of San Juan, home of the University of Puerto Rico. Eloy gazed at the central tower of the university, which, he had read, symbolized the lifting of the light of knowledge. This was going to be his home, he reflected with satisfaction. The *público* driver let him off at the gates next to the Facundo Bueso building, a fortunate stop because it was in this building that the laboratories of Dr. Nestor Rodríguez were housed.

Since it was early and he assumed no one was at work, Eloy waited outside the laboratory. He breathed in the aroma of strong Puerto Rican coffee mixed with the smell of laboratory chemicals and realized there must be someone inside even though it was only six in the morning. He hesitated before knocking on the door.

"*Adelante*," said a female voice.

Eloy entered and said hello to a woman in her early twenties working at a laboratory bench. She had short, auburn hair and green eyes and wore a white lab coat.

"My name is Maria," she said, as she extended her hand.

Distracted by the state-of-the-art laboratory, Eloy failed to acknowledge the welcome.

"Excuse me," he said, regaining his composure. "My name is Eloy Córdova Santiago, the new research assistant for Dr. Rodríguez."

"Oh, yes, my uncle sent you. Let me get my father. He's in his office. Sit down. Care for some coffee?"

"Yes," he said hesitantly, "*Café con leche*, please."

Eloy immediately felt self-conscious about his disheveled appearance and his body odor, the result of not showering for three days. He hoped the smell of coffee and chemicals would mask his scent.

"Welcome to our laboratory!" said Dr. Nestor Rodríguez as he bustled into the room. The resemblance to his brother was remarkable, down to the monklike hairstyle.

"My brother and his wife have told me a lot about you. I'd like to talk with you further, but you look tired and I'm busy. Maria, please take Eloy home. Let him clean up and rest. Work can begin tomorrow."

"*Gracias* for having me in the laboratory. I can't believe you have so much equipment. I'm very glad to be here," Eloy said nervously, continuing to sip his coffee.

"Thank you. We can talk about your work this evening and get acquainted then. Now go," he said, waving his arms toward the door. "*Vate.*"

Eloy's dark eyes filled with an expression of concern. He looked away from Maria. "Did I say something wrong?"

"Oh, don't worry. My dad is just like that. He means well; he's just preoccupied. At first he seems a little abrupt, but wait till you get to know him. You will like him as much as you like my Uncle Paul. Come on, let's go. You must be tired from your trip." Eloy finished his coffee, picked up his things, and followed Maria into the street.

Dr. Rodríguez and his family lived in Rio Piedras a few blocks away, to which they could easily walk. The narrow streets of the old town were beginning to come alive. The *piragüeros* had started hawking snow cones from their pushcarts. Mobile food stands sprouted along the sidewalks like mushrooms after a rain. Store owners unshuttered their shops. Workers commuted in cars or on foot to their jobs. And everywhere the people seemed alive, sociable. This was a city of vitality and charm. Eloy knew he would like it here.

As they walked, Eloy drank in Maria's beauty. Her facial features were strong and reflected her ancestry: the high cheekbones of the Indian, the smooth, light complexion of the Spanish, and the full lips of the African. She was truly enchanting. Her hair was the color of coffee with cream, accented by auburn highlights. It was cut short but framed her face delicately. When she turned around to point out the sights, Eloy caught her gaze, and he thought, those eyes are as green as the jungle and as deep as the lake. Eloy also admired her voice. She spoke slower than most Puerto Ricans, yet her tone was animated and her hands seemed to gesture with every word.

Eloy became aware of his loneliness. His life now seemed empty—empty of family, empty of home and, especially in this moment, empty of the love of a woman. His heart ached with the need. He even missed Iris. But would he ever know real love? And then there was *El Mal*. He shook his head.

The Rodríguez home blended Old World architecture with the new. The windows and doors were arched, typical of the Spanish style, but the floor plan was modern, with a sunken living room, a spacious kitchen, two bathrooms and a study. Maria showed Eloy around the home and told him that he was to have the bedroom that used to belong to her brother, before he got his own apartment.

Eloy placed his frogs on top of the dresser, showered, unpacked his suitcase, and arranged his books on the bookshelf. He lay down on the bed and within a few minutes fell asleep.

That evening at dinner, Eloy and the Rodríguez family had a wonderful meal of barbecued *lechón*, rice, black beans and bananas.

After dinner Maria and her mother, Rosa, remained in the kitchen while Dr. Rodríguez and Eloy retired to the study, which occupied a corner of the house in the back, overlooking the rock garden. Dr. Rodríguez had positioned a desk below the window on the right side, and two overstuffed leather armchairs sat on the left, with a side table and lamp for each. Tall bookshelves lined the walls. The sight filled Eloy with awe. Never in his life had he seen such a collection of books in a private home. There were hundreds. Nestor Rodríguez must truly be a man of knowledge, Eloy thought. Even more than his brother was.

"Eloy, sit here. Have a cigar, some rum," Dr. Rodríguez invited. The intoxicating smell of the tobacco and the smooth *ron de Barriel* warmed his heart and reminded him of home; it made him feel more at home here with Dr. Rodríguez, and he knew his future as a scientist was here too. At that moment Maria came to the door of the study.

"*Papá, teléfono.*" Maria looked at Eloy, then turned away when he returned the glance. The flirtation stirred his flesh, but the sound of shouting rudely interrupted his fantasy.

"*No, desgraciado.* . . . What a son. I will not lend you more money," Dr. Rodríguez yelled into the phone. "I will not help you anymore."

He returned to the study trying to look calm, but it was evident that he was angry.

"Here, take a glass of rum to your room. Now is not a good time to talk. It has nothing to do with you. It's a personal issue. And you're tired. Tomorrow we begin."

The next morning Eloy awoke to the fragrance of freshly brewed coffee. Little green *añoles* gazed at him from the window sill as he stirred. Their bobbing courtship behavior, which looked like they were doing push-ups, was amusing.

Rosa and Maria had prepared a breakfast of fruit, pastry, coffee and pineapple juice. Maria joined Eloy and her father at the table while Rosa retired to her bedroom.

"I'm sorry that we really haven't had time to talk about the lab. As you can see I've been very busy," Dr. Rodríguez said, trying to force a smile. "I've been trying to write a grant to submit to the National Institutes of Health. So if I've seemed a little cold, please don't take it personally. I'm very happy that you are here," he said, standing up to put a hand on Eloy's shoulder. "But it's getting late. Let's finish breakfast, and then we have to go to the lab." He gestured to Eloy that it was time to leave. As he walked to the study he said, "I'll be back in a moment, I just have to get my briefcase."

Eloy wondered about last night's telephone call. Dr. Rodríguez seemed to have forgotten his outburst. Eloy glanced at Maria. "Maria, is your father okay? I hope I'm not here at the wrong time."

"No, don't worry. He's just upset about my brother Juan. He's in the medical residency program at the Centro Médico."

Dr. Rodríguez returned from the study, shooting Maria a dark glare, and she immediately dropped the subject.

"*Vámonos*. It's time to go to the lab. Eloy, bring your frogs and an umbrella. It looks like rain," Nestor said.

Thunder clouds rose in the darkening sky, and before the trio reached the laboratory, a tropical shower began. As they made their way through the streets, the smell and touch of fresh rain on his skin gave Eloy a baptism of hope.

Eloy had never seen such equipment: centrifuges, mass spectrometers, computers, well-stocked chemical cabinets and something he hadn't ever seen before—cell culture incubators and chambers. Dr. Rodríguez told Eloy that the major objective of their research was to take the analysis of alkaloids and natural products a step farther than his brother had. Their work involved the extraction of active pharmaceutical compounds from various plants and animals, the analysis of their chemical structure, and the investigation of the effects of those compounds on actual living cells.

Eloy's first project was to analyze the effects of the toxins produced by his tree frogs on synaptic transmission in nerve cells. How did the batrachotoxins prevent communication between the motor nerve cell and the muscle that it affected? By what mechanism did this toxin cause irreversible muscle contraction? In preparation, he reviewed the textbook material on neurotransmitters and cell-to-cell communication in nerve cells.

The space between two adjacent nerve cells is called
the synapse or the synaptic cleft. Neurotransmitters
are chemicals housed in synaptic projections or knobs
found at the end of the axon. When the nerve impulse
reaches the end of the axon, the membrane becomes
permeable to calcium ions in the synaptic cleft and
releases the neurotransmitters. These transmitters
move across the synaptic cleft and bind to receptor
sites on the dendrite of the adjacent cell, or, as it is
called, the postsynaptic junction.

Eloy had learned that the action of neurotransmitters de-
pended on several mechanisms: the enzymes that synthesized
the neurotransmitters, the mechanisms that triggered the release of the neurotransmitters, and the postsynaptic receptors,
uptake mechanisms and enzymes that broke down the neurotransmitters.

From the work of researchers in the late 1970s, Eloy knew
that there were two major postsynaptic receptors for the neurotransmitter acetylcholine. One was the nicotine acetylcholine receptor found in the junction between the motor nerve
cell and the muscle. Nicotine was the neurobiologically active
ingredient in tobacco smoke that mimicked the effects of acetylcholine on skeletal muscles and some neurons. The other
acetylcholine receptor was called a muscarinic receptor, also
found in the junction of nerves and muscles.

One of the major research projects in the laboratory was
to determine which of the acetylcholine receptors bound to
the batrachotoxins. Eloy pondered this question for several
months and then devised a hypothesis that he could test using
radioactive isotopes and cell cultures.

Before Eloy could begin this research, however, he needed
to learn how to culture cells, so Dr. Rodríguez taught him the

proper technique. After some trial and error, he got his project started, and he ran several experiments over the course of the next nine months. Despite several failed experiments, the results began to look promising.

Then Eloy made a major discovery. He found that the toxins produced by his tree frogs bound to the nicotine acetylcholine receptors and that this prevented the acetylcholine from binding. This disrupted neural transmission, which paralyzed the muscles.

Dr. Rodríguez was elated, and Maria hugged Eloy joyfully and gave him a kiss on the cheek. Embarrassed, Eloy first hesitated and then returned the hug. He blushed self-consciously, and his cheek tingled where Maria's lips had pressed. Still, he felt a surge of desire with her body so close to his. The scent of her perfume made him ecstatic. Dr. Rodríguez broke the spell by slapping Eloy on the shoulder.

"We must celebrate tonight! I would like to invite you and Maria to join me for dinner in Viejo San Juan. What do you say?"

"*Seguro que sí.*"

Eloy anxiously waited for night to fall. This would be the most special night of his life. Not only would he be acknowledged by his mentor, but he would be close to Maria in a setting away from the lab.

The day's heat finally began to subside. The hurly-burly of street traffic and the noise of vendors dwindled as twilight descended on the city. A light rain shower freshened the air.

When they entered Viejo San Juan, the cobblestone streets glistened. This was Eloy's favorite part of the city, with its colonial architecture and magical richness of history. The balconies of the houses on Calle Fortaleza overhung the sidewalk like a canopy. In the walled area of Viejo San Juan, El Morró, the fort, guarded the headland overlooking the harbor, which was washed in color as the sun lingered on the horizon. The light reflected off of Maria's auburn hair, green eyes and yellow dress, enveloping her in radiance. It was a perfect evening. And Eloy was going to tell Maria his feelings for her—feelings he hoped she shared.

The narrow streets were lined with restaurants, but Dr. Rodríguez preferred the quiet atmosphere of the dining room in the Hotel Convento on Calle Cristo, an old convent that had been converted to a hotel. They walked through the courtyard to get to the restaurant. Paintings by Tufiño and Carlos Irizzary adorned the walls of the dining room, along with a mural depicting demented, bewildered old nuns watched over by God.

The waiter led them to their table, which was located opposite the mural. Eloy said, "I understand that this convent was a home for aged and mentally ill nuns."

"Yes, the nuns were described as having dementia, which we know today includes various neurological disorders."

This made Eloy think of his father. For a moment he remembered his suffering and felt sad, then he comforted himself with the thought that he had succeeded in uncovering one of the mysteries of the disease.

The waiter took their order. They began with piña coladas, then a main course of steak prepared Venezuelan-style with *arroz con habichueles*, and finished with coffee and sweetbreads.

After the meal, Dr. Rodríguez motioned to the waiter. "Champagne," he called. "To celebrate!"

"It's wonderful how successful you have been with your research," Nestor said a few moments later as he poured them all a glass of champagne.

"*Sí*," Maria acknowledged. "You have made a major contribution."

"Let's toast." Nestor raised his glass to touch Eloy's and
Maria's. "*Salud*. To health and success!"

One drink led to another and the bottle was soon empty.
The talk of science began to ebb, and Dr. Rodríguez perceived
that Eloy and Maria wanted to be alone. He said, "It's late—
almost midnight—and an old man needs his rest. *Mi hijita*,
you and Eloy enjoy the night. But be careful." He kissed
Maria's cheek and gave Eloy a firm handshake before walking
through the courtyard and out of the hotel.

Eloy and Maria wandered along the narrow streets. Music
emanating from bars and nightclubs filled the air. They went
from nightclub to nightclub dancing and drinking. Eloy loved
the graceful movement of Maria's slender hips as she moved
to the music. He placed his arms around her and led her off of
the dance floor to their table. Maria peered intently into his
eyes. She was smiling. He saw her breasts rise and fall. Was
she breathing hard because of the dancing, or was it something else?

Eloy looked at his watch and noticed that it was three in
the morning. Couples had started going home arm in arm.
Eloy longed to make love to Maria, but he still felt awkward,
especially with a woman as beautiful and sophisticated as she
was, and he didn't want to rush anything.

"Maria, it's late. We need to go," Eloy said.

"*Sí*, but I don't want the night to end," she replied. They
walked out into the street hand in hand. The sky was filled
with stars, and the warm tropical breeze felt refreshing after
the smoke-filled club. They proceeded down Calle Norzagaray
in the direction of the taxi stand, not saying anything, but
comfortable holding hands and sharing the awareness of their

affection. Eloy's heart raced in the certainty that Maria cared for him and in anticipation nevertheless of the difficulty he would have declaring his feelings to her, as he had planned. Slowing to a stop and turning to face her, Eloy took both of Maria's hands. Her eyes locked on his.

"Maria, this evening has been wonderful for me," he began.

"For me too," she interjected, giving his hands a squeeze.

"Most of all because of you," he ventured. "In fact, I want to tell you how much I . . . care for you."

Releasing his hands, Maria threw her arms around Eloy's neck and pressed herself to him. Their lips met, and they kissed passionately under the starlight.

Suddenly a man jumped out of the shadows, his eyes wild and his limbs twitching. He looked and smelled filthy, and his front teeth were missing.

"Give me your purse, *mamacita*!" he grunted. He held a knife to Eloy's throat and roughly grabbed Maria's purse. "Hey, baby, you are so fine," he said mockingly. "I think I'll take you to *mis* boys. You are too pretty to waste on this *puto*. *Mis* boys will love partying with you! *Cabrón*, don't you try anything," he warned Eloy. "We're just going to show your woman a good time. She needs to know what it's like to be with a real man," he said, grabbing his groin. His accent was Nuyorican, although more New York than Puerto Rico.

The thief was drug-crazed and dangerous. When he grabbed Maria roughly by the arm, Eloy felt a surge of protective anger, but the blade pressing against his neck told him it would be deadly to make a move.

The man guided them with rude shoves a block through the darkness toward the ocean and the infamous slum, La Perla, which huddled between the old city's walls and the Atlantic Ocean as if desperately grasping the edge of the city to avoid being washed away by the sea through the gates of hell. Prostitutes, thieves and drug dealers had taken over the area.

Screaming and struggling, Maria was dragged roughly by the thief into one of the nearby shanties. Eloy knew they were in serious trouble, but what could he do?

"I have money. Just take the money and let her go!" he shouted.

"We don't want your money, we already have it. We don't want you, we want your woman," he said with a leer as he grabbed her breasts and tore at her dress.

"Fucking bastard!" Eloy screamed, and he lunged at the doped-up kidnapper. His cry burst from his throat like the snarl of a cornered animal turning and attacking its tormentor.

Eloy caught the thief by surprise as he grabbed at the knife, and it fell to the floor, skidding across the room. The man let go of Maria to grapple with Eloy. They wrestled for the knife. The thief had Eloy pinned, but Eloy shoved him off, then jumped on top, reaching for his throat, only to be thrown back to the floor. The crook struggled to get back on top of Eloy, smiling his toothless grin, thinking he had overpowered him. The smile vanished quickly, though, as Eloy's knee caught him squarely between the legs. He doubled over, screaming in pain. He fell to the side and appeared to be unconscious.

"Let's go!" Eloy yelled, reaching toward Maria.

At the same time, the thief came to and grabbed them by the ankles as they ran past him. Caught off guard, they fell. Eloy searched the floor for the knife where he thought it lay, but it was too late. The thief had the sharp tip at Eloy's throat.

"*Maricón, puto!*" the thief screamed and backhanded Eloy across the face. Another man entered the room. Eloy's attacker shoved Maria toward the newcomer, who quickly tore off

Maria's clothes, ripping off her white bra and panties and rubbing his dirty body against her as he grabbed her from behind.

"*Chula*, such nice *nalgas*. I can't wait to put into you!"

Eloy felt the knife dig into his neck below his ear, as if his captor was going to slit his throat. Eloy thought he was going to die and Maria was going to be raped. Just then a familiar voice said:

"*Putos, cabrónes*! Leave him alone. He's too smart to kill. He can fix Amado's problem."

Eloy felt the knife ease away from his throat. Through eyes filled with anger he looked up and saw Manuel Cruz, his father's old friend, the friend who had gotten his papers for him and brought him to Puerto Rico. Why was Manuel here in this drug haven, in this shanty with these murderers and rapists? Then he remembered the bribe Manuel had used on the immigration officials.

Manuel pulled the lecher away from Maria and the toothless thief from Eloy. Eloy breathed a sigh of relief. Manuel had saved their lives . . . but for how long?

"*Mi amigo*, you are safe with me," Manuel said. "I have done you another favor. It is now time to return the favor, *mi amigo*."

Eloy wondered, how?

CHAPTER 7

Manuel took Eloy and Maria to another shanty to meet Amado. The Raven, as he was called, was a tall, thin man with a gaunt face framed by greasy black hair pulled into a ponytail, a large beak of a nose and dark, beady, close-set eyes. In profile he resembled the raven, a symbol of death. Amado dealt in death. Death through addiction. Eloy regarded him with disgust. Gold chains and a large crucifix encircled his scrawny neck. How blasphemous, Eloy thought, that a man who dealt in the devil's powder would wear a symbol of God.

"Manuel, I don't want anything to do with this bastard."

The Raven slapped Eloy. "You fucking piece of shit. You act so macho in front of the *señorita*, but you are my captive, *puto*. You do as I say or I kill you and I kill your girlfriend, understand? I have a problem for you to fix. It is only because you can help me that you are still alive and I haven't fucked your girlfriend and given turns to *mis amigos*." The Raven gestured toward his friends.

"What do you want me to do?" Eloy asked. "Just let me do it and let us go."

"*Mi problema* is very simple. Let me show you." He grinned. "Franco." Raven motioned to a fat man with a belly so large and legs so big it was a wonder he could walk. Franco was apparently Raven's bodyguard. He had a large tattoo across his right hand that said *El Oso*.

"Go get me *la puta*, Lolita."

El Oso went to the back room and brought in Lolita.

Lolita was young—only in her early twenties—a skeleton standing naked in front of them. Her large green eyes were sunk into her dark face. Her body, though young, had the aged look of a whore who had serviced too many men, and needle tracks ran up her skinny legs and arms like road maps of pain.

"Let me show you my problem. Come here, my little pussy," Raven motioned to Lolita. "Time for your candy." He took out a baggie of powder and cooked a hit with the expertise of one who had performed the act a million times before. He found a vein in one of Lolita's thin arms and pumped in a shot. As soon as it was injected, she appeared to come to life, euphoric for a brief moment, then she suddenly gasped. The pupils of her eyes were dilated to the extreme. Her bowels and bladder opened, releasing a stench, and as quickly as she had come to life, Lolita was dead.

"See, that is my problem. This heroin is shit! It is contaminated. It is poison. I have over a million dollars' worth of this shit, and it's not worth a damn penny. You can fix it, no?"

Eloy had to will his body to stop shaking from the horror before he could respond. He didn't want Raven to sense the fear and disgust he felt after watching him murder Lolita. He looked Raven straight in the eye and said as calmly as he could,

"I don't know. I need to know what the contaminant is. I need to do an analysis and see whether or not it can be removed without harming the heroin."

"What is this shit . . . contaminant . . . analysis? You think you're so damn smart. Little man, you can talk all you like, but if you ever want to see your girlfriend alive again, you better hope you're smart enough to actually fix it," Raven threatened.

"What do you mean?"

Just then Manuel interrupted, "Look, Eloy, you owe me. I helped you get to Puerto Rico. I gave that *cabrón* of an immigration official some *coca*. Are you so stupid to think that I only smuggled you here because of your father or a few *bolívares*? Hell, no! You are here because I knew you were a scientist and you could help *mi amigo* Raven."

"What if I don't?" Eloy challenged the old man. "I won't help you kill more innocent people!"

"It is very simple, Eloy," Raven continued, rubbing the plastic bag of heroin between his thin fingers. "Every day it takes you to fix my heroin, one of my men gets Maria to do with her as he pleases. *Comprende*? My men are *cabrónes* and are only pleased by drugs and pussy."

Eloy felt as if his soul had died. His sweet Maria . . . How could such a beautiful Friday evening, an evening of celebration, turn into this horror of a Saturday?

Eloy said quietly, trying to hide his anger and fear, "I need time. I need analytical instruments. I need a chemistry laboratory."

"Well, that's good, because you have one," said Raven. "Just use your lab at the university."

"I can't just go into the lab. Someone will see us."

"Look, it's Saturday. No one will be there."

"But Dr. Rodríguez will miss us. If we don't come home, he will call the police."

"Bullshit. He'll just think you lovebirds spent the night fucking."

Raven motioned to Franco, "Give Mr. Wizard the phone."

To Eloy he said, "Call Dr. Rodríguez. Tell him you and Maria are okay, and that you are spending the night with Maria's *puto* brother Juan. By the way, did you know he's one of my best customers?" Raven placed a knife to Eloy's throat. "Call him, *cabrón*," he ordered, "and tell him exactly that, but don't think of saying anything else."

Eloy dialed, and after three rings the phone was answered.

"*Hola*," said a sleepy voice.

"Dr. Rodríguez, I know it's late, but Maria wanted me to meet Juan. We are at his house, and will probably spend the weekend there."

"Juan's . . . Maria should know better . . ."

In the background, Eloy could hear Rosa saying, "Nestor, don't be so hard on Juan. They will be okay with him." Dr. Rodríguez placed the phone back on the cradle. Why did Eloy say *there* and not *here?* he wondered. Maybe I should call Juan, he thought to himself, then shook his head and lay back on the pillow.

"Good job, little man," Raven mocked.

"Franco, call Juan," Raven said, giving the phone to El Oso. "Tell him that if his parents call, Maria and Eloy are spending the weekend with him."

Franco dialed Juan's number. "*Hola, puto*. If your parents call, tell them that Eloy and Maria are spending the weekend with you, *comprende?* . . . None of your damn fucking business where they are, dopehead. Just do as Raven says if you want us to keep quiet about your nasty little secrets."

El Oso slammed the receiver down and said, "Well, that takes care of that. You two lovebird *cabrónes* are visiting Maria's brother."

Acid burned in Eloy's stomach, his heart raced, and his face flushed with anger.

"Here, let me give the señorita some love potion," Raven said, rubbing cocaine in Maria's nostrils.

"No!" she screamed, her eyes filled with terror, and Franco and his cohorts dragged her away.

All this time Manuel was watching. He placed a hand on Eloy's shoulder. "*Amigo*, fix his heroin and you and Maria will live."

"Fuck you, old man. I'm not your *amigo*," Eloy shouted, pushing Manuel's hand off of his shoulder. "And I don't trust you. You are no friend of mine or my father's," he said, spitting in the old man's face. He then lunged at Manuel, but El Oso tore across the room and restrained him.

"Maria, Maria," he shouted, struggling to free himself.

"Look," Manuel said, wiping the spit off his face. "It's only because you are the son of my dead friend that I don't kill you. Fix the heroin."

"Yes," Raven interjected, with an icy stare into Eloy's eyes, "fix the damn heroin."

Eloy had never felt so helpless as when fat Franco grabbed his hands and threw him into the back of Raven's black Mercedes. Franco motioned to Manuel to get in. "*Vamos*! We are going to the lab."

It was the Saturday of a long holiday weekend, and the campus was almost empty. Only the custodial staff and a few university police were on duty.

When Eloy, Franco and Manuel entered the gates of the university, they were confronted by a guard named José, who recognized Eloy. "Why are you working today? Don't you ever rest?" he asked. "Who are your friends?"

Eloy glanced at José's gun and nearly blurted out that he was being held captive. But one look at El Oso, and the thoughts of Maria being violated made him say, "Well, you know us lab rats, always working." José laughed and waved them through.

Once inside the laboratory, Eloy immediately got to work, taking the sample of the contaminated heroin and making it soluble for spectral analysis and thin-layer chromatography.

Please, God, make it simple. Let the contaminants be the work of ignorant chemists, he thought. But he couldn't concentrate. He pictured in his mind the vile acts that Raven's animals were doing to Maria—images that made him sick, yet more determined. Come on, he said to himself, I have to do this for Maria. Every second I waste is another second of torture for her.

He studied his analyses and the spectrographs. He saw that the contents very closely resembled morphine, but the two alcohol groups typical of morphine had been changed to ester structures by the reaction of the morphine with acetic acid, which formed heroin. The two ester groups made heroin soluble in the blood, so, as he already suspected, he had heroin.

But there was something else on the spectagraph, a belladonna-like compound he was familiar with because it contained one of the alkaloids he had been working on, an acetylcholine receptor blocker.

No wonder that poor addict, Lolita, died. The heroin had been poisoned with atropine, an extract of the belladonna plant, and it stopped her breathing and her heart. This also explained her extremely dilated pupils. Atropine was used in weakened solution to dilate the pupils for eye examinations.

The answer to the problem was simple. Chloroform would solubilize the belladonna toxin, evaporate, and slowly purify the heroin. He went to the shelf to obtain the chemicals and equipment needed to do the procedure.

Eight hours later he had isolated the contaminant. Eloy sighed with relief, knowing that the discovery would save Maria. Franco and Manuel were sitting in the corner. Franco watched Eloy's every move, with his gun at the ready.

"I located it," Eloy said, pointing to the spectral analysis.

"Good. It's about time," Franco responded. "I'll call the *jefe*."

"It's an alkaloid contaminant."

"Cut the *mierda*. Can you fix it?"

"*Sí.*"

Just then there was the sound of a key in the door. Franco grabbed Eloy and said, "Don't you say a damned thing or Maria is dead. We're just old *amigos*, me and Manuel."

The door opened and Dr. Rodríguez stared at Eloy in surprise.

"Eloy, why are you here, working in the lab? I thought you and Maria were spending the weekend with Juan," Dr. Rodríguez said, looking around the lab. "What are you working on? . . . Who are your friends?"

"I just thought I would recalibrate the instruments," Eloy said hesitantly, "and show my friends the lab."

"Why are you working today? I thought you and Maria needed time to be together. Where is Maria?"

"She is at Juan's."

"Who are your friends?" Nestor asked again.

"Dr. Rodríguez, meet Manuel. He is an old friend of my father's and an officer on the oil tanker that brought me to Puerto Rico. This is one of his friends, Franco, from the tanker. They call him El Oso," Eloy said.

"*Mucho gusto.* Nice to know you," Manuel and Franco said, nodding their heads.

"Yes, *mucho gusto.* Please excuse me, I have to pick up some papers from my office."

Dr. Rodríguez went into his office and closed the door. Franco gave Eloy a threatening look. "Remember Maria and *los hombres.*"

"Can you fix the problem?" Franco asked.

"I said I could," Eloy replied, his eyes glaring.

"Well, do it!" Franco ordered.

Dr. Rodríguez opened the door from his office and passed through the laboratory. "I have to go," he said. "Eloy, will we see you and Maria tomorrow?"

"No, no. We'll be staying with Juan in Isla Verde until Tuesday."

"Be careful. Have Maria call us when she can. I'll see you Tuesday in the laboratory. *Adios,*" he said, closing the door, then shaking his head.

"You did good, *mi amigo,*" said Franco.

"I am not your *amigo,*" Eloy retorted.

Franco called Raven. "*Jefe,* the little *hijo de puta,* Mr. Wizard, says he found the poison and can fix the heroin."

"Bring him here. Let him tell me how, and have him bring the clean shit. I want him to see his bitch try it. He may need some motivation," Raven ranted.

When they arrived at La Perla, salsa music flavored the Saturday night atmosphere like an air freshener masking the suffering and anguish of drug-addicted souls. Eloy promised himself that no matter what, he would not show his anger; he had to keep himself and Maria alive. He was prepared to be calm, to explain the contamination and the procedure to purify the heroin. Then he would negotiate their freedom.

When they entered the shanty Eloy could hear laughter.

"Come on, *coño* pussy. More."

Eloy thought he was prepared, but what Raven was doing to Maria was unbearable. She was naked, lying on a filthy mattress. Her eyes were swollen. Her face was bruised, her hair matted. She was high.

"*Mira*, look at me," Raven said as he thrust himself inside of her. "Now that she knows a real man, she'll never want a little *puto* like you."

"You bastard! I cleaned your goddamn heroin! Get away from her, you pig!" Eloy wanted to run to Maria, to rip Raven off her and kill him with his bare hands. His body shook with anger and horror. "Oh, God, Maria. I'm so sorry . . . I . . . , "Eloy turned away in disgust, his throat burning as he held back his anger. "Get off of her, you slimy bastard, or you can forget about me fixing your shitty drugs," Eloy shouted acidly.

"Shut up!" Raven said, giving Eloy the finger. He got off of Maria, zipped up his pants and grinned. "So tell me, *puto*, how are you going to clean up my heroin?"

Eloy tried to calm down. He knew that until he did what Raven wanted, he and Maria were his prisoners, and he had to get her out of there. He explained to Raven, "The heroin has been contaminated with an extract of atropine from the belladonna plant. Atropine inhibits muscarinic acetylcholine receptors, which causes smooth muscles to relax, leading to poisoning and death. That's why Lolita crapped all over herself, and that's why her pupils were so dilated."

"Cut the bullshit. I hate that science talk. Just fix my heroin. Can you do it or not?" Raven shouted.

"Yes."

"Well, then do it, *puto*, before I cut the tits off your bitch." Raven waved his knife at Maria.

Eloy, Manuel and Franco took the rest of the contaminated heroin and went back to the laboratory. It was late at
night, and José the guard said to Eloy, "*Hombre*, don't you
ever rest?"

"No, *mi amigo*. I am doing very important work," Eloy
replied.

Once in the laboratory, it was relatively easy for Eloy to
solubilize the atropine and, using differential fractionating
procedures, to separate the atropine from the heroin. The separation didn't take long, and he was finished before dawn. On
Sunday morning they returned to La Perla with the purified
heroin.

"Gimme the shit," Raven said. "How do I know it is pure?
Pablo, bring me the *puta*, Maria."

Pablo went to the back room and returned with Maria.
She was barely alive. She was drugged, naked and sweaty and
reeked of sex.

"Maria, I will get this Raven," he whispered. "I'll get him."

"If this is pure shit, then I can give it to your cunt," Raven
said. With that he prepared the heroin and started to inject it
into Maria.

"No, no," Eloy said. "No, give it to me."

"What do you think, I'm stupid? If you take it and it's
bad, you die. What good is that?"

Raven injected the heroin into Maria. She took on the
appearance of a heroin addict: a rush of euphoria, a soaring
high, and a look of exhilaration. But she didn't die.

"Oh, you are a good man. Gimme the heroin!" Raven
grabbed at the bags. "Kill the bastard. Kill the *puto* and his
little *puta*," he ordered Franco.

"No!" Eloy put his hand up to stop the men. "Before you
kill us, I want you to see something. You like gold, right?

Well, take a look at this." Eloy reached into his pocket.

Raven yelled, "The *cabrón* has a gun."

"Impossible. He don't have a gun," Franco said, his fat jowls shaking.

Just then Eloy pulled a tobacco leaf out of his pocket and in that leaf was a yellow gold frog, his Ranita. "Here Raven, here is a gift of yellow gold. A yellow gold frog."

"You bastard, I thought you had a gun," Raven said. "I'll kill you and your pussy and your damn frog, son of a bitch!" He reached over and grabbed the frog. Within moments Raven convulsed, went rigid and died.

El Oso was furious. He ran back into the shanty and screamed to Manuel, "Get the *cabrón*." To Eloy he growled, You'll never get off this island alive." Franco bent down to look at Raven and smashed the frog with his fat fist, the fist tattooed *El Oso*. Ranita was crushed by the blow. El Oso stood up, but suddenly fell to the floor convulsing, and then he stopped. El Oso lay still. Eloy hoped there was enough toxin left in his little frog to kill the big man.

Eloy picked up the keys that El Oso had dropped, ran over and lifted Maria, carried her up to the street, and jumped into the black Mercedes.

Manuel walked over to Raven's motionless body and kicked it. He pulled a gun from his pocket and shot the already dead Raven squarely between the eyes. "Take that, *cabrón*."

CHAPTER 8

"Maria," Eloy called as he drove her in the black Mercedes toward Rio Piedras and the Centro Médico. Maria was incoherent, her drugged mind and abused body devoid of soul. "Maria," Eloy called again. No response.

He drove past the Centro Médico and entered through the back near the Veteran's Hospital, passing by the heavy-walled prison, then turned into the emergency room parking lot. He parked the car hurriedly, blocking a police car, removed his shirt, and gently wrapped it around her. Eloy was filled with mixed emotions—guilt, anger, fear, revenge—but more than anything, love.

"Maria," Eloy said to her, "we're at the hospital."

He carried her into the busy emergency room. She groaned. The emergency room buzzed with activity, and doctors and nurses scurried about. Eloy tried to catch their attention, but to no avail. "Don't worry," he whispered into her sweaty hair. "I'll get you help."

He set Maria down in a chair, approached an overweight,

half-asleep security guard and punched him squarely in his protruding belly. The security guard came to and reached for his gun. "What the hell is your problem, *hombre?*"

"I'm sorry," Eloy replied, "but please help me. My girlfriend is dying. She's been raped and drugged. Get help."

The guard took one look at Maria and ran to get one of the medical residents on duty, who quickly wrapped her in a blanket, placed her in a wheelchair, and took her into the nearest examining room.

"Leave us alone," the intern said firmly. "We will take good care of her." With that he pulled the curtain around the bed where Maria lay, separating Eloy from the woman he loved. The woman he failed to protect.

Eloy sat down in the waiting room and bristled at the memory of Raven's savagery. He deserved to die for what he did to Maria, and El Oso too. *"Dios,"* he prayed, "please forgive me and my Ranita. Don't punish me with the curse. Don't let her die."

He knew he should call Dr. Rodríguez to tell him about Maria. He went to the telephone.

"Hello, Dr. Rodríguez. It's Eloy. I have something bad to say," he whispered, his voice breaking. "Maria . . . Maria . . . Maria is here. I'm at the Centro Médico in the emergency room."

"Qué pasa? What's the matter with my Maria?" Dr. Rodríguez's voice was edged with fear.

"Don't worry. They are taking good care of her. She will be okay. Please come. Hurry. I'll explain when you arrive," Eloy said.

He heard the telephone go dead. Dr. Rodríguez had hung up.

Just then a police officer approached Eloy. "Officer Rios,"

the man said by way of introduction. "We need to fill out a police report. Tell me what happened."

Eloy thought, If I tell him the truth, they will put me in jail, and all my hopes for the future will be destroyed. So he told the officer an elaborate lie about how Maria had been raped. The expression on the officer's face made it apparent that he knew Eloy was lying.

"Where is she?" Dr. Rodríguez demanded as he ran into the emergency room. "How is she? Where's my Maria?" Standing next to him was Maria's mother, Rosa. Her eyes burned with anger. "It is all your fault, you no-good-for-nothing *mestizo*. It's all your fault; whatever happened to Maria is your fault!"

"Don't pay attention to her. It's only her grief speaking," Dr. Rodríguez said, patting Eloy's shoulder.

Eloy pointed to the examination room where Maria was being treated and began to tell her parents what had happened.

"Dr. Rodríguez," Officer Rios interrupted, "remember me? I did a senior project with you and wrote a paper about the possible use of DNA to identify criminals."

"Oh, yes. Hello Rios. It's good to see you, but I can't talk right now. I must go to my daughter."

"Of course. I'm sorry I bothered you," Rios said apologetically and returned to his paperwork.

Dr. Rodríguez looked at the officer and asked, "What are you writing?"

"My report. My police report."

"Rios, is that really necessary? We don't want this made public. I'm afraid if the media get wind of this story they will ruin my daughter's reputation, and she doesn't deserve that, considering everything she has suffered. Please, *hombre*, can't you look the other way?"

"I'm sorry," said Officer Rios. "I have to fill out this report." He hesitated for a moment, considering.

As if he sensed the policeman was weakening in his resolve, Rodríguez laid his hand on the young man's shoulder. "Please. I would be forever in your debt."

The officer regarded him for a moment, then ripped the report form in half. "I hope you are not making a mistake, *señor.*" He nodded to Rosa Rodríguez and walked out the door.

While waiting for the doctors to give them a status report, Eloy told Dr. Rodríguez and Rosa the events that had led up to the present, omitting only Raven's death. He lied and told them that as he drove away he saw the police enter Raven's shanty. He didn't want them to fear for their daughter's life. He also remembered Franco's threat: "You will never get off of this island alive." Was his own life in danger? Was Maria's? Was El Oso alive, or did his Ranita kill him, too?

"Come," the doctor said to Eloy and the Rodríguezes. "Maria is sleeping now. We have examined her, and she will be okay except . . ." he hesitated and studied their concerned faces. "I must tell you she will never be able to have children."

"Oh, no. Why?"

"Because of the trauma to her uterus."

"No!" Rosa cried, "*Mi hijita*! It's all your fault!" she screamed at Eloy. "No man will ever marry my beautiful daughter. *Dios mio,* she can't have children! All because of you." She shook her fist at Eloy and hissed, "I hate you."

Dr. Rodríguez said, "Be quiet, Rosa. Maria needs rest. Come, let's go home. There's nothing more we can do here."

Juan ran into the emergency room and spotted his parents. "Papá! Mamá! I just heard from the intern that Maria was here. What happened? How is she?"

Nestor coldly responded, "Maria is fine, no thanks to you.

You lied for that drug dealer and told your mother that Maria and Eloy were with you. You are a disgrace to this family— don't you ever call me Papá. I have no son."

"Oh, *mi hijito*," Rosa said, hugging her son. "Don't listen to your father. It's okay," she said, stroking his brow. "It's not your fault, my son!"

"Let's go now!" Dr. Rodríguez abruptly turned his back on Juan and strode out the door.

The next day Eloy read an article on the back page of the *San Juan Star.*

DRUG LORD FOUND DEAD

Amado de la Cruz, known as the Raven, was found dead at his home in La Perla. One of his bodyguards, Franco Reyes, was found in a coma due to an overdose of drugs and is at the Centro Médico under police custody. The assailants are unknown, but the murder is believed to be related to the drug lord's turf wars on this island.

El Oso is still alive, Eloy thought. He is here in the same hospital as Maria. I should have made sure he was dead.

CHAPTER 9

Winter 1985

On the evening news, the silver-haired anchor announced, "Now we go live to the Department of Health and Human Services for a report from Dr. Cooper, the surgeon general."

"It has been twenty-one years since Luther L. Terry, former surgeon general of the United States Public Health Service, released his landmark report on smoking and health. In a press conference clouded in secrecy, he delivered the report to the media and the public on January 11, 1964, a Saturday morning, to prevent any precipitous reaction on Wall Street. The White House press secretary selected the auditorium in the State Department because of the state-of-the-art security system installed there after the assassination of President Kennedy.

"This was the first official recognition that cigarette smoking causes cancer and other serious diseases. On the basis of over seven thousand research articles connecting smoking to lung cancer and chronic bronchitis, the surgeon general concluded that cigarette smoking was a health hazard of sufficient importance in the United States to warrant appropriate remedial action. And what is appropriate remedial action? Your lawmakers took the correct approach in the Public Health Cigarette Smoking Act of 1969 by requiring a health warning on cigarette packages and by banning cigarette advertising in the broadcast media.

"Here it is 1985 and our public officials have done almost nothing to correct the single most preventable cause of premature death in the United States. Despite the overwhelming scientific evidence, your elected politicians—the very people who have sworn to act in the best public interest—have betrayed your trust. The federal government has allowed itself to be deftly manipulated by the tobacco industry because the politicians are afraid of angering the millions of voters who are addicted to nicotine.

"Allowing the cigarette industry to prosper from their victims is unconscionable. We must stop the powerful political and economic forces promoting the addiction of adults and children to this deadly product. The industry steadfastly refuses to admit any culpability for the health consequences of smoking. We must elect government officials who are not fearful of these powerful forces." After the surgeon general ended this passionate speech, he took questions from the assembled media.

With just as much passion, Senator Orville Reynolds snapped off the television. Shouting "We have to stop that S.O.B.!" he got up from his overstuffed leather chair and gently set his little terrier on the cushion. He waited patiently while the dog gleefully licked his skinny hand. Then he rubbed the dog's head. "You be a good boy, Benson. Daddy has to make an important call." From his office in the Hubert

Humphrey Building, an office that he had occupied for more than twenty years, Senator Reynolds called the president.

"Bob, did you see the surgeon general's report on television?"

"Yes," the president replied warily.

"Well, as I said to the administration before yours, and as I have told you several times, we have to do something to stop this antismoking crusade. Either you do something or I will! We need another surgeon general. We have to get rid of that self-righteous bastard! We need a woman, some token, some minority, someone we can manipulate . . . and by God I'll get one."

"You know that I support the tobacco industry. I won't jeopardize the livelihood of your constituency. Relax, Orville. Have a drink and a smoke." The president shook his head slowly as he hung up the telephone and turned to his Secret Service agent, Mark Wilson.

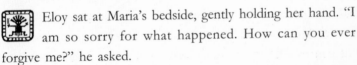 Eloy sat at Maria's bedside, gently holding her hand. "I am so sorry for what happened. How can you ever forgive me?" he asked.

She had remained in the hospital for three days, healing from her physical wounds, but she was a strong woman and knew that the physical scars would heal—all but one. She would always be barren. She felt sorry for herself and sorry for her father because she would never be able to give him a grandchild.

Maria looked up at Eloy. He appeared so sad, with his shoulders drooped and his eyes filled with sorrow. He is suffering too, she thought. "It's not your fault, Eloy. I know you did all you could. My father always says, 'You can't change the past, but you can change the future,'" she said, squeezing his hand. "I can't keep reliving what happened to me. I need something else to focus on. . . . I can't live like this. I have been thinking a lot about what I want to do next. I have been happy helping my father in the lab, but . . ." Her voice broke as she spoke of her father. "All his life he has wanted Juan and me to become doctors, to care for the sick. I earned my M.D. here. I elected not to do my residency because I wanted to do research and not clinical practice. My father always wanted to be a pediatrician. He loves children, and there is so much suffering on the island and in the world, and so much of this suffering is inflicted on little children.

"Because of everything, I've decided to accept the residency in pediatrics at the Hospital San Pablo in Bayamon. I love children, and if I can't have them, at least I can love and care for them as a doctor," she sobbed.

"Don't cry, *mi amor*. I will always love you. If we can't have children, it is because God wills it. What does it matter, having children or not?" Eloy felt a quickening in his stomach when he realized what he had said.

Maria looked at Eloy. "You love me?"

"I . . . I'm sorry. I should have waited . . . I just needed to say it to you. I promise I will protect you, Maria. No one will ever hurt you again."

"*Mi cariño*," she whispered as she gently touched his hand.

Eloy thought, With every bad event comes a good one. And thank you, God. I don't understand your ways, but I understand consequences. Did you do this to Maria so that the curse would end, that the Huntington's in my family would die?

At that moment, despite the sadness that filled the hospital room, Eloy's spirits lifted. He was free—free to truly love Maria. Before this he had always been afraid of loving a woman because he knew that he could never give a wife his children for fear that they might inherit the gene.

But now there was a commotion in the hallway, with loud shouting and the sounds of a struggle.

"Get him!" shouted a security guard.

"Get the bastard!" another guard shouted amid the clattering of carts being pushed over and glassware and medicine bottles crashing to the floor.

"What's happening?" Maria gasped. Eloy rushed to the door and peered into the hall. Two large security guards were trying to restrain a very burly man, who wrenched free and lumbered toward Eloy. Before Eloy closed the door, the last image he saw was the fat man's pudgy hand and the tattoo of the bear. El Oso was trying to escape.

Eloy didn't dare tell Maria.

"What was it?" Maria asked, looking up from her bed.

"Oh, it's just some addict having a bad trip," Eloy lied. "Don't worry, everything will be all right. "Eloy returned to the bed. "I'm going to the lab right now, and then tomorrow you get to come home. I'll see you then, *mi amor*." He kissed her forehead. Maria smiled, turned her head on the pillow and closed her eyes.

As Eloy walked out of the room he was assailed with doubt. He'd told Maria he would protect her, but could he? What would happen if El Oso tracked them down?

CHAPTER 10

It took Eloy three days to return to the laboratory. He found the work area where he had analyzed the heroin and its atropine contaminant exactly as he had left it. Small remnants of the contaminated heroin still remained on the lab table, and he wanted to clean them off before Dr. Rodríguez returned, as much to expunge the memory as to restore order.

Dr. Rodríguez and his wife were at the hospital with Maria, readying her to go home, but Rosa was very mad at Eloy, so it was probably best that he wasn't there. Because Maria's exposure to the heroin had been brief, her withdrawal symptoms were minor. The doctors felt that an outpatient methadone program would see her through withdrawal satisfactorily and that Maria could go home. She was very fortunate. Was it her physiology, or was it her determination and strength of character that allowed her not to suffer more? Eloy wondered, remembering her condition at the time he finally got her to the hospital.

Eloy immediately shook the scene at the hospital from his mind and got back to work. He snapped on his latex gloves and proceeded to the cell culture chamber to continue processing his culture of embryonic nerve cells. In a couple of hours he finished the procedures, and felt that he had done enough. The hospital had released Maria that morning, and he was anxious to get home to see her. When he arrived there, Eloy rushed to her bedside and gently kissed her.

"I'm so glad that you're home."

"Me too, *mi amor*," Maria whispered.

Dr. Rodríguez looked approvingly at the couple and was pleased that his daughter was bringing this man into her life. Eloy would make a good husband, he thought. They would give him a lot of grandchildren to comfort him in his old age. Then, as quickly as that thought had come, it was swept away by the reality that there would never be grandchildren from his daughter. Nor from Juan, but that was another problem.

Rosa looked away from the sight of Eloy holding Maria. How could her Maria love him, she wondered, this weak man who allowed those drug addicts to rape her? What a good-for-nothing excuse of a man.

Later that night, the sounds of Rio Piedras settled into the darkness, and a fresh breeze carried the scent of the recent evening rain into Eloy's room. The moonlight filtered through the ornamental iron covering his windows, forming strange images on the far wall. The sounds of the small coqui frogs floated through the air. Eloy thought of his Ranita, and the events of the past week. He could not believe how much had happened since last Friday. He thought of his research, his father and his brother. In a jumble of thoughts, sleep finally came.

"Kill the bastard! Don't let him near Maria. I will cut his heart out!" Eloy cried. "El Oso must die!"

El Oso caught up to Maria and grabbed her. He began to hit her. Blood spurted from her face. He cut at her abdomen and ripped her open. Eloy was frozen, as if his strength had been sucked away. While he looked on with horror, the Raven emerged from Maria's bloody womb. He screamed as if his soul were being torn out of him through his mouth.

Eloy woke up bathed in sweat and shaking from the nightmare.

As the days went by, he felt increasingly uncomfortable living in the Rodríguez household. Dr. Rodríguez and his wife were constantly fighting, and many nights Eloy had to put his pillow over his head to muffle their shouting. The aftermath of the rape was taking its toll on them all. He knew that he had to find another home and thought about moving to student housing. However, when he approached Maria about it, she assured him that everything would be okay and that he should continue to live with them. She said that the problems her parents were having weren't because of what happened to her but because there had been a lot of family conflict since Juan left.

"Eloy, come into my office a minute, will you?"

He set down the pipette and went into Dr. Rodríguez's office.

"What's bothering you? You look troubled."

"Almost two months have gone by, and I'm still confused about my results. I can't understand why the fetal nerve cell line—the embryonic cells—are dying in culture. No matter what I do, I can't get active acetylcholine production or uptake. I have reformulated the media. I have checked CO_2

levels and pH, and I've looked for fungal or bacterial infection. This just doesn't make sense."

"There has to be an explanation. You're working too hard. You need a break. . . . This has been too much for all of us," Dr. Rodríguez said. "Let's stop work for the moment. How about if we go across the street to the Burger King and have a cup of coffee."

"*De acuerdo*," Eloy responded.

Crossing the street, Eloy felt that someone was following him. Out of the corner of his eye he saw a large shadow running toward him.

"Oh, no!" Eloy screamed. "*Cuidado*! It is El Oso!" He picked up a fallen tree branch to protect himself and Dr. Rodríguez. Just as he was about to swing the branch, he recognized Oswaldo, a graduate student from Dr. Morales's organic synthesis laboratory down the hall. Embarrassed, Eloy dropped the branch and mumbled a greeting. Dr. Rodríguez regarded Eloy with concern.

"I didn't mean to surprise you. Is everything okay, Eloy?" Oswaldo asked.

"Yes, I'm sorry. Please, join us for coffee," Eloy said, his face burning with embarrassment.

"Thanks, but I'm late for an appointment. Good to see you," he said and walked on.

"Eloy, why so jumpy? You have been acting real nervous lately."

"I keep thinking I see . . . I keep thinking of La Perla."

"Well, why don't you and Maria take a short vacation? Spend a couple of days on the island of Vieques, stay at a country inn and just relax. I know it's not like a father to suggest that his unmarried daughter go away with a man, but I trust you, even in light of recent events. I know it wasn't your fault—you would never hurt Maria," he said, rubbing his bald head. "And she needs to get away too."

"*Sí*," Eloy sighed, "that's a good idea. If Maria feels well enough, we will go this weekend."

El Parador was a traditional hacienda converted into an inn. Originally it had been the main house of a colonial tobacco plantation, and it was renowned for its old-fashioned elegance and bucolic charm. The intimate setting was sure to help them grow even closer, Eloy felt. On Saturday, he and Maria spent a wonderful day relaxing on the beach, sipping piña coladas and eating barbecued pork on a skewer. Everything was perfect.

They sat in their room that evening and watched the sun set over the Caribbean. The colors reflecting off the water reminded Eloy of the sunset on the day that he, his father and Miguel first discussed *El Mal.* He thought of his vow to his father, his work at Dr. Rodríguez's lab, and where his research was headed. Why, he wondered, were the cells in his cultures not producing or taking up acetylcholine? Eloy was perplexed. Why weren't the cells communicating?

"What are you thinking about?"

"Oh." Eloy realized he had once again let his work occupy his thoughts. "I'm sorry. I just started thinking about my cultures again."

"Please try and forget about the lab for a while. Look at that incredible sunset."

Eloy slipped Maria's arm through his and led her toward the railing on the veranda.

"I'm so sorry about everything, Maria," he whispered softly. He held her hand gently and touched her warm skin.

"I want to take care of you," he said and pulled her close. His breath was in her hair. She pulled away, trembling.

"Eloy," she said. "I love you, but I'm afraid. . . . I'm not ready. It's too soon."

Sensing her uneasiness even before she spoke, Eloy gave her a warm smile. "*Mi amor,* I understand. I want you to know that I love you. What those animals did to you, I . . . I will never force myself on you, and I think you know that. I only wish I could change the past."

Eloy sensed Maria's body relax. She turned her head toward him, her mouth toward his, and brought her full lips to his. He had kissed her before, but this time he wanted more. He sensed that she did too.

"Do you feel we . . . "

"Yes, yes," she whispered, taking his hand and leading him to the bed. Maria continued to kiss Eloy, cupping his face in both her hands and with each kiss becoming more and more passionate. "Undress me, *amor.* I'm ready," she murmured.

He began to undress her, gently kissing every inch of freshly exposed skin. She returned each kiss, first gently, and then with hungry lips.

She lay on top of his naked body and gently led him into her. Eloy was caring and tender. He didn't want to hurt her. Their limbs entwining, they clung to each other with mounting passion. They were lost in the world of their love. Their breathing quickened, then the moment came when time stood still, and they were one.

Smiling with pleasure, they lay together afterward. Tears pooled in Maria's green eyes. Eloy reached over and stroked her smooth skin and kissed the salty tears from her cheek. He held her closer, and there in the tropical moonlight, on their bed in Vieques, their hearts found peace, the peace that only true love can bring.

A couple of hours later they were awakened by the sounds of the coqui and the gentle lapping of the waves on the shore.

They dressed and walked out to the veranda. Maria sat in a large, white wicker chair with an overstuffed floral cushion. Eloy poured them each a glass of wine and then sat down on a chaise next to her. They drank wine and watched the waves slowly roll up on the shore of Sun Bay. Eloy looked at Maria. He felt closer to her than ever, with a rare sense of complete contentment. Maria arose from her chair and curled up next to Eloy on the chaise.

"It's so beautiful here, so peaceful. I wish we could stay here forever."

"Then let's stay here. I would do anything to make you happy, Maria."

"You say that now, but I know you, Eloy. You want to get back to your research. You were probably thinking about it just now!"

"Well, I just have this one concern . . ." he replied with a roguish smile."

"I knew it!" Maria laughed. "What's the problem?"

"I can't understand why I can't get the embryonic nerve cell lines to produce acetylcholine. Why is there no chemical transmission? In the past it's been easy. I've checked again and again to make sure that the environmental conditions are optimal in the growth chamber. I've rechecked the culture media, and I don't know what to do next."

"*Mi amor,* it could be that there is an external contaminant. Have you checked the purity of the water? Did you use sterile techniques in your transfers?" Maria asked.

"That's another thing I love about you. Not only are you

strong and beautiful but you're so smart and you love science." Eloy pulled Maria to her feet and held her close. For a moment they became silent, as their bodies and souls communicated wordlessly. Eloy looked into Maria's eyes and saw his own eyes reflected in her pupils, which the darkness had enlarged.

"That's it," he said. The romantic spell was broken.

"What?" she asked in surprise.

"Atropine! Remember, the heroin was contaminated with the atropine extracted from the belladonna plant. I must have been sloppy when I went back to the laboratory to clean up. I must have contaminated my gloves with atropine. Remember, weak solutions of atropine are used as eye drops to dilate the pupils during eye examinations. And before victims of atropine poisoning die, they experience a general loss of memory and disorientation, symptoms similar—yes—to those of Alzheimer's disease."

"Yes, and . . ." Maria said, "Alzheimer's victims suffer memory loss and, upon autopsy, show massive destruction of the basal forebrain that contains the acetylcholine-producing neurons."

"That's it!" Eloy said. "My nerve cell cultures have been contaminated with atropine. They have Alzheimer's!"

CHAPTER 11

Once back home, Eloy could hardly wait to tell Dr. Rodríguez his hypothesis. It would be a major finding if it could be replicated.

"Great. Let's try to estimate the concentration of the atropine contaminants," Dr. Rodríguez urged.

Eloy did the calculations on the computer and determined the concentration. They repeated the experiments and verified that atropine was interfering with acetylcholine transmission—but why? Why were the cells dying? Eloy wondered.

"Is atropine interfering with acetylcholine production or blocking acetylcholine muscarinic receptors?" Dr. Rodríguez questioned.

"I tend to believe that, because we still find acetylcholine present, atropine is probably blocking the acetylcholine muscarinic receptors," Eloy said, picking up his yellow legal pad and starting to write. "We should use the following logic if indeed the atropine is binding to the receptors:

"One: If atropine can produce such dramatic effects on

acetylcholine transmission and result in changes in memory
and muscular coordination, we must demonstrate that atropine binds to acetylcholine receptors.

"Two: If we label the atropine with radioactive hydrogen,
^{3}H tritium, then the distribution of the atropine in the brain
of experimental animals should be found in the highest con-
centrations in the region of the brain with the most acetylcholine receptors, the basal forebrain.

"Three: If indeed the atropine is blocking the muscarinic
acetylcholine receptors rather than the nicotinic acetylcholine receptors, we would find inhibition of cyclic adenosine
monophosphate, or cAMP, one of the chemicals needed for
some energy metabolic cycles."

After running several experiments for three weeks, Eloy
and Dr. Rodríguez determined that atropine bound to
the receptors on the postsynaptic junction of the neurons in
the region of the basal forebrain. Also, because the cAMP levels decreased, they determined that atropine binds to the muscarinic acetylcholine receptor. From this finding Eloy speculated that the blockage could be one cause of memory loss in
patients with Alzheimer's disease.

When Eloy told Maria about the results of their investigation, she recognized their importance.

"You must publish your findings. This is significant. You
have to present a paper at the neurobiology meetings in Washington."

"Okay," Eloy said hesitantly. "But Maria, I don't know.
Do I really have something to say? . . . you know, to leaders in
the field?" he finished somewhat dubiously.

"Look," Maria said, "I wouldn't jeopardize your career.
This is significant."

"Okay, but . . . oh, I don't know . . . I need your help."

"Of course," she said, and kissed him on the cheek.

"Great. We'll write the paper together and submit an abstract for publication."

During the following months Eloy, Maria and Dr. Rodríguez worked to get their research ready for publication and presentation. They prepared slides and analyzed data on the computer and soon had it ready for submission to the journal *Nerve*. They would also submit the abstract to the Society for Neurobiology.

September 1986

 Senator Orville Reynolds stormed into his office, slamming the door behind him. "Joe, get Dave on the telephone. I need to talk to him right now."

"Sure, boss," Joe drawled, picking up the phone.

The senator grabbed the phone and bellowed, "How's that research coming along? I wanted that new tobacco strain months ago!"

"Hmmm. As you probably already know, we ran into a little problem," Dave replied sheepishly.

"Look, we need progress. I want you in my office this afternoon. See you at one o'clock, and bring your seeds!" Orville slammed the receiver down and turned to Joe. "This bullshit has to stop. We've been supplying that bastard with federal research funds since 1972. He promised us a high-nicotine-yield tobacco. We cannot continue to divert federal funds to this son of a bitch under the guise of producing a low-nicotine cigarette without results."

Dave really didn't want to meet with Senator Reynolds and face his explosive temper again. Arriving at the office, he was immediately ushered in. Orville was obviously upset, but tried to display a look of paternal concern on his thin, ruddy face.

"Dave, it's almost 1987, and all you can produce are these jars of tobacco seeds," the senator lectured. "Your techniques are too old-fashioned. Why aren't you using more modern techniques like anther culture, tissue culture, hybrid sorting or protoplast fusion?"

Dave registered genuine surprise. Where had Orville learned about such advanced procedures? "Hmmm, I guess I just didn't think of it."

"'Didn't think of it' my ass. Give me those seeds and get out of here." Orville grabbed the package in Dave's hands and pushed him toward the door. "I said, get your ass out of here."

Dave needed no further encouragement. He rushed out of the office, glad to be leaving.

"Joe! Call our friend in the Secret Service. I think we can help Dave get his early retirement."

Less than twenty-four hours later, Dave was found dead from a gunshot wound to the head outside a bar in Beltsville.

Orville sent the seeds to the Kentucky Green Tobacco Company in Louisville. Within two months, using a combination of conventional and genetic-engineering techniques, their scientists produced a strain of high-nicotine-yielding tobacco, code-named Y-1. Its leaves contained over 6 percent nicotine by weight—more than two times the normal amount. The tobacco industry finally had what it wanted, and the seeds from Y-1 were shipped to Brazil for cultivation.

"Joe, get on the telephone. I need to talk to Stu Brown at Kentucky Green!" Orville's friend and former classmate was the CEO of Kentucky Green.

"Orville, you ol' son of a bitch. Good to hear from you.

You are a devious bastard. Thanks for taking care of our problem two or three months ago. I understand that a certain government scientist retired early."

"Yeah, real early." Orville broke into a hearty laugh that ebbed in a choking, mucus-heavy cough.

Stu echoed his old friend's laughter.

"Stu, what do you think about the new Y-1 strain? I understand that you are getting ready to put it in your cigarettes. Remember, if we ever have any congressional inquiries or lawsuits, the only reason you are using high-nicotine-yield tobacco is because it produces less tar, and of course, the tobacco industry is only looking out for the health interests of its consumers."

"Hell, with this new tobacco we can rev up our campaign to reel in the young folks. Hook 'em while they're young, isn't that how the saying goes? What do you think of the new campaign? Our advertising and marketing people say that we should appeal to kids by featuring a camel or a tiger or a lion or something to get to them. Almost sounds environmentally friendly. What do you think?"

"Sounds good to me," Orville grinned, dragging deep on a Lucky Strike. "Sounds real damn good to me."

November 1986

Eloy was anxious. He had never been to the mainland or presented a research paper at a major convention. He had only given seminars to colleagues in Dr. Rodríguez's lab, but never to investigators of this caliber.

The thought of flying to Washington both excited and frightened Eloy, chiefly because this would be his first flight. He knew that flying was safe, but he couldn't forget the crash he had seen as a fifteen-year-old. He wondered what had become of Karen.

"Are you ready? Do you have your suitcases packed? Don't forget the slides and other material for your presentation," Dr. Rodríguez reminded him as he opened the door to leave. "*Apurense.* We have to get to the airport; the taxi is already here."

At the Luis Muñoz Marin Airport in Isla Verde, Eloy tried to look relaxed. However, when he handed Dr. Rodríguez his ticket to give to the ticket agent to get his boarding pass, his hand trembled.

"What's the matter, Eloy? Afraid of flying? How about a drink before we board the plane? You need to relax," Dr. Rodríguez teased as he put his arm around Eloy and steered him toward the lounge.

Despite the terror of takeoff, Eloy was surprised to find that flying could be uneventful. He began to relax a bit, and shortly thereafter drifted off to sleep. Before he knew it, the pilot was announcing their descent to National Airport.

Dr. Rodríguez, Maria and he checked into their rooms at the Hyatt Hotel next to the convention center. Eloy and Dr. Rodríguez shared a room, and Maria had an adjoining one with a door between them. The hotel room was large and fresh-smelling, with green plush carpet and charming French country-style furniture. The bathroom offered thick towels and a hair dryer. The cedar-lined closets were first class.

That evening, tired from the flight from Puerto Rico, the three of them went to bed early. Eloy knew that the next few days could be the turning point in his career. He thought about his quest for the cure for Huntington's. He was becoming an authority on Alzheimer's, which wasn't his focus, but he knew that neurodegenerative disorders from Alzheimer's to Huntington's were all related.

The next morning they ate breakfast at the hotel restaurant. After sipping the coffee, Eloy remarked, "This is very weak."

"Yes, in America they like their coffee weak," responded Maria and took a bite of her croissant.

Dr. Rodríguez looked up from his plate of fruit and began to discuss the plans for the day. "Let me think. You don't have to present your paper until tomorrow, right? We should attend the opening session, have lunch and listen to the presentation on receptors. Then later on in the afternoon, why don't we go to the Smithsonian Museums?"

Eloy, who had been perusing the meeting program, said, "I would also like to attend the meeting on Huntington's, the session that Don Romano and Karen Williams are chairing. I haven't seen them since I was a teenager in Venezuela. It would be interesting."

Maria flinched as she looked at the picture of Karen Williams in the meeting program. "Remember, Eloy, the reason you are here is to present your research paper, not to visit with old friends," she said with a sting in her voice. She then looked away as if she were just as surprised as Eloy by her tone. Eloy stared at Maria. Tension filled the space between them.

To break the awkwardness of the moment, Dr. Rodríguez said, "Come on, let's go across the street to the convention center. It's time for the opening address. Eloy, don't worry, you will have plenty of time to rehearse. Your practice presentations went fine, and I have no doubt that your paper will be well received."

The opening address was given by a Nobel Prize laureate, who welcomed the participants and discussed the mechanism by which the part of the brain known as the hypothalamus regulated the activity of the master gland, the pituitary. Eloy thought that the presentation was excellent. Very high-quality science. As they left the auditorium to go to lunch, a female voice called out.

"Eloy, is that you?"

"Yeah, that's him," said a deep voice. Don and Karen rushed up to Eloy, and Karen gave him a big hug. Overjoyed at seeing his old friends, Eloy introduced them to his companions.

"You ol' son of a bitch!" Don couldn't contain his Italian enthusiasm. "It's so good to see you. Are you open for lunch? We have some time. Our session isn't until one. Let's catch up."

"How about Chinese?" Karen said, running her fingers through her blonde hair. "I know a wonderful restaurant around the corner."

"Sure, let's go," Eloy said.

Maria hesitated. "I would love to go, but . . ."

"Oh, come on. We want you to join us," Karen said.

Their conversation at the restaurant was lively. Each rushed to tell as much about their lives as they could. A lot had happened during the ten years since they had seen each other in Venezuela.

"Yes, Dr. Soto has related how well you were doing with Dr. Paul Rodríguez."

"That's my brother," Nestor interjected.

"I have heard many wonderful things about you over the years, Eloy. I'd love to hear your paper on the atropine blockage of muscarinic acetylcholine receptors, but I'm afraid I can't," Karen said.

"What?" Eloy exclaimed.

"I'm sorry, Eloy. Tomorrow Don and I have to go back to the NIH. Maybe you could come up after your presentation and tell us about your work. We want to tell you about all the things that we have been doing, too," she said, smiling. "For example, I've documented and established a pedigree for over ten thousand individuals from the villages around Lake Maracaibo. And what's really exciting is that a couple of years ago Don found a genetic marker for Huntington's disease on chromosome four. Today he'll be discussing not only the marker but his search for the gene!"

"The gene?" Eloy said, his voice rising in excitement. People in the restaurant turned to stare. "The gene?" he repeated more quietly. "I have to know more."

Although excited about Eloy's enthusiasm, Maria acted as if she felt awkward and out of place. "Please excuse me. I am tired, and you know, Papá, I'm allergic to monosodium glutamate."

"Here, Maria. Let me go with you," Eloy said, getting up.

"*No, mi cariño*. You stay here."

"Yo, your *cariño*," Don mimicked. "Aha! Eloy has a girlfriend."

Eloy blushed.

As Maria walked back to the hotel, she struggled to understand herself. Why was she behaving like a jealous schoolgirl? It was so contrary to her nature.

She knew that she had a lot of thinking to do. She had to decide what to do with her life. Should she enter the residency program in pediatrics? Should she allow her relationship with Eloy to grow or would it only add more conflict to her life?

In order for her to accomplish her professional goals she would need freedom from a relationship. She wouldn't want Eloy to sacrifice his scientific career and quest for the cure because of her goals. She brushed away a tear. It would just be easier if she and Eloy had never met and fallen in love.

Suddenly, Maria felt like she needed a friend. Maybe she should call Reuben, her old colleague from medical school. He was working down the street in the Department of Health and Human Services in the office of the surgeon general. When she got back to her room, she called him.

Eloy could hardly wait to hear Don's paper. He was so excited that he completely forgot about rehearsing his presentation. After lunch he said, "Dr. Rodríguez, I can't go to the receptor session. I have to hear about Don's research." Turning to Don, he grinned and said, "Just think of it, you ol' son of a bitch. You might find the gene."

Dr. Rodríguez and Karen stared at Eloy, surprised by the swearing. It was out of character for him.

Eloy went to Don's session, and Dr. Rodríguez attended the session on receptors. After Don gave his presentation, Eloy's excitement turned to concern. "Do you mean that it will soon be possible to detect the presence of Huntington's? That it's possible to develop a test to locate the killer gene?"

"Yep," Don said.

Eloy knew what he had to do. He would develop the test to help others and maybe even himself. "I'll go to NIH and visit you and Karen tomorrow."

"That's great. Good luck with your presentation," Don said.

CHAPTER 12

Barely able to contain himself, Eloy rushed back to the hotel. Eloy entered his and Dr. Rodríguez's room and went to the door that adjoined their room with Maria's. He knocked loudly.

"Eloy, is that you?" she responded in a sleepy voice.

"Yes. I need to talk to you."

"Come in." Eloy walked into her room.

"Guess what? Don thinks he found the markers for Huntington's disease on chromosome four. And one day he might find the gene."

It was obvious from Maria's weak response that she didn't share his enthusiasm. "Oh, that's nice."

"Oh, that's nice?" he mocked. "This is the most significant finding of the century relative to Huntington's, and all you have to say is 'that's nice'?"

"What's the matter? Why are you raising your voice to me?"

"I'm not. I'm just excited."

"Well, I'm tired. I need to rest." She rolled over in bed, turning her back to him.

What's the matter with her? he thought.

The door to Eloy's room opened, and Eloy heard Maria's father come in. "Dr. Rodríguez, Don found the markers, and he might have found the gene—yes, the gene—and I have some ideas about developing a test to detect it. Then people will know if they have Huntington's."

"What do you have in mind?"

"Remember at the hospital when your old student, Officer Rios, said he did a paper for you on the use of DNA for identifying criminals?" he asked. "Well, that may be it! I have to work with Don. After my presentation, I'm going to talk to him about using polymerase chain reaction modifications to develop a test for the presence of the Huntington's gene or its markers. Isn't that great?"

Listening through the door of the adjoining rooms, Maria thought, I don't know about Eloy. If he loved me, he would be here with me rather than talking to my father about some dumb police officer who had done a paper on DNA. Has he forgotten the hell I've been through? He's not thinking about me at all.

She knew she was being unreasonably jealous, but she couldn't shake the feeling as hard as she tried. Soon she heard another knock on the door. It was her father. Maria pulled herself up off the bed and opened the door.

"Come, *mi hijita*," he said. "It is time to go to visit the museums."

"I don't feel good, Papá. Go without me." She didn't feel well, but it wasn't because she was tired. She sensed that she was going to lose Eloy either to Karen, to his work or to her own career.

"Okay, if you're all right by yourself. We'll be back around seven."

The men left to catch the Metro to the Smithsonian Museums. When they came up the escalator from their stop, the air felt brisk, and they saw that the few leaves remaining on the trees had lost their color. They walked in the direction of the Capitol past the old Smithsonian buildings, the Hirshhorn Museum and across Seventh Street to the Air and Space Museum.

Eloy was glad for the chance to visit the museums, but his mind was focused on Don's research findings. He was also concerned about Maria. Why was she acting so strangely? He couldn't think of anything he had done to offend her. Women. Why were they so complicated?

As if he noticed the distant look in Eloy's eyes, Dr. Rodríguez touched the young man's arm. "You're preoccupied. What's the matter? Are you nervous about your research presentation tomorrow?"

"Yes. I'm sorry," Eloy said. "I've had a busy day . . . *muchas cosas*. I need to rest and think about my presentation. Maybe we should forget about the museum and go back to the hotel."

Dr. Rodríguez said, "That's understandable. You go on back. I told some of my old friends I would meet them in Georgetown for dinner."

When Eloy turned to walk back to the Metro station, he called after him, "See you tomorrow. Sleep well."

Entering the hotel, Eloy decided to go to the bar and have a drink, motivated more by a desire to avoid Maria than by thirst. He didn't understand why she was being so cold and distant. He hoped she wasn't jealous of Karen—they were just friends. Did she blame him for the rape and her inability to have children? Maybe she simply stopped loving him. But how did that happen?

Eloy ordered a piña colada. The man sitting next to
him said, "Order a man's drink, my friend, not a woman's
drink. Here, have a whiskey on me. He extended his hand
to Eloy, saying, "My name is Joe Ray. I'm a congressional
aide in the office of Senator Orville Reynolds." The lanky
man wore black snakeskin cowboy boots and had a handlebar mustache, reminiscent of a villain in an old cowboy
movie.

"Mind if I smoke?" Joe blew smoke out of the corner of
his mouth toward the ceiling.

"It's okay. Go ahead. Everyone else is."

"Hey, partner, that sounded a little sarcastic. I'm just trying to be a good neighbor."

"Oh, sorry," Eloy said. "I've had a very full day."

"You're here with that bunch of scientists?"

"Yes. I do research on neurotransmitter receptors associated with Alzheimer's."

"Sorry, fella, I don't understand all of that scientific
malarky, but I do have a grandma in a Florida nursing home
who has a memory problem. Poor lady. She don't remember
a damn thing."

Eloy finished his whiskey and said, "Thank you for the
drink. I have to go and get ready for a research presentation
I'm giving tomorrow. Please excuse me."

"Good luck," Joe said. "Oh, by the way, what was your
name?"

"Eloy Córdova Santiago."

"Eloy Córdova Santiago? That's a foreign-sounding name.
Where ya from, partner?"

"Venezuela," Eloy replied as he got up from the bar stool
and walked toward the elevator.

"Eloy Córdova Santiago . . . Alzheimer's. I never forget a

face. I never forget a name." Joe stroked his mustache and picked up his glass.

When Eloy entered his room, he saw that the door to Maria's room was closed. He started to knock but then thought better of it. He didn't want to argue. Anyway, he had to review his notes.

The caliber of the speakers he'd heard earlier made him nervous about his own abilities. Dr. Rodríguez said he was professionally on a par with the other scientists at the convention, but was he really? Eloy still felt ashamed of the lack of letters after his name.

Eloy sank into the soft sofa and looked at his slides and notes for what seemed to be the hundredth time. Enough was enough, he decided. He was as prepared as he was going to be. All he needed now was rest.

Drifting off to sleep, Eloy heard the outside door to Maria's room close. Had she gone out, or had she come back? He got up to check, then sat back down on the bed. The muted sound of a television wafted through the wall. Maria must have just returned from somewhere, he concluded. It was probably best not to disturb her. He knew that she was still upset. But he didn't know what else to say or do to comfort her. He certainly didn't need any more stress before his professional debut. After tossing and turning a few times, he finally fell into a fitful sleep.

 "Are you ready?" Dr. Rodríguez called, as Eloy went over his notes one last time.

"*Sí*," he said.

"Maria, are you coming?"

"No, I'm sorry. I think I'll just stay here or go shopping," she said. "I don't feel like a meeting."

"What's got into her?" Eloy muttered. She was completely ignoring him. After the conference they would have to talk, but not now. "See you later," he said quietly and closed the door.

The moderator of the research panel was Dr. Zoren Krekorian, the director of the Alzheimer's research programs at the National Institute of Aging of the National Institutes of Health. After Dr. Krekorian introduced him, Eloy began his presentation by showing slides and listing the evidence that led him to the conclusion that atropine blocked acetylcholine muscarinic receptors. Eloy speculated that this could be one of the many causes for the memory loss associated with Alzheimer's. After he finshed the lecture he answered questions from the audience. Applause filled the room as he left the stage.

Zoren returned to the podium. "This, I think, is a very significant finding with respect to Alzheimer's." The audience applauded again. Eloy was happy but uneasy. Should he continue working with his Alzheimer's research, or should he try to work with Don and Karen to develop a genetic test for Huntington's? He tried to shrug his worries off, since he hadn't even been asked to work with his old friends. But he found himself hoping that they would.

When he left the room, several colleagues gathered to question him about his research and requested prepared copies of his research article. Eloy answered their questions politely, but he was in a hurry to visit Karen's and Don's laboratory, and quickly excused himself. Before he could get away, however, he felt a hand on his shoulder.

"Eloy," a voice said with a slight accent. It was Zoren. "I was very impressed with your paper. Here's my card—call me at NIH. I'd like to talk to you about your research. NIH is very interested in what you're doing. At the moment I am in somewhat of a hurry to get to the Metro to get back to my office. Please excuse me."

"I'm going to NIH too," Eloy said.

"Good. We can ride together and talk a bit."

"I would like that, but can you give me just a few minutes? I need to call Don and Karen to see if it's okay for me to drop by."

"Sure, no problem. I have to step into the men's room."

Eloy called Karen. They agreed to meet at her lab in Building 27 around one o'clock.

A few minutes later, Eloy and Zoren were riding the red line to the Medical Center station.

"Tell me a little more about your research," Zoren said.

Eloy explained his research protocol again, and he could sense Zoren's excitement. He kept interrupting Eloy to ask questions.

Then Zoren said, "You know, we at NIH would like to support your research; however, if you apply for a grant for this project, the paperwork and review would take at least a year, and we couldn't guarantee that you would be funded. Research funds are very tight right now, although we do have expert consultant positions available and could bring you aboard to work in some of our research laboratories." Zoren buttoned his trench coat. "Do you have a coat?"

"No, just this," Eloy responded, smoothing out his sport coat.

Zoren continued, "Just think, you could use your procedure to produce an Alzheimer's-like condition in primates, or even in human cells. The implication of such a research tool is astronomical! What do you think?"

"It would be significant," Eloy said.

They got off the Metro and walked to the long escalator

leading from the subway tracks to the station entrance above ground. Leaves blew into the entrance of the escalator shaft borne on a brisk breeze that tunneled into the station and caused Eloy to shiver. Leaves littered the grounds of NIH. Squirrels scurried across the brown, dormant lawns foraging for food.

"What is that large red brick building there toward the center of campus?" Eloy asked.

"That's Building 10, the Clinical Research Center. That's where the majority of our clinical research occurs. Well, I have to go this way." Zoren nodded to the right. "My office is in Building 31 on the fifth floor in wing C, room 5C31. Make sure you stop by after you have talked to your friends.

"Can you direct me?"

"Building 27 is straight ahead past the Clinical Center. It's one of the more modern-looking buildings on your left, facing Old Georgetown Road."

Eloy continued walking in that direction. When he got closer he asked a dark-skinned woman in a lab coat, "Please, could you tell me where Building 27 is located?"

"Sure, follow me. That's where I'm going." She led Eloy to the building.

When Eloy entered Karen and Don's suite of laboratories, Don was viewing an electrophoretic gel. He dispensed with the formalities of a welcome in his rush to share what he had discovered with Eloy. "Here, Eloy. Let me show you where I found the marker," he said. "There it is, that son of a bitch." He pointed to a dark smear on the polyacrylamide gel.

"Don," Karen interrupted, "not so fast. Let him catch his breath. You didn't even ask him about his presentation."

"It went well," Eloy grinned.

"That's great, Eloy. It's so nice to see you. Welcome to our laboratory." She gave him a hug. Pressed close to her, the aroma of her perfume flooded his senses. For a moment, Eloy thought she held him a little longer than customary and that the embrace communicated more than friendship.

Eloy pulled back and said, "What a lab. I've never seen such equipment."

"Yes, the problem here at NIH isn't equipment, it's space," Karen said, and she gestured to her lab and office in the adjoining room. "We're cramped. Don takes up all the space. You know how equipment-dependent wet bench research is. All that genetic sequencing and separation takes up a lot of valuable laboratory space; but you know, the less important the research, the more equipment required," Karen joked, playfully pinching Don on the arm.

"Yeah," Don retorted, "those of us who do *real* research need equipment. Those number-cruncher statistical types who think they are scientists just because they collect data know nothing about *real* science."

Eloy laughed at their good-natured banter. "Oh, you two, will you ever change?"

How relaxed they are, he thought. How familiar with each other they seemed. How better equipped this laboratory was compared to the laboratories in Venezuela and Puerto Rico.

Now seated at her desk, Karen gestured to Eloy and said, "Come over here. I've got something to propose to you."

Karen's desk was cluttered, in contrast to her neat laboratory back in the old schoolhouse on Lake Maracaibo. Data filled the screen of her computer, and spreadsheets littered her desk, cascading to the floor. She swept some papers from a small, gray, government-issued metal chair with a green naugahyde seat. "Sit down. I just received a call from Zoren at the NIA. He suggested that you be appointed an EC assigned to both NIA and NINDS."

"What?" Eloy's eyes widened. "The government has so many acronyms."

"Yes," Karen smiled, "we love acronyms. Let me translate. An EC is an expert consultant. NIA is the National Institute of Aging, and NINDS is the National Institute of Neurological Disorders and Stroke. You get it? In simple English, will you work with us here at NIH? We're offering you a job."

Eloy's brow wrinkled. "Let me think about it. I would love to, but I need to talk to Dr. Rodríguez. I'll let you know tomorrow."

Eloy was filled with conflict and self-doubt. In his heart, however, Eloy already knew the answer. He was being offered the chance to work toward the cure. He would take the job. No matter what the cost.

CHAPTER 13

When Eloy got back to their room, Dr. Rodríguez was on the telephone, and Maria had the door open to her room. She lay on the bed reading sightseeing brochures. She looked up at Eloy with a smile. "I'm glad you're back, Eloy. I've got something to tell you," she said.

She seemed like her old self. He wondered if she would still treat him so warmly when he told her about his decision.

"I need to talk to you and your father," he replied. "I have some great news, and I need your advice."

Eloy could overhear Dr. Rodríguez on the phone. "Yes, she wants to. She thinks that would be good for her career. Well, Eloy's back. I have to go. *Te amo. Adios.*" Dr. Rodríguez hung up the phone and turned toward Eloy.

Maria came into the room and said, "I have news, too."

"Well, I feel left out," Dr. Rodríguez said. "Eloy, you first."

"Karen, Don and Dr. Zoren Krekorian want me to work at NIH," Eloy blurted. "They are ready to bring me aboard as soon as possible. Dr. Krekorian wants me to help develop an animal or cell culture model for Alzheimer's," he said, smil-ing. "Isn't that great?" He paused to catch his breath. "I want to work with Don and Karen to develop a technique to locate the Huntington's gene. But the sad part," Eloy slowed down, "is that I would have to leave Puerto Rico."

He searched Maria's face for clues to her feelings. Did she care? Did she still love him, or was she relieved that he might be leaving her? She didn't show a hint of emotion.

Dr. Rodríguez clapped his hands. "That's wonderful! We'll miss you, of course, but this is the opportunity of a lifetime!" Then he said, "Maria, tell Eloy your news. I have to go back to my room for something. I'll be back in a couple of min-utes." He walked away, closing the door behind him.

Maria looked down at her clasped hands. "You may have noticed that I have been acting strangely . . ."

Strangely, Eloy thought, that's an understatement.

" . . . But I want you to know that my behavior was not because you had done anything. It's because I have a conflict I've been trying to resolve. I was trying not to like you so that it would be easier for me to leave you."

Eloy's stomach sank. It seemed that she did want to end the relationship.

Maria's eyes widened at the look on Eloy's face. "No, no, let me put this another way. I'm going to be joining the public health service, and I'll probably be working here in Washing-ton in a couple of years, after my residency."

Dr. Rodríguez returned to the room and noticed the look of concern on her face. He put his arm around Maria's shoul-ders. "*Mi hijita*, you look worried."

"Not worried, but I had been thinking that my real strength and interests are in research and administration. I've always had leadership strength. I just talked to my old friend Reuben from medical school. He's now an administrator in the public health service and works just down the street at 4th and C. We had lunch today. He told me about the public health service and said that after I finished my residency in Bayamon, I can work with him here in Washington. Papá, that's why I was so preoccupied."

"You know that I only want what's best for you. Don't think that this old man wants to live his dreams through you. It was long ago that I wanted to be a pediatrician. I'm very happy with my life and research, *mi hijita*. You have your own path to pursue." Dr. Rodríguez kissed his daughter on the forehead and, sensing that she and Eloy wanted to speak in private, left the room.

"Eloy, *mi amor,*" she said, turning her head toward him. "I don't want to leave you."

"I'm so happy for you . . . happy for us. God works in mysterious ways. It even looks like we might be able to be together again one day." But then, realizing the demands of their careers, he added, "Maria, don't take what I'm saying the wrong way. I love you very much, but separation is hard. I don't think it's fair for us to expect to feel obligated to each other. If God wants us to be together, then we will. A love can only grow if it is true."

Feeling that she needed to defend herself, Maria said, "You know how demanding residency programs are, being on call thirty-six hours at a time. We would probably not have time to see each other anyway. Besides, I would never want our relationship to stand in the way of our career goals, especially yours. You're getting close to finding the cure."

Maria continued, "It's only a three-and-a-half-hour flight from San Juan to Washington. We can talk by telephone and see each other when the opportunity arises." She threw her arms around Eloy. Eloy returned the hug weakly. He knew it lacked sincerity, but could she tell? he wondered.

The moment was interrupted by Dr. Rodríguez, who appeared at the doorway and inquired, "Shall we have dinner?"

When they entered the small French restaurant in Georgetown, the smell of garlic and other spices promised an evening of culinary delight. The dinner was excellent and the evening perfect. Eloy couldn't help remembering the dinner in Old San Juan that had started so well but had ended in tragedy.

The conversation flowed freely. Maria seemed to be in good spirits. Eloy and Dr. Rodríguez discussed the time line for Eloy to end his research projects and to train one of Dr. Morales's doctoral students to continue the work.

Eloy and Maria began talking about their own time line. She would begin the residency after *Las Navidades*, the Christmas season. Eloy decided that he could begin his move to NIH around the first of December, in just a couple of weeks.

As they left the restaurant, a cold wind blew off the tidal basin and the Potomac River. The three of them huddled close together for warmth and hailed a cab.

When they arrived at their hotel, Dr. Rodríguez said, "Would you like to have a nightcap before we go to our rooms?"

Eloy sighed, "I'm sorry, Doctor. I'm too tired. And besides, I have to call Karen and tell her my decision."

Maria raised her eyebrows. "Will she be in the laboratory this late?"

"I don't know," Eloy said, "but if she isn't, I have her home number."

"Her home telephone number?" Maria's question had a sharp edge to it.

Eloy sighed. It seemed he couldn't say anything without upsetting her.

"Well, good night, Eloy. I'm going to have a drink," Dr. Rodríguez declared. "Maria, would you care to join me?"

"Sure," she said.

"See you in the morning." Eloy turned and walked toward the elevator, deep in thought about the day's events and Maria's puzzling behavior.

In his room, he called Karen at home and told her he would take the job.

CHAPTER 14

O rville glared at the president sitting so smug and distant behind his desk in the Oval Office.

"Bob, when are you going to put a stop to this antismoking campaign by those public health zealots of yours? You're fooling yourself if you think you were reelected because of your accomplishments. We did it for you. We got you elected. Bob Winston, are you listening to me?" Orville shouted at the president, who slouched in his chair and distractedly drummed his fingers on the desktop. Joe Ray eyed Orville in his rage with a bemused smile.

"By God, sometimes I think you just use your hearing problem as an excuse. Sometimes I think I am just talking to a puppet. I'm serious. We have to do something to shut up your damned surgeon general. Just last year the fool announced the goal of a smoke-free society by the year 2000. What's next? Is the Department of Health and Human Services going to establish smoke-free environments and not allow people to smoke in the workplace?

Joe Ray licked his handlebar mustache and drawled, "Yeah, we need you to get rid of that damned surgeon general."

Joe stopped speaking as Vice President Ray Cole strode in. "What's this? Get rid of Cooper? I couldn't agree more. That Cooper has become a royal pain in the ass. Believe me, if I ever become president, he can kiss his appointment goodbye. Don't you think it's time, Bob?" he said, turning to the president, who didn't respond. His eyes were closed.

"Damn it," Orville snapped. He flashed the sleeping president a dark look and stood up. "What kind of bullshit is this, Ray? Come on, Joe, let's get out of here."

"Shit," Joe said. "If I didn't know better, I'd say this president is going to sleep his way through his entire term."

"Whatever. We'll just have to solve this problem our way." The senator reached the door, and the president's Secret Service agent opened it for him. "Yeah, we'll handle it *our* way," Orville repeated to Joe with a sly smile as they exited.

The flight to Puerto Rico was uneventful and productive. Eloy and Dr. Rodríguez finalized plans for a smooth transfer of Eloy's research projects to the new research assistant. Eloy and Maria discussed the separate but parallel paths they would take in the coming months. As excited as Eloy was about returning to the United States, and as happy as he was for Maria, in his heart he dreaded the moment they would say goodbye.

When they arrived home, Rosa Rodríguez welcomed her husband and daughter warmly. Eloy didn't even receive a polite hello. Over coffee and pastries, Rosa learned of Maria and Eloy's plans. Rosa regarded Eloy superciliously as she clasped her daughter's hand. "You are so smart to move on with your life, *mi hijita*. You deserve only the best!" Her words sliced Eloy's heart.

Over the next several days, Eloy showed Oswaldo, the doctoral student, the cell culture procedures and research protocols necessary to continue with his project.

His relationship with Maria was another matter. One moment she seemed very close and loving, the next moment she acted distant and cold. Their strained relationship kept him in constant confusion. In some ways Eloy felt eager to leave. He was anxious not only to begin his new research career but to put some distance between him and Maria.

On the day of his departure, before he left for the airport, Eloy took Maria in his arms and held her close to him. "I don't know how to say this. . . . you probably feel the same way. I don't know what's happening to us. One moment I sense that you love me, but the next I don't know."

"*Sí*, I feel the same way. I'm unsure." Maria hesitated, then turned away from him. "Maybe it's good that we spend some time alone. The separation will allow us to see more clearly what direction we are each going." She looked deeply in his eyes, then hugged him tightly.

"Oh, Eloy, it's so hard."

"Don't worry. I love you." Eloy kissed her forehead. "I'll write and see you when I can. Besides, I'll be coming back to Puerto Rico in the spring during *Semana Santa*."

"Eloy, come on. It's time to go!" Dr. Rodríguez bustled into the room. "Maria, are you coming with us?"

"No," Maria replied. "Please, Papá, just give me a moment with Eloy."

"*Sí, mi hijita*."

When they were alone, Maria looked at Eloy intently. Her large green eyes sparkled with fervor. "Oh, Eloy, I do truly love you. Please remember our love and our two years together. If our love is to die or if our love is to live, it is in the hands of God. *Lo que Dios quiera.*"

"Yes. *Adios, mi amor,*" Eloy said and parted from her with a final kiss. He picked up his suitcase, bit at his lip and left with Dr. Rodríguez.

CHAPTER 15

December 1986

It was snowing when the airplane landed at National Airport. He had never seen snow before. This had been a month of so many firsts: his first plane ride, his first major scientific meeting, his first romantic contretemps, his first experience in a non-Latino culture, his first research project on his own. That is, from now on his research responsibilities were his and his alone; they would not be directed by a research mentor.

And now his first snow. He reached out to touch the snowflakes with his hands, tasted them with his tongue, and felt their cold softness. But a rude woman brought him back to reality as she pushed through a group of people waiting to catch a taxi, muttering, "Go on, move it. Get out of my way. Foreigners."

The air smelled fresh, despite the heavy airport traffic. Eloy couldn't believe how cold it was. The cold penetrated his thin sport coat and settled deep in his bones. He shivered. Was it due to the weather, or was it a coldness born of loneliness—the aloneness he felt in this new place on this new adventure?

Eloy found the shuttle to the Metro station. The crowd pushed him on board, and the windows quickly fogged over with their warm breath. The bus was quiet, an unnerving contrast to the públicos in San Juan or the subway in Caracas. People didn't even say hello or acknowledge each other.

Eloy boarded the Metro and took the blue line to Metro Center, where he transferred to the red line to Shady Grove.

When Eloy exited at the Medical Center station, he looked around at the snow-covered campus of NIH and saw Karen waving to him from across the street. He ran to the van she was driving, his hands freezing. He had never needed gloves before.

"I'm so glad you're here. Welcome to NIH." She gave him a big hug, again embracing him a little longer than expected.

"It's so cold here," Eloy exclaimed, abruptly pulling away.

"Get in." Karen opened the passenger side door. The van was as cluttered as her office. Ream after ream of computer printouts, journal articles and fast food wrappers littered the floor and seats.

"Here, sit down." She pushed some journal articles off the passenger seat.

"Zoren has reserved a room for you at the Marriott Hotel," she said, turning left onto the Rockville Pike. The NIH campus extended to the left. The large, red brick clinical center was dusted with snow. On his right rose the Naval Hospital, its imposing tower piercing the dark gray sky.

Just before the beltway, Karen turned left onto Polk's Hill Road and into the Marriott Hotel. "Forgive me, but I only have time to drop you off. I have to get back to the lab and home before the snow gets worse. You have no idea how horrible Washingtonians drive in the snow. Zoren will pick you up at eight tomorrow."

"No problem. I'm just glad to be here."

"Sleep well," she replied. Did she wink or was it a twitch?

Precisely at 8 A.M. Zoren met Eloy in the lobby of the hotel. "Go ahead, finish your coffee. We don't need to rush."

"I just can't get used to this American coffee. It's so weak and tasteless. I have to find some good, strong Puerto Rican coffee."

Zoren chuckled. "Weak coffee probably won't be the only change. How do you like this weather?" They chatted aimlessly as they drove to the NIH parking lot off Cedar Avenue behind Building 31.

Zoren introduced Eloy to the personnel administrator, a heavyset black woman with a no-nonsense attitude. She shoved a stack of papers at him and instructed him to fill in all the blanks.

Zoren shook Eloy's hand before departing. "Well, good luck! Call me this afternoon when you're through. I'll be in my office until 5:00, then I can take you back to the hotel."

Eloy looked puzzled. Would it really take all day just to fill out papers? He was anxious to talk to Don and Karen. He only wanted to work. His fears of a mountain of paperwork to complete were soon realized.

The personnel administrator said firmly, "I said, 'Fill out these papers.' Do I have to repeat myself?"

Eloy hurriedly filled out the papers, and within thirty minutes returned to the administrator looking hopeful. She raised an eyebrow and sized him up, then scanned each page, looking for any blanks he had missed. "It looks okay." She shrugged almost with disappointment, but when Eloy turned to leave she grabbed his arm roughly. "Wait a minute! You're not through yet. Go down to the basement. You have to be fingerprinted and have a federal government security background check."

Eloy froze. He'd been told nothing about a background check. Would his dreams finally be shattered after coming all this way? Did Manuel's friend in Puerto Rico prepare the papers properly, or would the government discover his secret?

"I said, 'Go down to the basement, get your fingerprints and background check.' When you have all of that taken care of, then catch the shuttle to Westwood building 673 to fill out your paperwork for NINDS. Here, give the personnel officer at NINDS these forms."

When Eloy didn't move, she waved him toward the door. "Go on! You'll never get done if you don't start moving!"

Eloy moved, but fear still gnawed at his gut. Exiting the elevator at basement level 3, the heels of his shoes clicked on the hard, black marble floor. The echo sounded to Eloy like cries of fear.

The clerk, a rather large, heavyset woman who looked like the sister of the personnel administrator he just left, grabbed Eloy's hand to ink his fingers and thumb. He hoped she wouldn't notice how much he was perspiring.

"Boy, you sure have sweaty palms. What did you do, run down the stairs to get your security check?" she asked.

"No. I'm just a little nervous. All of this paperwork."

"Don't worry. It's a formality. Most of this stuff just goes into a file unless you do something wrong or need to do sensitive classified research."

"Oh, I see."

Eloy caught the Westwood building shuttle. The ride gave him time to calm down. They passed large homes on palatial lots. Some of the homes were decorated for Christmas. Thoughts of the holidays with his family back home in Maracaibo warmed him inside, despite the feeling of homesickness stirred up by the memories.

The process at the Westwood building was just as complex as at NIA. Why couldn't he simply copy the forms he had filled out for the NIA? Why repeat this entire process for NINDS? It was just wasting his time, he thought, and increasing his chances of getting caught.

Arriving at Zoren's door precisely at 5:00, Eloy complained, "What a day! I can't believe the amount of paperwork I had to deal with. Why did they need my fingerprints?"

"It's just routine," Zoren smiled. "At least that part's over."

"I sure hope the daily work is easier than coming aboard."

"Working here at NIH is like going to college. The registration process is worse than the actual course work. Now that you've finished the paperwork, you can start your research."

"You know, I didn't even get a chance to talk to Don or Karen."

"That's okay. I've already met with them and the chief of the Alzheimer's research intramural program, Dr. Roger Atkins. I scheduled a meeting for tomorrow to discuss your role here at NIH."

It sounded so official to Eloy. He again wondered if it had been a good idea to come here.

"Let's go," Zoren urged. "I want to get home before the weather gets much worse. Traffic is unbearable. Look. The snow is already beginning to fall."

After Zoren dropped him off at the hotel, Eloy stepped into the restaurant and had dinner. When he returned to his room, the message light on the telephone was blinking.

CHAPTER 16

The next morning Eloy waited in the hotel lobby, eager for his first day at NIH to begin. Maybe today, he thought, I can start working, or at least find out where I am going to work and with whom.

Zoren arrived promptly at eight, but Eloy was already pacing outside. The snow had stopped, and the air was crisp and invigorating. For the first time, Eloy felt optimistic about his new home, the climate, and even the city's strange people.

"Did you get my message last night?"

"Oh, no," Eloy groaned. "I remember seeing the message light flashing on the telephone, but I forgot to retrieve it. Was it important?"

"Well, I wanted to tell you a little about Roger Atkins, the chief of Alzheimer's research, before you meet him. He is not the easiest person in the world to work with. He's a good scientist but lacks any social skills, and his ego is much larger than he is. But don't worry, if things go as planned, in a couple of years we may be able to find a laboratory for you."

Eloy tried to make light of Zoren's comments. "Yes, with every good comes a little bad," he quipped.

"It's not as bad as that. Roger means well. He's just difficult to work with. He's very short in stature, but in his mind he's a research giant. Don't tell him I said this, but we refer to him as Napoleon." Zoren's accented voice crackled with a touch of laughter. "Oh, by the way, Karen thinks she has found you a condominium in her building. It seems that one of her neighbors who works at NIH is going on leave for a couple of years. Karen says it's a nice one-bedroom on one of the higher floors with a view north to Gaithersburg toward the Parklawn building and not too far from a Metro stop."

"Sounds good. I can't wait to settle in and start working and buy myself some warm clothes, especially gloves."

Zoren reached into the glove compartment to retrieve a pair. "Here, you can use these."

"You're probably the only person I have ever known who actually keeps gloves in the glove compartment," Eloy said with a chuckle. He tried to use humor to lessen the nervousness he felt about the impending meeting with Roger. "Thanks for the gloves," he added.

"Well, here we are," Zoren said as they turned into the parking lot. Walking up to the doorway of Building 31, Eloy was surprised to see a large group of people huddled outside in the cold, smoking.

"Why are they outside?" Eloy asked.

"The Department of Health and Human Services is trying to institute a smoke-free environment in all of the HHS facilities. Rumor has it that this policy is to be in place by 1987, but I doubt it."

"Boy, these people must really be hooked if they are willing to freeze out here just to smoke."

Don and Karen gave Eloy a warm welcome. Dr. Roger Atkins stood up and stared awkwardly at Eloy, who couldn't help noticing how short the older man was—even shorter than Eloy. Roger was wearing his laboratory coat, and his posture was rigid. "Welcome to NIH," he said, his mouth forming a sarcastic smile, and didn't offer to shake Eloy's hand. Eloy shuddered and forced a smile. Zoren's description had been an understatement. Karen tried to break the ice.

"Eloy, coffee?" Karen asked as she handed the coffee pot to him.

"Yes, thanks." Eloy poured some coffee into a styrofoam cup and wrapped it with his hands to warm them. It's going to be a long, cold meeting, he thought.

CHAPTER 17

Eloy didn't like the tenor of the discussion. Every time he interjected an idea or suggested a new research direction, Roger countered with a reason why it wouldn't work. It appeared that Roger was deliberately trying to make him look naive and inept. Whenever Eloy referred to his hypothesis that the clue to inducing an Alzheimer's state in an animal model was best approached at the molecular or cellular level, Roger dismissed the idea with a wave of his hand.

"How can you say that your atropine studies demonstrating blockage of the muscarinic receptors and the resultant lower levels of acetylcholine and cell death have anything remotely to do with the memory loss in Alzheimer's? How pedestrian."

"Roger . . . ," Eloy began to protest.

Roger snapped his crooked teeth. "My name is *Doctor* Roger Atkins, a title I have earned, a title I deserve. You haven't earned a doctorate, and your limited formal training was done in Third World countries. I don't understand how you dare think of yourself as a professional. I must say, Zoren, in all honesty, I don't have as much faith in this young man as you do. His lack of a Ph.D. and postdoctoral training are an insult to the NIH. An insult."

Eloy had no idea that Roger would be so difficult. He had tried to smooth things over by quietly stating, "I only think it's time for a new approach if we are ever going to produce an animal model."

"Are you implying that the years I have used surgical techniques to attempt to produce an animal model are wasted? How dare you!" Roger waved his fist in the air.

Zoren intervened, holding his hand up. "Roger, calm down. Eloy is here to work with you as an expert consultant in the lab. He's here to work with Don and Karen on developing a diagnostic test to detect the presence of the gene for Huntington's. We need to welcome Eloy, to work as a team."

"I don't want him as part of my research team," Roger snorted. "We have been developing Alzheimer's models surgically for years. You've seen the results of our work—they are significant. Producing surgical lesions in the fimbria fornix of the rat brain has induced the degeneration of the acetylcholine cells. Our model is tried and true. Zoren, you of all people know that the fimbria fornix corresponds to the basal forebrain in humans, which is a major site of acetylcholine degeneration in Alzheimer's."

"Well, yes," Zoren said, "but Roger, it doesn't work when you try it in a primate model."

Roger huffed and glared at Zoren. "Damn it, Zoren, you always bring that up whenever you can. We are trying very hard to produce the same results in primates, and every chance you get you remind us of our failure. It's those damn monkeys . . . they're all lab monkeys. Those damn animal care facilities are probably contaminated with God knows what. Discussion over. I'm going back to my lab. I will not be subjected to ridicule." Roger rose up and strode in a huff to the door. "And, oh, have the 'expert consultant' report to my postdoctoral student, Donna. I won't waste my time with him. These molecular-cell types . . . what do they know about real nerve research?" He slammed the door.

Eloy blew out his pent-up breath. "Zoren, I think this is a mistake. I don't think I can work in their lab."

"Let me talk to the director. It might be best for you to work with Don and Karen first, and then you can work on the Alzheimer's model. Why don't we just split up the year— six months with Don and Karen, six months with Roger's group?"

"Sounds like a good idea to me," Eloy responded.

"Yeah, same with us," Don echoed.

"I know Roger," Zoren continued. "After he realizes you are here to stay he'll be more agreeable. He sees everyone as a threat, especially young scientists such as yourself."

"I hope you're right."

"Okay, meeting adjourned." Zoren slapped the tabletop with the palm of his hand. "Don, take Eloy over to your lab and get him started. I know he'll hit the ground running. I'm looking forward to his assistance in finding the Huntington's gene."

"Before we go back to the lab, let's stop for an early lunch," Karen suggested.

"Sounds like a good idea. I could eat a horse," Don said.

"Be careful what you say," Karen joked, "because for all you know, in that cafeteria, what you eat might actually be a horse."

On their way to the cafeteria Eloy sidled up to her and said, "I want to thank you for recommending your friend's apartment at the Forum. I don't have to see it. Just tell the real estate agent that I'll take it. You said you had the key, right?"

"Yes."

"Good. I think I'll sleep there tonight. Would that be okay?"

"Sure. You can either sleep there," she said teasingly, "or you can always sleep at my place!"

"Oh, no, that would be inconvenient," Eloy replied seriously.

"You old dog," Don said. "Don't believe Karen. She was just teasing. She wasn't really inviting you to spend the night. Right, Karen?"

"Who knows?" she said, winking. "Oh, before I forget, we need to get you some warm clothes. When we go home tonight, we can stop off at the mall." She looked at her watch. "I have to go back to the Building 31 conference room. They are getting ready for some grant reviews, and I have to look at a couple of proposals. See you around four."

Eloy looked around the large cafeteria filled with white-coated scientists and lab assistants and felt better, more at home with his peers.

After lunch, Eloy pushed his tray aside. "Don, what's with that little Napoleon?"

"I see, my little *amigo*, you've figured out why we call him Napoleon. Just ignore the bastard. You don't have to even think about working in Roger's lab until the summer, if Zoren gets his way. And you'll like working with Donna. She's a quality researcher, and it will be productive. See that good-looking, dark-haired woman, the one with glasses, the one who fills those white pants . . . what an ass. *Que bella*. That's Donna. I would introduce you to her, but it looks like she is getting ready to leave, and we have to go too."

That afternoon Don told Eloy a little bit more about their research project. He mentioned how back in 1983 he first suspected that he had found a marker for the Huntington's gene on chromosome four. Finding the marker was almost as good as finding the gene. He was pretty sure that he had also located the gene.

"Well, if you *have* found the marker, it should be relatively easy to develop a procedure to identify either the marker and/or the gene."

"One would think so, *mi amigo*, but, as you know, to go from theory to actual development can be a long, hard road."

"What techniques have you used?"

"First we had to take a sample of blood from the individuals in question. Because Karen located so many affected people in your village, it was easy for me to extract the DNA. Then, using various techniques, including polymerase chain reactions, I made literally billions of copies of the gene fragments I wanted to study. I used restriction enzymes to cut the DNA molecule at specific locations in the nucleotide sequence, and I took those DNA fragments to polymorphize the DNA segments. This is what they call the RFLP techniques; you know, *riflip*. Are you familiar with it?"

Eloy nodded, "You know, I thought I was up on my techniques, but I've never really done RFLPs or PCRs, and I'm anxious to learn."

"I guess we have a place to start, then. Tomorrow I'll have one of the technicians take you through the procedures. Before you know it, you'll be an expert at it."

Putting his arm around Eloy, he said, "It's good to have you here. Who knows, *mi amigo*, you may find the cure. If not the cure, at least the way to determine whether the gene is present or not."

After Roger's cold reception, Don's warm words were like a balm to Eloy. Zoren also called Don to confirm that Eloy could start working with him and Karen.

Karen returned to the lab. "Don gave you an overview of his research?" she queried Eloy, then instructed him, "Come into my office. I need to get my purse. Where are my keys? We can go to the White Flint Mall to find you some warm clothes. Boy, it's getting cold out there."

In Karen's office, large pedigrees were laid out on display boards attached to the walls, along with numerous pictures of the villagers, the people of Eloy's home, some friends. The familiar faces brought a wave of nostalgia. Then he noticed the shaded circles and squares in the pedigrees, symbolizing the individuals who had the gene.

Karen noticed the distance and sadness in Eloy's eyes. "Homesick?" she asked. She rubbed his back, then winked. "Don't mope. A little shopping, a good drink and my company will cheer you up!"

Eloy had thought that the shopping center in San Juan called the Plaza de las Americas was upscale. But he had never seen so many fashionable stores in one place as in Washington, D.C.

"You know, I don't need anything fancy," he protested. "I just need a warm coat and gloves. Why don't we go down the street to K-mart?"

"K-mart my foot. You're a respected scientist, and we're going to dress you like one!"

They went into Bloomingdale's, and Karen took charge, making sure that Eloy was not only warm but that his apparel was top of the line.

"I'm sorry," he said, "but I haven't been paid yet. I can't afford all these things."

"Don't worry, I'll pay. Here." She gave her credit card to the cashier. "It's on me."

"No," Eloy said firmly as he tried to retrieve the card. "What do I owe you?"

"Think of this as a gift, a favor between friends. You owe me nothing."

A favor between friends, he thought, remembering Manuel and the old oil tanker. A favor between friends. Was Karen like Manuel? No, she couldn't be. She helped him, but she was acting strange. Eloy vowed to repay the debt as soon as he received his first paycheck.

CHAPTER 18

K aren lifted her martini glass and looked around. "Where's the waitress?" she whispered, and moved her head closer to Eloy. She sucked on an olive and played with it in her mouth. When the waitress came to their table, Karen drained the rest of her martini. "Two more martinis, please."

"No. No more for me," Eloy said.

"No problem. I wanted both of them anyway."

"I think you've had enough," Eloy said, handing the empty glasses to the waitress. She soon returned with the martinis, and Eloy watched as Karen removed one of the olives, popped it into her mouth and toyed with it suggestively as she looked at him.

"Come on," he said, "it's time to go home."

Her fingers tightened around the stem of the glass while she quickly drank it down. She immediately swallowed the second martini in one quick gulp. "Now I'm ready. Let's go." Trying to get up from the table, she fell toward Eloy and he caught her. She pressed herself against him, but he pulled away from her.

"We'd better get home. Tomorrow will be a busy day."

"Not as busy as tonight!" Karen teased with a sly smile.

Uh-oh. I think I'm in for trouble, Eloy thought. "Do you mind if I drive? You've had a lot to drink."

"Good. You drive. I'll give directions." She dropped her keys into his outstretched palm. "Just go north on the Rockville Pike. You'll see it on your right."

As they drove up the Rockville Pike toward the Forum, Karen put her head in his lap. Eloy didn't know if it was an attempt at seduction or just the effect of the alcohol. He breathed a little easier when she made no further moves, and they reached the apartment complex without incident. But when they caught the elevator to go up to her floor, Karen staggered. Eloy held her arm as they entered her condominium.

"Where is the key for my apartment?" he wanted to know.

"In my purse," she slurred. "Come in for a night cap first."

He noticed that she was trembling as he backed out of the doorway. "No, I don't think so."

"Don't go. Come in." She pulled him back into the apartment. "Sit down while I go tinkle. Pour yourself a drink. I'll be just a minute."

Her apartment was tastefully furnished, but finding a place to sit was a problem. Her apartment was as cluttered as her office.

"Eloy," Karen called from the bedroom, "please bring me a glass of white wine."

Eloy's stomach fell as he struggled to reply. "Sorry, but I have to go. Have a good night's sleep." He grabbed his shopping bags and quickly closed the door behind him, then broke into a brisk walk toward the elevator.

He couldn't understand Karen. What did she want from

him? For a moment he thought he should return to her apartment. Maybe he should sleep with her. After all, he was a man, and she was willing. But he didn't want sex. He wanted Karen as a friend. Why did sex change things? he wondered. Never mind. She had probably already passed out. He thought suddenly about Maria . . . , but enough about sex, enough about women!

Eloy felt the apartment on the eleventh floor was a refuge even though it was the first time he had seen it. He liked it, and he would sublet it. Not only was it furnished, but it came with a complete library of books on every topic, from protein biochemistry to self-help psychology to investing. He lay on the couch, turned on the ster-eo and listened to music.

As he teetered between sleep and wakefulness, he thought about Karen and her strange behavior. Was she coming on to him, or was she just drunk? How would he deal with her when he saw her again? Why was she so disorganized? He had never seen such a messy office, car or apartment. Tomorrow he would pick up his things from the hotel and move in, but now he just wanted to sleep.

The next day Eloy left his apartment and boarded the Metro for the short ride to the Medical Center station. The walk across the campus to Building 27 was exhilarating. It was cold, but he was dressed warmly, thanks to Karen. He wondered about the events of the previous night. Karen knew he was in a relationship with Maria. But was he really in love with Maria? How sure of his feelings was he? Did Karen sense that he might have sexual feelings toward her? He entered the lab more confused than ever.

Don was busy as usual. "Here, *mi amigo*. Come in. Let me introduce you to our technician, Tyrone. He's working here for a couple of years to earn a little money to go back and finish his Ph.D. in biochemistry and molecular biology at Purdue."

Tyrone was a lively African American with an infectious smile. He loved to talk and tell stories, Eloy eventually learned.

"Tyrone, I want you to teach Eloy some RFLP and PCR techniques. *Comprende?*"

"Yes, boss," Tyrone joked. "Welcome to the lab," he said while shaking Eloy's hand. "First, we use some restriction enzymes to cleave our DNA sample at specific nucleotide sequences. Then we place the fragments on one end of our polyacrylamide gel, turn on the current and, because the phosphate groups in the DNA have a charge, the DNA fragments move through the gel. Large pieces move slower, smaller fragments move faster. As they separate they form bands. In essence, we are just using a modification of electrophoresis. The DNA has been labeled with a fluorescent dye, so these fragments form a luminous banding pattern that can be viewed under ultraviolet light. Because there are variations in the length of these restriction fragments—polymorphisms—we can compare the variations from one person to another. These procedures can be used to develop a unique DNA fingerprinting test that allows us to identify the source of the DNA."

"Oh, yeah. I remember talking to my former mentor, Dr. Rodríguez, about DNA fingerprinting."

"Remember," Tyrone said, "be careful of electrical current when running a gel."

"Eloy nodded. "I'm familiar with electrophoresis, both two-dimensional and western blotting and several variations. I have also done a lot of chromatography," he said. "I'm familiar with the manual techniques, and now I can see that a lot of the separation can be automated with the instruments you have here in the lab."

Tyrone smiled approvingly. "You'll learn easily."

"Where's Karen?" Eloy asked Don.

"She called in and said she would be working at home today. There are some advantages to doing paper-and-pencil research rather than real wet-bench research like us. We need equipment and instrumentation. All Karen needs is her computer and some data to do her number crunching," Don said facetiously.

"Yeah, good ol' Karen." Relief flooded over Eloy. He didn't want to see her today. He couldn't figure her out.

Two weeks later, Eloy decided to give Maria a call from the laboratory. He still hadn't taken the time to have the phone in his apartment transferred to his name. He couldn't believe that in the two weeks he had been at the NIH, he had only called Dr. Rodríguez once to say he'd arrived and to give him his laboratory phone number and address and to ask him to contact his brother to say he was okay. He hadn't even taken the time to give them his new address. His life was lived in the lab.

Maria answered the telephone with a cheerful *"Hola,"* but when Eloy responded, her voice turned cold.

"Oh, hello, Eloy. Is that you?"

Uh-oh, Eloy thought, here we go again. In spite of the tension, he quickly brought her up to date with the work in the laboratory. Maria told him about her preparation to begin her residency at Hospital San Pablo in Bayamon. The conversation was very businesslike, with very little talk about personal issues. Eloy thought he could probably get a warmer reaction from Dr. Atkins.

"I have to go," Maria said as the conversation faltered.

"So do I . . . *adios*," Eloy said, more confused than ever.

That evening when he arrived at his apartment there was

a note on the door from Karen, inviting him to a Christmas party in Potomac, an exclusive community in Montgomery County near Bethesda. The party was on Friday night. She also asked him to stop by for a drink when he got home. Eloy took the elevator down to the lobby and called Karen from the pay phone.

"Hello, Eloy. Did you get my message?" He thought she sounded as if she had already been drinking.

"Yes. I don't think I can go to the party. . . . You know I'm busy."

"Oh, come on. If you don't, I'll come right up there and force . . . ce . . . ce you," she stammered.

"Okay, I guess. Yes. I would be happy to go to the party. See you tomorrow night," he said with some reluctance.

"Can't you come over tonight?"

"No, sorry. I'm very busy, and I have things to do—moving in and all. I haven't even transferred the phone to my name yet. I'm calling from the lobby."

"You still haven't settled in? Can I help? I wish you could come over."

"Thank you, but I have to go," Eloy said, hanging up the phone.

On Friday, the pace of work was slow. Eloy couldn't believe that Christmas was only two days away. At least he would have time to get himself and his apartment organized. In Puerto Rico Fridays were *Viernes social*, devoted to social events with family and friends. Here in the United States, people seemed indifferent. For Eloy, however, tonight was *Viernes social*. He was going to a party with Karen.

The party was given by an old friend of Karen's, a Senator Blackman from New York, whom she had met when she went to school there. Senator Blackman served on the board of directors of the Woodie Guthrie Foundation, which had funded her first research trip to Lake Maracaibo among other projects.

The gray stone house was huge, and looked more like a palace than a home. An attendant parked the van. Eloy and Karen could hear the sound of music and festivities emanating from the house. Inside, a large foyer led to a large room gaily decorated for the holidays. Karen wore a simple cocktail dress that revealed her figure. Eloy thought she looked stunning. He wore his best suit, which actually seemed to him a little too casual for this event.

"I didn't realize that this was going to be so formal. I don't know any of these people. I must be the youngest person here. I really feel out of place."

"You look just fine. In a moment I'll introduce you to Senator Blackman. I had a special reason to bring you to this party."

He wondered what she was referring to, but didn't ask.

"Have a glass of bubbly." Karen lifted two champagne flutes off of a cocktail tray carried by a passing waiter and handed one to Eloy. She quickly emptied her glass and picked up another.

She pushed her way through the crowd in search of their host. She stopped when she reached a very distinguished-looking gentleman with a full head of gray hair who looked like Phil Donahue. "Come here, Eloy."

"Karen," Senator Blackman said as he gave her a kiss on the cheek, "I'm so glad you could come. Did you bring him?"

"I sure did." Karen gestured to Eloy to step forward. Eloy had never met such a dignified person. Senator Blackman had an aura of power about him.

"I want to introduce you to Senator Blackman," Karen said.

"Pleased to meet you, sir," Eloy said.

"Pleased to meet you!" Senator Blackman extended his hand and gave Eloy a strong, firm handshake. "Karen has told me a lot about you," he said, motioning to the band leader to stop the music.

Stepping to the microphone, Senator Blackman said, "Ladies and gentlemen, I have a special announcement to make. I would like to introduce you to Eloy Córdova Santiago from the Lake Maracaibo region of Venezuela, now working as a neurological disease researcher at the NIH.

"Before I get to the reason we are here tonight, I want to say something about the Woodie Guthrie Foundation. The foundation was created by the family and friends of the famous folk singer, who died of Huntington's disease in the late 1960s at Creedman State Hospital in Queen's Village, New York.

"Back in 1978, Gene Stein, one of our grant administrators, told me about a young, passionate, determined investigator who had called him. She complained that the federal agencies had turned down her research on familial genetic histories of Huntington's in the native peoples of Lake Maracaibo because she was a self-taught geneticist. The NIMH said that because she was young and inexperienced, she would have to establish more of a research record in order to be funded. That's why we have our foundation. We don't have to deal with that federal red tape, which sometimes delays scientific progress because of the layers of bureaucracy to contend with. I'm glad to say that we funded that young researcher, Dr. Karen Williams. Her contribution toward finding a cure for Huntington's makes us all proud." Senator Blackman put his arm around Karen.

"Oh, as usual, I digress. As I said before, I want to introduce you to Eloy Córdova Santiago." He walked over to Eloy.

"Years ago Eloy rescued Karen from an aircraft that had crashed into Lake Maracaibo and was sinking. He risked his life to save Karen, and she in turn taught Eloy and inspired him to follow her in the quest for a cure for Huntington's. At his young age, Eloy is already on his way to making major contributions to our understanding of neurological degenerative diseases like Alzheimer's, Huntington's and others. Thank you for your work. And to everyone, Merry Christmas and happy holidays!" he said, raising his glass to drink a toast to Eloy. The crowd applauded.

"Thank you," Eloy said, slightly embarrassed, then turned to Karen. "So that's why you wanted me to come to the party."

"I am so proud of you. Ever since I told Senator Blackman about you, he has wanted to meet you. He insisted that I bring you tonight."

Senator Blackman patted Eloy on the shoulder. "I wish I could spend more time talking to you, but I have many people to greet. Enjoy yourself. Eat, drink, and dance." A thin elderly man with glasses approached Senator Blackman.

"Oh, by the way, Karen, Eloy," the senator said, "I would like to introduce you to Senator Orville Reynolds. Orville, meet Karen Williams and Eloy Córdova Santiago."

"Nice to meet you," Senator Reynolds said, his bow tie bobbing on his prominent Adam's apple. "This is my aide, Joe Ray."

"I think I met you, my little friend, at that scientific meeting at the Hyatt before Thanksgiving. You're a brain scientist from Venezuela," Joe said, twisting his mustache.

"Yes. You have a good memory."

"Well, yes, I do have a good memory, but it's probably only because my grandma has a poor memory. That poor little thing has dementia, you know. Remember I told you?"

"Yes," Orville added pompously. "Joe has mentioned his grandmother's health condition several times. I only hope your scientific experiments are fruitful. We would all like to see a cure for those dreadful neurological disorders."

"Let's dance!" Karen interjected and abruptly pulled Eloy to the dance floor. It had been a while since he had last danced with Maria. He had forgotten the scent and the touch of a woman. Karen looked attractive and sexy. She pressed her body close to him and then even closer. He responded by caressing her smooth skin. She trembled.

"We should go. I'm getting tired," she muttered. Karen's face looked weary, her neck muscles were tense and her hands jerked. "I think I drank too much. Please drive me home. I don't feel well."

The drive was silent. Karen had fallen asleep with her head in his lap. He couldn't help but notice her long graceful neck leading down to her breasts, and he gently ran his hand through her beautiful blonde hair. Oh, my friend, my friend, he thought, why do you drink so much?

CHAPTER 19

The holidays were lonely for Eloy. He missed his family. He wanted to call them, but Mamá didn't have a phone at home—the only phone in the village was in the church—so he had only been able to communicate with them through letters. He looked forward to the new year and returning to a normal work schedule. He decided to read, organize his apartment and spend time in the lab. Karen and Don invited him to several parties, but he thought it would be best to keep his friendships more on a professional level, especially with Karen.

Eloy felt sorry for Karen. Maybe she drank to forget her uncertain future. Maybe his sorrow was not only for Karen. She was older, and she would know sooner than he would. The uncertainty of genetics was a terrible cross to bear.

Toward the end of January 1988, Eloy and Tyrone made a major breakthrough. He told Don, "I think we have developed a diagnostic test with the potential to detect the presence of the marker for Huntington's. It's a modification of the gel electrophoresis technique that you developed."

"Great," Don said, "but *mi* little *amigo*, why so sad? I thought you would be happy to find more markers for the gene."

"Oh, I'm happy," Eloy responded with forced enthusiasm.

"But you look preoccupied," Don said.

"Let's show Don what we're finding." Eloy motioned to Tyrone to get the gels.

"I've been so damned busy trying to run this lab and deal with all the bureaucratic bullshit that I haven't kept up with your research," Don said.

Tyrone returned with the gels and handed them to Don.

"Tell me about your procedure," Don said.

"You know how you were first able to find the marker? We used a similar technique," Eloy said. "We modified the position between the base sequences in the DNA, then we used the restriction enzyme to cut the DNA at specific nitrogen base sequences. Finally, using gel electrophoresis to separate the fragments, we locate the gene or its marker by comparing the lengths of the bars on the gel. Here, Don, look at this gel . . . you can see that the male, the father, has Huntington's. Here it is." He pointed to a fluorescent spot on the gel.

"I see it."

"His wife is homozygous normal. Look at her pattern—no Huntington's. Now look at this. This is the blood that was drawn from their unborn child, using amniocentesis." Eloy handed Don the gel and continued, "Because the father had Huntington's and the mother was normal, the probability of their developing child having the disease is 50 percent. Look at this gel . . . this is the column of the child."

"*Mi amigo*, I know why you're concerned! The kid has the fluorescent blur. It has the marker."

"Yes, he has Huntington's," Eloy said quietly. "But now that we know, what do we do with that knowledge? Should we tell the parents that their child has Huntington's and will die from it? Or shouldn't we? Is death the end to it?"

"Yeah, what good is knowing if we can't offer a cure? How do you lead a normal life? Would you want to know?" Don asked Eloy. "Oh, shit, *mi amigo*, forgive me. I forgot that your father had the gene."

"At least now I can find out if I have it."

Tyrone looked at Don and Eloy. "Come on, you guys. This is getting way too serious."

"Yes," Eloy said.

"Let's go over to Tacoma Park, and take Eloy to see his *compadres*," Don said. A lot of Central and South Americans lived in the Tacoma Park region on the Maryland/D.C. line, and there were many ethnic restaurants and shops. "You need to get some good Latino food."

Over lunch Don said, "Let's not talk shop, okay?" He glanced at Eloy. "Eloy, lighten up. Life isn't just work. Look at all of those good-looking *señoritas* giving you the eye. Hell, you need a good woman to get you out of the blues. Tyrone, let's take my *amigo* downtown and find him a girlfriend."

"Nah," Eloy said hesitantly. "You know, I have Maria."

"Sure," Don said. "If you really loved her, you'd be calling her up, writing to her, talking about her. Hell, you've done nothing. You spend more time with Karen than with Maria. Come with us."

They took Eloy to one of the many strip bars that catered to the luncheon crowd of federal workers and out-of-town conventioneers on M Street near 14th. The smoky bar was filled with bored-looking men staring at equally bored, naked, gyrating dancers.

"Let's have a round of drinks," Don said to the topless waitress. "I'll have a gin and tonic," he said, eyeing her breasts intently. After Eloy and Tyrone ordered their drinks, Don asked, "Have you ever seen such perfect tits?"

Eloy, pretending to be interested, said, "Oh, yes, what a fine woman!"

"'Fine woman,' *mi amigo*? If that's all you can say, I think you've been away from women too long—or never with one!" Don teased.

The topless waitress wanted to perform a lap dance for Eloy. It was as if she could sense his disinterest. "Come on, let me sit on your lap," she said, shaking her shapely hips and breasts in his face.

"At least give her some money," Don said, reaching over and slipping a five-dollar bill into her green-sequined G-string.

Eloy remembered Maria, their love making and her beautiful body. He shook the memory out of his mind and ordered another round of drinks. He began to think maybe he did need a woman. It had been a long time. And the distraction of a love affair, even if only a night of passion, would take his mind away from the nagging question of the ethics of using the diagnostic test for Huntington's. Was innocence bliss? Did anyone want to know? Did he want to know? Why worry? he thought. It was for the NIH ethics committee to decide if the test should be approved, not him.

Eloy was getting drunk. Don said, "Let's take Eloy to 14th Street and find him a woman. Our little *amigo* needs to get laid."

"No, no. Let's go home. I think I drank too much."

They walked up the stairs and staggered out of the bar. Day had turned into night, and the complexion of the street had changed from federal workers to night people in search of entertainment. Hookers paraded on 14th Street.

"Let's go home. The Metro is going to stop running pretty soon," Eloy said.

"Hey, boys, you want a good time?" one scantily clad hooker after another asked them as they meandered the street. Eloy wondered how they could stand the cold.

Don and Tyrone kept daring Eloy to go with a hooker. When a young Puerto Rican woman approached him, Eloy thought, hell, why not?

Eloy staggered towards her. "Come on, *mi amor.*"

"*De acuerdo. Vámonos a mi cuarto.*"

"*Amigos,* wait here. I'll be back in an hour."

"What? Wait in the cold for an hour?" Don laughed. "Shit, that's crazy. You'll be back in five minutes."

The woman swayed her ample hips as she opened her coat, revealing that she was naked underneath, except for a tiny red thong. She had beautiful well-formed breasts. When they got to the room, however, she wanted to talk business before she let Eloy sample her pleasures.

"It's fifty for a straight fuck. What do you want?"

"What?" Eloy said.

"I think you don't want a woman."

"How did you know? Don't tell my friends. I just came up here so they would stop teasing me."

"Look, you little bastard, I'm not here to make you look good to your friends. If I spend time with you, whether we fuck or just talk, it's fifty dollars for half an hour." She laid her naked body on the bed and rubbed her flanks seductively. "Come here," she purred, motioning him to the bed. But when she raised her arms, he saw heroin tracks on her skin.

Oh, God, he thought, flashing back to Lolita at La Perla. "I have to go," he said as he threw the fifty dollars on the bed and ran out the door.

"That was fast," Don laughed.

"You were right. I feel better now," Eloy said, looking away.

"At least you started the new year off right. You got laid, and you found a diagnostic test for Huntington's. Oh, shit. I said we wouldn't talk shop," Don said.

CHAPTER 20

Fall 1988

T he day after Labor Day the Bethesda-Rockville area had already begun to take on the look of autumn. The mornings were cool, and the promise of the end of the long, humid summer hung in the air.

"Clear diagnoses of general conditions are important and essential. The techniques of modern recombinant DNA technology allow us to develop therapies and treatment modalities that will give the affected individuals a higher quality of life," Fred Anders said to the recombinant DNA Medical and Ethical Committee at NIH. He took a sip of water and continued his discourse.

"Not only can we use the DNA technology to produce important products from growth hormones to insulin, but we have now arrived at the point where we can perform gene replacement. We can take a gene that produces a particular protein product, splice it into a bacterial plasmid, clone those spliced genes, and literally have thousands of copies of the gene. Now we can take that gene and insert it into the cells of affected individuals, producing the missing protein, such as an enzyme or a gene regulator or another missing protein, and reverse the genetic conditions."

Eloy listened. Gene therapy had the potential to reduce the suffering and death of individuals affected with genetic diseases like Huntington's, he thought.

Fred Anders continued, "We propose to use gene therapy for the first time in humans. We are asking this committee to begin the process of establishing guidelines to allow us to do so. We will have enough data to introduce laboratory-produced genes into the cells of human patients in 1990 and actually insert genes into a patient to correct an immune system disorder in 1991."

"Not so fast," yelled a small man from the back of the room. "Dr. Roger Atkins from the NIA, Chief of Alzheimer's research. I am sick and tired of you and your research dreams. This technology is flawed, and it will never work in humans. Just because you can identify the gene and clone it in laboratory animals, what makes you think you can develop a delivery system? How the hell do you think you can get the cloned gene into every affected cell and have enough of the defective protein product produced in the cell to reverse the genetic disorder? I'm tired of the NIH diverting important research funds to these ludicrous, pie-in-the-sky dreams. This is bullshit!"

"Please, Dr. Atkins," the committee chairman said, "this is a committee on ethical issues, not the appropriation of research funds, and we will not tolerate foul language."

"You know what I think? You bastards can take your high ethical issues and stick them you know where," he said, and he stormed out of the room.

Eloy watched the spectacle and realized how lucky he was

that Zoren was able to delay his working with Roger again. He was an ass.

"Please excuse the interruption," the chairman said. "Our last agenda item is the ethical issue of making available to the public a diagnostic protocol using RFLPs to detect the presence of the Huntington's gene or its marker. We of the committee recommend that this protocol be approved with the following condition: That the decision to be tested be voluntary. No mandatory testing, and results must be strictly confidential. We don't want potential employers or insurance companies to have this information. You can understand the ramifications if this information is misused. Regarding the question of maternal or prenatal screening and testing and the right to abort the affected fetus, each state will be responsible for determining the legal rights of the fetus in accordance with local laws."

"Well, *mi amigo*," Don slapped Eloy on the back. "We're approved. We can do the test."

The *Washington Post* carried an article about diagnostic tests for Huntington's, and before Eloy and Don knew it, they were on CNN and various morning news shows discussing their tests. They were prepared to answer the scientific questions, but the number of ethical questions surprised them. Nonetheless, their visibility increased substantially because of the media exposure.

Eloy answered the telephone in the laboratory. It was Karen congratulating them on their research. Her words were slurred again. God, Eloy thought, something was seriously wrong with Karen. She had hardly come into the lab in the last nine months. She was almost always at home, and the few times that Eloy had seen her she seemed very preoccupied. They had hardly spoken to each other during the past year.

As Eloy and Don left the laboratory there was a commotion outside Building 27. Security guards were trying to control a crowd of about a hundred people who were carrying antiabortion placards and screaming, "No genetic screening! Genetic screening kills!" The placards showed graphic pictures of late-term abortions. "Death to the killers of the young and innocent," the protesters shouted.

Eloy and Don tried to get through the crowd but were stopped by the mob closing in on them. Television camera crews on hand to tape the demonstration turned their focus to a large man and a woman attacking Eloy and Don with their signs, and on the security police who were trying to restrain them. The man pushed past them and grabbed Eloy by the shoulders.

"You son of a bitch!" Don screamed as he pushed the heavy brute away from Eloy. The police took him into custody. The woman spit on Eloy, calling him the devil and screaming that he should burn in eternal hell. The demonstration escalated until the security guards had to call in the Maryland State Police to help control the crowd.

In the meantime, Karen showed up. She couldn't have picked a worse time, Eloy thought. Pushing through the crowd to get to Don and Eloy, Karen fought with the mob, which surged around her and forced her to the ground. The protesters began to kick at her. A security guard and Don pulled them off of her, and Eloy and Don helped her up. They quickly walked her back into the lab.

"Are you okay?" Eloy wiped the blood off her face with a cloth and dropped it on the lab table.

Karen looked blankly at Eloy. "Who are you?"

"Eloy."

"And who are you?" she asked Don.

"Hey, Karen, quit kidding," Don said as he held her. "Are you okay, or did those bastards give you a concussion?"

Karen's eyes suddenly widened. "Eloy, Don. What happened?"

It must have been just a temporary memory loss, Eloy thought, but then all of a sudden she started to wave her arms, the muscles in her neck tightened and she smacked her tongue against her lips.

"Oh, no," Eloy groaned. "Look, Don. I'm worried. I think she has it," he whispered.

"No, *mi amigo*, you're overreacting. She's just hurt," Don said, turning away. "Let's get her to Building 10. They can take a look at her."

Karen's injuries were minor. The doctor said not to worry. They would just let her rest for a couple of hours and then see to it that she was taken home. He told them they should leave, since there was nothing more they could do.

"No," Don said. "We'll wait here, and I'll take her home."

The television in the waiting room was turned to the local news. The headline story was about the demonstration at NIH and the attack on Eloy and Don. Eloy flipped the channel and saw that the national news was also reporting the demonstration.

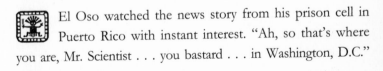 El Oso watched the news story from his prison cell in Puerto Rico with instant interest. "Ah, so that's where you are, Mr. Scientist . . . you bastard . . . in Washington, D.C."

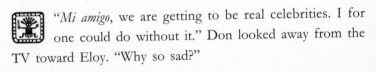 "*Mi amigo*, we are getting to be real celebrities. I for one could do without it." Don looked away from the TV toward Eloy. "Why so sad?"

"Oh, I'm not sad. I'm just tired, and I'm worried about Karen. You know, I think I'll go back to the lab. I can't do anything here. Call me if her status changes. See you Monday."

Eloy knew what he had to do. He went to the lab, sat down at his bench, selected some reagents and prepared to run a gel to do another test. He picked up the bloody rag that he had used to wipe Karen's cuts and prepared to extract a blood sample. This test was special. Never had he been so anxious for the results. But should he do it? He was curious as hell, but he felt torn. He remembered his promise to God never to use his knowledge for evil when he used his Ranita to kill Raven, but this was different. He ran the gel, placed it under the fluorescent light and looked for the marker. He looked again. There it was . . . Damn it. No wonder Karen was deteriorating. The downhill slide had started. Did she know? Should he tell her?

CHAPTER 21

The telephone rang, waking Eloy. He glanced at the clock—it was two A.M. Who would be calling at this hour? he wondered. He picked up the receiver. On the other end of the line a female voice cried to him.

"Eloy, I need to talk to you. Please come down to my apartment," Karen sobbed.

"What's the matter?"

"I'd rather not talk on the telephone. Please come."

A few minutes later, Eloy knocked on her door.

Karen's apartment was even more messy than usual. Not only did she have papers scattered all over the floor, it looked like she hadn't cleaned her kitchen in months. Dirty dishes filled the sink. The stench of rotten food tainted the air.

"What's the matter?" he asked as he looked at her and the bandage covering her forehead.

Confusion darkened her face. "Eloy, I can't go on. I have to tell you something. I've been trying to hide it, but I know that you can tell." A roach scurried across the floor. "Please excuse the house. I haven't been myself lately." She drew a deep breath. "I have Huntington's," she sobbed.

Eloy wrapped his arms around her. This time he didn't pull away.

"Oh, Eloy!" she cried. Catching her breath she said, "I've suspected for a long time, for at least a year, but I've been in denial. That's why I haven't gone to work. I've been talking to my friend, Senator Blackman. I've decided to spend my remaining days in New York at the Creedman State Hospital in Queens Village."

Eloy's eyes filled with tears. Was this his fate? Did he have five or ten years of health before it started? Should he test himself and find out? Should he tell Karen that he had tested her and already knew? That he had found out just a few hours earlier that very night?

"How can I help you?" he asked.

She wiped away her tears. "You can't help me. You know that. But you and Don have given people a choice. A choice that I never had. I wouldn't have taken the test myself. I couldn't have lived a normal life knowing—that's just the way I am. But others *do* want to know in time to achieve their goals, to plan their lives, to decide whether or not to have children."

Eloy gently held her. "Shh, Karen. Not so much. Rest."

"No, Eloy. Let me continue. Time is so important. I never married because I never knew if I had the gene and could pass it on to my children. But by using your test, people now have the chance to see if their children might have the gene. I didn't have that choice. I just rushed through life obsessed with finding a clue, any clue, that would lead to a cure. Part of my passion was selfish. I didn't want to die like my mother. But at least I know now. As sad as I am, just knowing is a relief."

"I understand," he said to her, but he asked himself if he would be relieved if he knew tonight. "Karen. Oh, my Karen, my friend!" he cried.

"Stay with me tonight."

"I will." They lay on the couch and hugged through the night. Finally peace came to them and they slept.

The next morning, Eloy watched Karen sleeping soundly. She appeared very peaceful. Who would guess? he mused.

He went into the kitchen to find some coffee, to no avail. There was hardly any food in the cabinets. The refrigerator was a mess. Eloy threw away some spoiled milk, lettuce and other leftovers in various stages of decay. Karen had given up on living, he thought. She was ready to face her fate. Was he? Eloy wrote Karen a note saying he would be right back, and went up to his apartment to make some coffee to bring back down to her.

When he returned, he woke her gently and offered her a cup.

"Eloy, I need to tell you how much I appreciate everything you have done for me," she said. Her hand trembled, and she spilled coffee on her night clothes.

"I feel that my life has been productive, so don't feel sorry for me, but sometimes I only wish that I would have done other things to make it more personally fulfilling. I'm sorry for talking so much, but there is so much I want to say. Don knows. He has suspected, as I assume you have, since the new year. Now the year is almost over, and I don't know how many more new years I'll see.

"The Guthrie Foundation will pay for my stay and treatments at the hospital until . . . it's over." She started to cry again, but fought back the tears. "My family will take care of the few assets that I have. My estate will go to the Guthrie

Foundation so that even after my death I can help in some small way to find the cure. Please don't feel sorry for me; just pray for me.

"As strange as it may seem, I would like you to stop working on Huntington's for a while. Let Don and the other researchers work on it. Focus your talents and potential on developing a research model for Alzheimer's. Roger will never accomplish that goal. He is so narrow-minded, thinking that the only way to produce a model is surgical, and so lacking in molecular techniques. Talk to Zoren. See if he can convince NINDS to let you have my lab space.

"Eloy, leave me alone now. You have to go to work."

Eloy leaned down to give her a kiss of blessing on the forehead. A million thoughts spun through his head. He wanted to say something—anything to make her feel better—but he knew words would fail. Maybe prayer would work. All he could say was, "*Adios, mi amiga.* I will do it. I'll be thinking of you."

CHAPTER 22

The next three months were hectic. Eloy continued working with Don, but the laboratory was not very productive. The entire team knew of Karen's condition. The news had even shown up in articles in the *Washington Post*. Her lab was empty— as empty as the place in Eloy's heart. Zoren continued to process the paperwork, and finally, during the Christmas holidays, he announced to Eloy that Karen's old lab space would be his. Eloy was simultaneously elated and saddened.

He decided to drive to New York to see Karen. He had talked to her on the telephone regularly since she entered the hospital, and it was obvious that her health was failing. He thought the trip would give him more time to be alone and to think.

The drive to New York was only four hours, but it seemed longer because of all the holiday traffic. The skies were dark and threatened snow. When Eloy arrived at the state hospital, its gray stone façade gave it the appearance of a giant tombstone standing at the head of the long greensward from the entry gate to the front door through which he had to drive. The attendant who greeted him doubted that Eloy would be allowed to see Karen. He had to wait at his hotel until the next day to see if Karen's doctor would allow her to have a visitor.

"Typically," the doctor said the next morning, "death doesn't result from Huntington's until ten to fifteen years after onset, but in Karen's case progression has been unusually rapid. Her heart is weak, although we feel we can control that. Her involuntary muscle movement is increasing. She is becoming more dependent on constant care, and she is losing musculoskeletal control. But I am much more concerned about her depression. At times we have to restrain her. As you know, the dementia can disrupt the personality. She has become careless and very untidy, and let me warn you, she can be obstinate. I'll let you see her, but remember, she is not the person you knew just a couple of months ago."

Eloy emotionally prepared himself for the worst.

Karen was restrained, her eyes lifeless, her once beautiful blonde hair matted. She constantly smacked her tongue. She tried to speak, but her speech was slow and indistinct. Even though she was restrained, her hands had started to wither. Her neck muscles kept contracting spasmodically. He looked at her; she grimaced back.

"Oh, Karen. I am so sorry." She couldn't respond. Flashes of his father in his final days assaulted Eloy's mind.

"Is there any hope?" he murmured to the doctor.

The doctor sadly shook his head. "It's just a matter of time. Like I said, we've used the accepted treatment modalities. She's had tranquilizers as well as antipsychotics, Thorazine, Haldol, and Tofranil. The drugs help control her involuntary movement, but she has reached the point where she no longer has the will to live."

Karen lay supine and inert. The doctor motioned to the nurse. "You can remove the restraints. Ms. Williams is resting soundly."

"Karen; oh, Karen," Eloy whispered as he approached her. He put his arms around her. He was saddened when he touched her weakened body. He knew that she didn't have much time left.

Eloy held her even tighter. She had been so important to him. "Remember the day we met in the waters of Lake Maracaibo and you thanked me for saving your life and you asked how you could repay me? Karen, you have more than repaid me. You gave me a new life, you have given me friendship, and you have given me hope that maybe one day we'll beat this disease. Oh, Karen, I love you so much. As a friend and more than a friend. I love you for giving me purpose in my life." Tears filled Eloy's eyes as he said goodbye. He gazed into her eyes, then kissed her gently on the cheek. "Goodbye, my good friend." The doctor and the nurse exited the room. Eloy caressed her face and then he, too, went out.

After the door closed, a tear formed in the corner of Karen's right eye. Her expression soon turned to one of resolve. Karen let her right hand drop over the side of the bed as she pulled at her hair with her other hand. With all of the control she could muster, she reached for the bed frame. Her fingers walked up the angle iron that supported the headboard until it met with a little shelf that held a collection of pills. She selected an orange bottle that held about forty tablets. She managed to open the bottle, but spilled the contents on the bedspread in front of her. With all of her determination, she forced her trembling hands to clutch the pills and bring them to her mouth. Her neck went rigid, but she managed to slowly get the pills to her lips. As she swallowed them, tears rolled down her cheeks.

CHAPTER 23

Fall 1990

 tu Brown had invited his old friend Orville down to
Kentucky for a little visit. As a good host, Stu offered
him some of the Tennessee sipping whisky that he knew the
senator liked and a few cigarettes. He escorted Orville into his
private office and pointed to a pair of burgundy leather armchairs.

"Have a seat, Orville," Stu said, setting down his whiskey
and taking a drag on his cigarette. "We have to put an end to
this damn antismoking bullshit. You said that you would
handle it."

"I know, and I am. Our new advertising campaign aimed
at young people is working, and we're hooking more people
every day," Orville said. "We're gaining about three thousand
smokers under the age of eighteen every day. Even with the
decline of tobacco use in adults, more than 30 percent of teen-
agers smoke. Orville laughed. Who gives a shit about the old
smokers anyway? They'll just die, and the dead don't buy cigarettes.

"But let me get to the point. We have gotten rid of that old puppet of a president who did nothing for any of us, especially us in the tobacco industry. President Cole will help us remove the surgeon general and quiet down the government about smoking. But we have a problem on your turf in the D.C. area. Those asshole lawmakers in Maryland have decided to pass a law to make restaurants set aside a portion of their rooms for nonsmokers, and, what's more, the city council in Tacoma Park has decided to ban smoking in restaurants altogether. The tobacco industry can't live with that. You know why? Because when the *Washington Post* reports it, every damn lawmaker on the hill will read about it. Secondly, all of those bastard bigwig politicians live in Montgomery County, and thirdly, if they set a precedent on banning smoking in restaurants, it might catch on.

"Shit, I just about puke every time I think of Cooper making the entire offices of Health and Human Services smoke-free. We need to stop this antismoking movement, and we need to make sure that surgeon general gets replaced. We need to put out the fires in Tacoma Park."

"Joe and I will solve this problem before you know it," Orville said determinedly. He set down his empty glass and left the room.

Joe called John Barker at the Tobacco Industry Institute. John was one of the most powerful tobacco lobbyists on the hill. He was a retired Maryland politician, and he had gained a reputation for being tobacco's best strategist. He was a skilled and persuasive lobbyist.

"The problem is very simple," Joe explained. "We have to stop the Tacoma Park bill. We need a strategy."

"I've got some ideas," John said. "I'll be meeting Orville

this afternoon to discuss the situation." John hung up the phone and sat down at his desk, rubbed his square chin, and began to make notes on a legal pad.

Later that afternoon he arrived at Orville's office.

"What's your plan, John?"

"Orville, this is war. The best general is the one who never does battle but who's able to outmaneuver his enemy."

"So? What's the solution?" Orville asked.

"The solution is simple. Tacoma Park is home to a lot of Central and South Americans, and, hell, all of those Latinos smoke like a '67 Pinto with bad valves. Just identify the Latinos who own restaurants inside Tacoma Park and those who own restaurants just outside the D.C. limits.

"Can you imagine? You're a smoker. You go to your favorite restaurant in Tacoma Park and you can't smoke. So, what the hell . . . you just cross over the D.C. line to your favorite restaurant and eat and smoke to your heart's content. What are those restaurant owners in Tacoma Park going to do? You divert media focus from regulation of smoking to how the antismoking law would force these poor Latino immigrants—who came here to pursue the American Dream—out of business."

"You devious son of a bitch. You always have answers," Orville said as he petted his terrier, Benson.

A couple of weeks later, all the Latino restaurant owners were contacted about the important bill under development. Many of them went to the Montgomery County courthouse and demonstrated at the hearing. They waved signs and screamed in Spanish and broken English: "Racists. Stop anti-Hispanic laws!" They protested so vigorously that the bill was killed on the floor of the Maryland Senate by an overwhelming majority.

Two years passed. Eloy had lost contact with Maria after Karen committed suicide. When Maria heard the news, she sent Eloy a sympathy card, but it lacked any personal touch; it was just a polite condolence. They hadn't communicated after that.

However, Eloy had communicated many times with Maria's father. They talked shop, and Dr. Rodríguez occasionally gave him a status report on Maria's career. She had done extremely well in her residency. Her supervisors had recognized her administrative skills, which they needed more than her clinical skills. She was made chief resident immediately after beginning her program and just recently had been asked to oversee a national committee established by the Public Health Service of Health and Human Services. The committee was to study the decreasing quality of health care among children, especially the low rate of inoculation, drug-addicted newborns and the increasing number of children born with AIDS, and propose solutions.

Eloy learned that Maria had traveled to Washington several times, although she never contacted him. He knew he should just forget her, but still he wished his old love the best and felt a pang of longing when he remembered the taste of her lips.

Later he heard that Maria had become a public health administrator in Puerto Rico. Then the governor appointed her to one of the highest positions on the island, in effect the surgeon general of Puerto Rico.

The progress in Eloy's laboratory was slow. When he first found out that he would have his own laboratory, he was filled with high expectations of getting to work on the Alzheimer's cell model. But almost a year passed before he finally got all of his equipment, supplies, computers and research staff together.

Don and his research team, on the other hand, had continued to refine the Huntington's test. In their initial tests, the level of accuracy was far less than desirable. The marker, Don's team discovered, was probably 3 to 5 million DNA subunits away from the actual gene, and because they still hadn't identified the specific gene for Huntington's, this distance could lead to false positive tests. With horror, Eloy imagined himself telling someone that he had the gene and then discovering he was wrong.

Don and his research team halted all testing until they improved the accuracy of the test significantly. Having only the marker but not the actual gene, they could never be 100 percent certain that they had the gene or that they didn't. The closer the marker was to the gene, the less probable that recombinations could occur, giving false positives. Don, Tyrone and collaborators from all over the world had found additional markers—markers on both sides of the gene—that increased the test's accuracy to 99 percent, thereby making it valid enough for genetic counselors to share results with their patients.

Eloy felt frustrated by the delays in getting his laboratory up and running. A critical piece of equipment he needed to culture embryonic nerve cells had been delayed for months, and he couldn't understand why. When he called the purchasing department, they said that they had never received the P.O. and that they couldn't order the equipment until they did. Eloy called Zoren at NIA several times, and each time his secretary said that Zoren was in conference or otherwise unavailable. Eloy finally decided to walk across campus to Building 31 to see Zoren and take matters into his own hands.

When Eloy entered Zoren's office, he could hear muffled

voices coming from the closed office door. Zoren's reception-
ist looked up, "Hi, Eloy. Is Dr. Krekorian expecting you?"

"No, I just thought I would drop by. I need to ask him a
few questions."

"He's busy right now, but he should be finishing up soon.
You can sit down and wait here," she said, motioning toward
a chair.

The sounds behind the door grew heated. Eloy heard yelling and fists pounding on a desk. Dr. Roger Atkins stormed
out of Zoren's office and brushed past Eloy, glaring. When
Zoren emerged, his face was flushed; it was apparent that the
meeting with Dr. Atkins had not been pleasant.

"What are you doing here, Eloy? I wasn't expecting you,
but come on in. What can I do for you?"

"I just thought I'd stop by and see if you could have lunch
and discuss the delays in equipping my lab. I'm crazy with
frustration."

"Me, too," Zoren said, taking a deep breath, "with Dr.
Atkins."

"I don't think I've ever met anyone more disagreeable."

They took the elevator down the C wing and left the building on the east side facing Rockville Pike. They proceeded
quickly toward the cafeteria. The large Naval Hospital loomed
across the street.

Zoren sighed heavily. "The delays are actually why I was
talking to Roger. Because he's chief of the Alzheimer's research intramural program, his office has to approve your
purchase orders. The bottom line is that he hasn't signed some
of them. When I asked him why, he said at first that he was
too busy, but when I said that was a pretty flimsy excuse, he
came clean and confessed that he wanted everyone to know
that he was dead set against your appointment. You were lucky

that Karen's lab space was dedicated to NINDS and not aging, or he would have prevented you from ever getting a lab."

"So that's the reason for the delay?"

"Yes. I told Roger that I wouldn't tolerate his tactics. From now on, every request that you make will bypass his office and come directly to my office for signature. We want you to get to work on your model for Alzheimer's."

They went into the cafeteria. Lunch hour was almost over, and more people were leaving than entering. As Zoren and Eloy entered, a short man on his way out jostled Eloy.

"Get out of the way. Watch where you're going," the man said. It was Roger.

"Oh, sorry," Eloy said.

Roger scowled back and looked at Eloy with disdain. "You foreigners should all go back to your own damn countries," he muttered.

"Did you hear what he said?" Eloy asked Zoren.

"I don't pay any attention to him. I don't know if he was talking about you or me or both of us. Let's just ignore him and enjoy our lunch," said Zoren.

CHAPTER 24

A couple weeks later, Eloy received an e-mail from the Public Health Service in downtown Washington. The reply-to address showed that it had come from the office of Dr. Reuben Rosario in the office of the surgeon general for the Public Health Service. The message was from Maria, asking if it would be possible for them to get together for dinner that evening. He was surprised to hear from her, partly because he didn't even know she was in town, but mostly because it had been so long since she had contacted him. She apologized for the short notice and said it was very important that she speak with him, but she understood if he had other commitments. She also apologized for the lapse in communication.

Eloy wondered what could be so important that Maria had finally decided to contact him. He had almost forgotten her—almost, but not quite.

Eloy sent a message back saying, yes, he would meet her for dinner.

Maria suggested that they meet at 7 P.M. at the Potomac
Fish Market Restaurant, which was located along the shore of
the channel connecting the Potomac River with the tidal basin. She wrote:

> I hope the location is okay. I picked it since it's near
> Reuben's downtown office and not too far from my
> hotel.

Reuben, Eloy thought, an all too familiar name. He remembered Reuben Rosario as an old friend of Maria's from
medical school. Reuben had served as vice president of the
student organization when Maria was president. Now Reuben
worked directly with the surgeon general, a step up from
when Reuben was just working in the Public Health Service
office. Reuben was obviously a go-getter. Eloy had to admit
that his thoughts about Reuben were tinged more with personal jealousy than professional envy. Was Reuben seeing
Maria?

The evening was gloomy and overcast, and the air was
cold. The wind whipped across the tidal basin, causing the
boats moored there to bob like apples in a tub at a children's
Halloween party. Eloy entered the Potomac Fish Market Restaurant and searched the crowd for Maria—finally he saw her.
She was as beautiful as ever, even dressed in the Public Health
Service uniform. Standing next to her was a tall man, also in
uniform, with piercing eyes and a chiseled face that conveyed
a rugged self-assurance.

"*Hola*, Eloy. It's so good to see you."

Eloy approached Maria to give her the customary *abrazo*,
but she just extended her hand for a handshake. Confused,
Eloy complied. He didn't know what he was feeling. He was

happy to see her, but since she was with Reuben, he felt awkward and out of place.

"Let me introduce an old medical acquaintance of mine, Dr. Reuben Rosario. You might remember I talked to him when we were here at the neurology conference. You know, when I decided to join the Public Health Service."

"Oh, *sí*. Glad to meet you."

"*Igualmente*. The feeling's mutual," Reuben responded.

"Let's go into the bar and have a drink while we wait for a table," Maria suggested. She does have a take-charge attitude, Eloy thought as he followed her to the bar. It was packed and very smoky. They managed to find a table, but the two couples seated next to them were all smoking.

Once seated, Reuben said, "I can't stand this smoke. I wish we could go outside and sit on the veranda." Just then, however, a gust of wind made the canvas awning outside snap and tear, and it blew over the plastic chairs and tables.

"Oh, well. I guess no veranda tonight," Eloy quipped, and then he gazed fixedly at Maria, remembering the love they had shared on the veranda in Vieques.

They ordered drinks and began to catch up with each other's lives. Eloy told Maria about the significant developments in his life: the refinement of the diagnostic tests for Huntington's, Karen's death and the establishment of his own laboratory. Maria told Eloy about her residency, her appointment as the director of public health in Puerto Rico and her participation on the Public Health Service Committee in regard to the problems of declining health care for children, especially disadvantaged children. Reuben said the committee both valued and appreciated Maria's contribution. He added that she had impressed the surgeon general with her insight, dedication and determination. As

Reuben praised Maria, he reached over and took her hand with warmth and familiarity.

"Dr. Maria Rodríguez, party of three," came the announcement over the restaurant's public address system.

"That's us," Maria said. "Let's go."

The trio ate, drank, and talked, and as the evening wore on, Eloy began to feel more comfortable. He found Reuben to be a vibrant, intelligent man with a zest for life and a sense of humor. Eloy also enjoyed the company of other Latinos. For the first time in a long while, he felt like he belonged, and it was a relief to speak in his native tongue, to gesture, to use expressions that reflected their upbringing.

Reuben was very proud of his involvement in health care legislation and the current antismoking campaign. He talked about the 1988 report from the surgeon general's office that concentrated exclusively on the addictive properties of nicotine. He had been instrumental in convincing Congress to pass a bill that banned smoking on all domestic airline flights of less than two hours. This year, he said he had to convince Congress to modify the law to prohibit smoking on all domestic airline flights of six hours or less, which would effectively ban smoking from all domestic air travel.

He was also very busy assembling documentation for the surgeon general that would arm the secretary of health and human services with data to denounce the tobacco companies for targeting the "Downtown" brand of cigarettes specifically at blacks.

"Can you believe how merciless those jerks in the tobacco industry are?" Reuben asked. "The percentage of older Americans who smoke decreases, so what do they do? They target the young. We pressure them not to sell to the young, so what do they do? They see that the rate of smoking among blacks is low and not increasing, so they aim their advertising at blacks. Who knows what they will do next. I wouldn't put it past them to increase the nicotine content of the tobacco or to add ammonia to their cigarettes to deliver a bigger jolt."

He continued, "But those guys are sly. They killed a bill to prohibit smoking in all restaurants in Tacoma Park by convincing the Latino restaurant owners to demonstrate at the congressional hearing and by convincing state lawmakers that the ban on smoking was racist." He smacked the table for emphasis.

Later that evening, the focus of their discussion shifted from Reuben's work to Eloy's Alzheimer's research. When they had exhausted that topic, Maria finally brought up the reason she had asked to meet with Eloy. "I know that you have been writing to your brother at my uncle's laboratory in Venezuela. But you know how hard it is sometimes for mail to get through or to call Venezuela. A couple of weeks ago my uncle visited us and wanted me to give you this letter from Miguel."

Oh, no, Eloy thought. Something's wrong.

"There's another thing I want to tell you before you open that letter. Remember my brother, Juan? I'm afraid that situation has gotten worse," she said, taking a deep breath. "His drug problem is worse, and Juan has contracted AIDS from his lover."

"What! Juan is a homosexual?"

"Yes. He never shot drugs, but he tried to convince my father that he contracted AIDS from a needle stick at the hospital."

"What did your father do?"

"He checked the hospital records. My office has mandated that all needle sticks be documented, but there was no report of an accidental needle stick."

"What happened then?"

"My father knew about the drugs and about Juan's lifestyle, of course. But it recently turned ugly and very public. There was a horrible double murder in the condominium where Juan lives. One of the men killed was my brother's lover. Several witnesses claimed to have seen my brother with the victims, and now he's the primary suspect. The newspapers suggested jealousy as a motive and reported that both of the deceased had tested positive for the HIV virus. My father was devastated by this. My mother had a mental breakdown and is undergoing therapy.

"From my perspective, they have blown this story all out of proportion, focusing undue criticism on my office," she said, playing with the brass buttons on her jacket. "The religious right on the island has started a movement to have me removed from office. They say that I have encouraged immoral, criminal behavior by promoting needle exchange programs, HIV testing and the use of condoms to control the spread of AIDS. And now the political and personal pressures are almost unbearable.

"My world is falling apart," she said, shaking her head. "I love my brother, and even though symptoms of AIDS have not . . . it is only a matter of time. Eloy, I know you understand . . . because of the Huntington's. Oh, excuse me, Eloy. I got carried away. Excuse me for making an analogy between your health condition and HIV. It was cruel," she said, lowering her head. Please excuse me. Forgive me." She stood up from the table and embraced him emotionally.

Eloy thought that Reuben recognized the depth of feeling in Maria's hug. "Oh, I am sorry," she said, trying to hold back the tears.

"Me too. Is there anything I can do for you and Juan?" Eloy asked.

"No, thank you."

She sat back down. "My father and I have had long conversations. It seems that the best thing for me is to resign and take a position in Reuben's office working as an assistant to the surgeon general. I'll be moving to Washington, D.C., after the first of the year."

"That's good. Contact me when you get settled. It's been so long . . . I would like to become reacquainted." He shouldn't have said "reacquainted," Eloy thought. Would Maria think he wanted to resume their romance? He supposed he wanted to subconsciously, but there was Reuben.

"It's getting late. I have to go," Eloy said finally. He didn't really want to go; he just wanted the opportunity to open the envelope from Miguel.

"Oh, forgive me. I have burdened you with all of my problems and not even let you read the letter. Go ahead. Open it," Maria urged.

Eloy's hands trembled as he took the letter out of his jacket pocket. He recognized Miguel's perfect penmanship on the envelope. He opened the letter and began to read. After the polite salutations and brief paragraphs of sundry events, Miguel broke the news: their mother was very ill. But Miguel said not to worry. Tia Isabel was taking care of her, and he would go back to the village every couple of weeks to make sure that everything was fine.

"*Mi madre, pobrecita.* Oh, my poor Mamá *está mal.*"

CHAPTER 25

Eloy couldn't wait to contact his brother. But how? Mail to Venezuela was so slow and unreliable. He could call, but it was too late to reach Miguel in the lab, and Dr. Rodríguez was probably at home asleep. Maybe he should try e-mail, he thought. After all, it was faster, and surely someone at the University of Venezuela had access to e-mail. It didn't take long for Eloy to find a chat room of Venezuelans and someone who could forward a message to Miguel Córdova Santiago at the university.

A few hours later, Eloy checked his e-mail and was relieved to find a communication from Miguel. The e-mail was short but told Eloy everything he needed to know about his mother. She had developed emphysema, but with rest her condition had improved since Miguel had written the letter. Miguel didn't feel that her health was threatened or that it would be necessary for Eloy to return to Venezuela, especially because of Eloy's concern about his immigration papers. He said he would arrange for their mother to call in a couple of days. But it wasn't until the day after Christmas that Eloy received another e-mail from Miguel stating that at 5 P.M. their mother would phone him at the laboratory.

Waiting for the call, Eloy got a lump in his throat. Would he ever get to go back and see his mother? Was she more ill than she let on? He remembered the many times that she was ill and pretended that nothing was wrong. He truly loved his strong little Mamá. He wished he could hold her. Finally, the telephone rang.

"*Mami,*" Eloy said.

"*Sí, mi hijito!*" It was wonderful to hear his mother's voice. It sounded strong and full of joy. "Oh, *mi hijito,* I am so happy to talk to you. Don't worry, I'm okay. . . . I just had a little trouble breathing. It's the price of getting old and smoking so many cigarettes. Miguel has told me all of the wonderful things you are doing. I'm so proud of you, *mi hijito.* Your Papá would be proud of you too." When she mentioned his father, her voice broke. "I still miss him. I miss you too. I know that you can't come here as often as you would like because of *la Migra,* but I'd like to see you."

"I'm not worried about *la Migra,* Mamá. Things have been very well here. *Estoy muy contento.* I enjoy my work and I have many friends." Eloy told her more about his experiments at NIH, his friends, Karen's death, and the fact that Maria was going to move to Washington. He ended by saying, "Mamá, please take care of yourself. I love you. Take care of Miguel. When I get the chance, I'll try to come and visit."

"*Adios, mi hijito.* I love you. Please call or write when you can."

"*Adios, Mamá. Te amo.*"

Eloy looked around his lab and felt empty. He thought of how far he had come from the shores of Lake Maracaibo to the NIH. It was a long way in terms of both distance and experience, and the journey had been filled with many adventures. He mused how little his family knew about his life. They didn't even know about the Raven and El Oso.

Eloy went back to his apartment and felt even lonelier. It was the holiday season, and he was homesick. He fixed himself a rum on the rocks and leaned back in his easy chair in front of the fireplace, thinking about holidays spent with his family as a child and about simpler days, until he fell asleep.

Eloy didn't do much during the Christmas season. He just stayed in his apartment catching up on his reading. Sometimes he felt lonely, so he took the Metro to Tacoma Park and had a nice meal of rice and black beans and *caraotas* that reminded him of the food his mother cooked. He also liked to go to the Cafe Caribe for Puerto Rican coffee. Despite his loneliness, the holidays eventually passed.

In January, Maria sent Eloy an e-mail saying that she had moved to Washington and that after she settled in she would like to visit. A month later, she called him on the phone to tell him she had an appointment the following Monday with the secretary of health and human services in the Parklawn building in Rockville, and since she would be near NIH, she would like to have lunch with him. She mentioned that she also wanted to see his laboratory, so Eloy asked her to meet him there.

At the designated time, Maria entered Eloy's laboratory with Reuben in tow. Eloy was surprised, since Maria hadn't mentioned that she would bring him. Nevertheless, Eloy showed them around his lab and introduced them to his colleagues. He was proud of the lab, and especially proud of the experiments they had devised to develop the Alzheimer's model. Eloy explained how he and his technicians had concentrated their findings on the molecular aspects of acetylcholine synthesis inhibition and receptor uptake. He also noted that as he researched the literature, he had observed some interesting linkage to acetylcholine-producing nerve-cell death and various nerve-growth factors. He speculated that they would continue to investigate the role of nerve-growth factors as a possible mechanism of nerve-cell death in neurodegenerative disorders.

During lunch Maria mentioned that she and Reuben had just come from an important meeting with the secretary of health and human services. They had written a persuasive message for the secretary to deliver on television denouncing the "Downtown" cigarette brand and the advertising campaign aimed at young blacks. She also mentioned that Juan was still being held on a murder charge and that it didn't look good. Her father had decided to go to Venezuela and visit his brother because he needed time to sort things out.

"I am also relieved to have resigned my position in Puerto Rico," she concluded. "I know it will be so much better here working in the office of the surgeon general and being with Reuben," she said and gave him a playful squeeze.

That hug spoke volumes. What Eloy had suspected was true.

"There that shit goes again," Orville said. "Hey, Joe, can you believe what the secretary of health and human services just said on television? Here, put this tape of the speech in the VCR."

"Sure, boss," Joe said. He stopped polishing his boots and turned on the VCR.

The secretary stared intently from the TV and spoke somberly. "Each day in America more than six thousand children under the age of eighteen begin smoking. Over half of them will become addicted and become regular smokers. When looking at the percentage of young smokers by ethnic group, the lowest percentage of cigarette smokers in the United States is among young black Americans. So what does the tobacco industry do? They develop a multimillion-dollar advertising campaign targeted directly at black children. The development of a specific brand called 'Downtown' to hook these children is truly unconscionable. It is yet another example of the extremes the tobacco industry will go to for profit.

"I denounce the activities of Kentucky Green Tobacco in this regard, and I am asking for the formal and immediate cessation of the production and marketing of this product. I propose that the government seriously consider an all-out ban on smoking and begin investigating the inner workings of the tobacco industry."

"Turn off that damned VCR!" Orville bellowed. "I'm tired of this shit. I'm going to get rid of this fucking surgeon general. You know damn well that report was generated in his office. Get me the president on the phone. That lazy son of a bitch is the most ineffective president we've ever had. At least Bob Winston just slept through his term and did no harm, but this bastard thinks he actually is a president and can have an impact. I also want you to find out who in the surgeon general's office is responsible for that report. I want to know who the bastard is!"

A few moments later Joe said, "I have President Cole on the phone."

Orville stomped across the room and grabbed the receiver from Joe's hand. "I thought you said that you would support the industry's interests. How can you mean that if you still allow that damned surgeon general and the secretary of health and human services to denounce us and, even worse, demand an investigation? Where in the hell will this bullshit go? There is no way in the world the tobacco industry institute will allow your administration—or any administration—to declare an all-out ban on smoking. Why don't you take on another health issue? Hell, you have all those faggots wanting more money for AIDS. Cater to them!"

"Calm down. Look, you know we have a public image to protect, and you know I'm still seeing to it that the industry has its special budget to continue research."

"Look, I'm sick of repeating myself. I want this antismoking bullshit to stop. Or, as I have said before, I will take matters into my own hands."

The president's voice bristled through the receiver. "Orville, who the hell do you think you are? You can't speak to me in that tone of voice. I am the president of the United States. I could stamp out your sorry little ass in a moment. I will not tolerate your offensive outbursts!" Raymond Cole slammed down the phone.

"That bastard. He's going to pay for this. Him and his cronies in the surgeon general's office. Joe, find out who is responsible for this, and do it now!"

CHAPTER 26

Winter 1993

In the year since Maria had moved to Washington, Eloy had had very little communication with her. But even though he hardly talked to her, he was well aware of her activities as the special assistant to the surgeon general. He could hardly avoid it, since she seemed to appear in the media on a regular basis. Day after day, various AIDS groups would demonstrate in Washington, D.C., for more federal services, and AIDS had become a political football. On the evening news, Maria was one of the major government spokespersons for increased research on AIDS drugs, development of treatment guidelines and rapid FDA approval of anti-AIDS drugs.

Orville looked at Joe through a cloud of cigarette smoke as he sat back in his leather chair, stroked his dog and finished his glass of whiskey. "Pour me another."

"Yes," Joe drawled.

"And pour one for yourself. We should celebrate. You have to admit," Orville continued, "that John Barker is a hell of a strategist. Ever since we put him on this problem, the amount of press coverage directed against smoking has decreased, and more and more attention has been given to those fairies and queers and their homosexual disease. Shit, it was almost too easy. Once John stirred them up about the lack of attention that the Department of Health and Human Services— and especially the surgeon general—was paying to their cause, they keep getting more hot and bothered with every passing day." Orville set down his glass and ran his hand between the ears of his dog.

"Hell, every day we see letters to the editor that say 'Get rid of Cooper.' The time is right to replace him, and that Puerto Rican, Maria Rodríguez, is a godsend, but we have to get rid of Rosario, the guy who has been so proactive with Cooper in all that bullshit about smoking and health risks. Call John Barker," Orville pointed toward the telephone, "and tell him to make sure we get our special ending at the Parklawn demonstration tomorrow. Rodríguez and Rosario are sure to be there."

The coalition of AIDS activists that organized the demonstration had planned well and big. They had brought in thousands of demonstrators from all over the country, and they had alerted the media, who arrived in droves. Orville and Joe watched events unfold on television.

"This is Lisa Chin for CNN, outside the Parklawn building in Rockville, Maryland. The demonstrators are orderly but vociferous in demanding that the secretary of health and human services oust the surgeon general and replace him with someone more willing to increase AIDS research and drug testing. Tell me, sir, why are you here?" the newscaster asked one of the demonstrators.

"To demand that Health and Human Services do more AIDS research, streamline procedures for clinical trials, take stronger action on testing AIDS drugs, and encourage the FDA to speed up the process of drug approval."

"We demand, we demand . . . " The chant started to become continuous. "We demand that Cooper be fired. We demand a new surgeon general. Fire Cooper. Fire Cooper. Fire Cooper." The crowd numbered more than a thousand and became increasingly irate as they chanted.

"Just a moment, ladies and gentlemen. Surgeon General Cooper and members of his staff have exited the Parklawn building, and he is going to speak. Let me see if I can get closer." The news reporter pushed her way through the crowd of demonstrators and news reporters.

Cooper approached the microphone with Reuben and Maria at his side.

The crowd continued waving signs and screaming, "Murderers, murderers. Cure AIDS, cure AIDS!"

On the twenty-first floor of the west wing of the Parklawn building, Secret Service agent Mark Wilson looked out the window at the crowd. He had a clear view of the surgeon general. He looked above him and to the side to be sure that the other agents were in place so that the government officials were adequately protected. None of the agents could see his location. He punched the combination into the locked file cabinet, opened it, and retrieved the special sharpshooter rifle. He checked to make sure it was loaded. He adjusted the high-tech scope and scanned the officials standing on the podium. He centered the cross hairs on the surgeon general, then on Maria, then on Reuben. He placed his finger on the trigger, aimed, and murmured, "Say your prayers."

The sound of muffled shots filled the air of the empty

office in quick succession. Reuben's head snapped back as the top of his skull blew off and his chest sprouted two red florets, and he fell backward to the ground.

The crowd erupted in panic and chaos. Demonstrators ran for cover. Secret Service agents swarmed around the surgeon general and Maria and rushed them to a waiting limousine.

"Oh, my God. He's been shot. I have to see him. Let me go," she screamed. "I have to see him! Reuben, my Reuben!" She pushed the agents aside.

"Sorry, ma'am," one agent said. "He's gone. There is nothing more that we can do except protect you. Hurry, get in the car."

"Who could have done this? Why?" Maria shrieked.

The surgeon general said, "I don't know, but I know the bullet was meant for me. I've been receiving death threats . . . this is the last straw. I can't have innocent people killed because of my policies regarding who knows what . . . for my failure to act more aggressively and support AIDS? What does an AIDS victim have to lose if he kills me? He's going to die anyway. Eliminating me makes him a martyr for the cause."

Maria was not really listening. She was in shock.

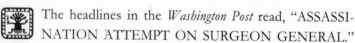 The headlines in the *Washington Post* read, "ASSASSINATION ATTEMPT ON SURGEON GENERAL." The story explained that the FBI was investigating leads that the death of Reuben Rosario was the result of the assassin missing the surgeon general and hitting his special assistant by accident. The killing was believed to have been perpetrated by an extremist homosexual group that had vowed to force the government to increase its war on AIDS. A suspect had been arrested, a twenty-six-year-old gay prostitute, Andrew King. According to the newspaper, he had already confessed to the crime.

"Good job. I knew I could depend on your intervention," Orville said to John Barker as they lunched at a Roy Rogers fast food restaurant.

"I would like to think so. This is war, and you and I are on the same side. We have to see to it that this administration and these antismoking fanatics are put in their place once and for all. Don't hesitate to call if I can do anything else for you," John said as he left the restaurant to return to work, while the senator stayed to have a smoke and a cup of coffee.

After Eloy saw the assassination on TV and watched replay after replay of Reuben being shot, he telephoned Maria.

"I'm so sorry, *mi amiga*. I'm so sorry for what has happened," he told her, his voice breaking with emotion.

"Why did he have to be killed? *Por que*? I'm cursed when I love. . . . why is life so unfair?" she cried.

"I don't know, Maria. God works in mysterious ways. But know that I'm your friend, and that I will always be your friend. How can I help? Do you need help with the arrangements for Reuben?"

"No, thank you. Reuben's family has made all of the arrangements. They plan to fly his body back home to Puerto Rico." Maria began to cry—deep, heavy sobs that flowed from the depths of her soul. "Eloy, I miss Puerto Rico so much," she managed to say. She cried some more, then blurted, "I never told you about Reggie, but we were sweethearts in high school, and he drowned when he was seventeen. He drowned while swimming in the ocean at Isla Verde near the condominium where my brother lived. *Dios mio*," she cried, "I'm sorry. I have to hang up. I'm so upset."

"Yes, I know. When can I see you?"

"Not now. I hope you understand, but I just need to be

left alone to think about Reuben and my future." Maria hung up the phone.

Eloy looked out his laboratory window at the gray skies of Bethesda.

A week later the surgeon general announced that he was resigning and that the president had appointed his assistant, Dr. Maria Rodríguez, the interim surgeon general.

A couple of months after Reuben's death and Maria's appointment, Eloy tried contacting her, but she was too preoccupied. Eloy suggested visiting, but she was always too busy with her work. She was using it as an escape from her personal problems. He could understand. Poor Maria. She had been through so much: La Perla and that horrible rape, her brother's arrest, the death of her friend and lover, Reuben, and now the tremendous responsibility of the position of acting surgeon general. It was almost too much.

Eloy picked up his jacket and left the apartment. He walked to the drug store and bought a "Thinking of you" card to send to Maria.

The presidential elections were over and the incumbent, Raymond Cole, had been defeated. In an address at a meeting of the tobacco institute, Orville noted, "The best thing that ever happened to us is that the president, Raymond Cole, was so ineffective that there was no way in hell he could ever be reelected." A young, charismatic governor from the South, Clint Walker, had beaten him. The tobacco industry was pleased to see that a Southerner had been elected and that his vice president, Ted Daniels, was from North Carolina. After all, Southerners knew the importance of tobacco to the economy. Orville and his group breathed a sigh of relief.

CHAPTER 27

Fall 1993

Stu Brown sat at his large oak desk rubbing his hands together. His brow furrowed as he thought of the increasing antismoking campaign and the impending congressional inquiries that would probe many of the tobacco industry's trade secrets.

His gaze focused on a picture of his mother. He picked up the photo and drew it closer for a better view. Her eyes were sparkling and full of life. Stu longed for the old days. He ran the fingers of his other hand through his gray hair and pictured how his mother looked yesterday at the Louisville Convalescent Home. Her eyes were lifeless; she just stared at him as if he weren't there. Sometimes he wished that she would just die and end this living hell. Alzheimer's was such a horrible disease—the mind was gone and memory was erased, but the body remained whole. Yesterday his mother didn't even recognize him. What a cruel act of God, he thought. He stroked the picture and set it back down on his desk.

He wished that Atkins would hurry up and find a cure. In

the years that Kentucky Green had financed his Alzheimer's research team, the results had been nil. He remembered how excited he had felt when Dr. Atkins approached him and convinced him and the board of directors that they needed to diversify their resources and to invest money in research on diseases associated with aging. He had described his research as "cutting edge" and "on the verge of a major breakthrough." What breakthrough? When would that little twerp stop wasting their money and develop a cure? It was already too late for his mother, he thought.

In the years Roger had been working on an Alzheimer's model, the best that he and his research team could do was to replicate the experiments they had already conducted at NIH. All they had to show for the millions of dollars of research money invested was that surgical lesions in rats produced memory loss. Not only was Roger failing to produce any progress with the research, but due to falling tobacco sales, money was becoming scarce. Kentucky Green's board of directors was pressuring Stu to close the Alzheimer's research laboratory. He had delayed doing so because he still hoped Roger's research group would find a miracle cure. But he knew that it was just a dream. Roger would never discover a cure, at least not in time to save his mother. Stu picked up the receiver of the phone.

"Marge, get me Roger Atkins at NIH."

After three rings, a mousy voice responded, "Dr. Atkins—NIH."

"Roger?"

"Yes?"

"I'll get right to the point. Roger, you and your research team have let me down."

"No, no we haven't. We are on the verge of . . ."

"Look," Stu said forcefully, "I won't stand for any more excuses. We need results. It's as simple as that. You know that I have supported you, but you let me down. You let my mother down and all the other victims of Alzheimer's. When are you going to make some progress?"

"We have demonstrated that surgical lesions in the fibria fornix induce degeneration of the acetylcholine-producing cells."

"Hell," Stu said trying to remain calm, "you've been feeding me that garbage ever since I've known you. All you have done is punched a hole in a rat's brain. Bingo—there goes the memory. Of course if you put holes in the brain memory is going to be lost."

"We have done more than that," Roger insisted.

"Listen to me. At this stage we have to 'put up or shut up.' I understand from your assistant, Donna, that the new researcher, that little Indian-Mexican . . ."

"You mean the *mestizo* from Venezuela."

"Same thing," Stu replied. "Look, I'm losing my patience. Don't interrupt me. Just listen, do you understand?"

"Yes."

"Good. Okay. I understand that this *mestizo* . . . what's his name . . . ?"

"Eloy Córdova Santiago."

"Yes, Eloy, has been making excellent progress, and as a matter of fact, he has almost developed the model. Am I right?"

"Well, not completely. His science is flawed."

"What? My patience is rapidly disappearing," Stu shouted.

"As I said, his science is flawed."

"With all due respect—hell, with no respect—you wouldn't know good science if it bit you in the ass. People say you have done everything in your power to derail that guy's research.

As a matter of fact, I understand you have continuously challenged his work and erected barrier after barrier to delay his progress. You should be encouraging him!"

"Oh, I couldn't do that," Roger shouted back. "No, I won't!" he said like a spoiled child.

"Okay, then, the solution is simple. I'll find a way. I'll find someone to approach Eloy and add him to the company payroll. Remember, you are only the director. We own you. Hell, what does he make at NIH, sixty or seventy K? We could double that!" Stu said. "You're on notice. We need results fast, or we'll get rid of you fast, and I think the only way we are going to get results is to get new ideas. Yours are going nowhere. Do you understand?" Stu said, slamming down the receiver.

Then, picking it up again, he said, "Marge, get me Orville Reynolds at the Capitol."

"Hello, Senator Reynold's office," Joe Ray drawled in his deep voice.

"Joe, is that you? I need to talk to your boss. This is Stu. Tell him it's urgent."

"Sure, just a moment. He is on the floor in a committee hearing. Hold on."

After several minutes, Senator Reynolds picked up the phone. "Stu, this better be important. I'm in a real hurry here because the shit is about to hit the fan. That bastard president isn't going to help us."

"We need to get rid of Roger Atkins. His research is going nowhere. I want Joe to recruit that hot shot researcher Eloy Santiago away from NIH. Do whatever it takes, got it? We need him to work for us."

"I'll have Joe get on it right away. I have to go," Orville said, coughing as he hung up the phone. He turned to Joe.

"Stu wants us to get Eloy Santiago on board our Alzheimer's program. Take care of it," Orville said, straightening his bow tie as he walked out of his office back to the hearing.

Joe stroked his handlebar mustache and knitted his heavy eyebrows. This is going to be a tough one, he thought. He left the office and headed west toward the National Gallery. He wanted the exercise, and he needed time to think about the problem. The little bastard didn't seem interested in money. Maybe they could blackmail or threaten him. But how would that encourage him to think and do research? The guy could just refuse. Oh, the hell with it, he thought, as he approached a pay phone in the National Gallery. I'd better give John Barker a call.

When Barker came on the line, Joe drawled, "Say, John, this is Joe Ray. How are you doing?"

"Just fine. And you?"

"Real good. My people sure are happy with the way you handled that little problem with the surgeon general."

"Well, thanks. But enough bullshit," John replied. "What do you want?"

"Umm," Joe drawled, "Orville wants you to help us with another problem. You all remember my grandma is senile and Stu's mother has Alzhemier's, and you know about Kentucky Green's Alzheimer's lab."

"Yes. What's your point?"

"Okay, hold your horses. The point is that Roger Atkins . . ."

"That man is an embarrassment."

"Well," Joe continued, "Roger is not making any progress, and Kentucky Green's board is ready to shut down the lab, but I would hate to see that research come to an end all of a sudden and so would Stu—you know, with his mother's Alzheimer's and all."

"Okay, get to the point."

"There is this hot shot at NIH named Santiago who's on the verge of a major breakthrough in Alzheimer's. Even Donna says so. We want you to help us bring him on board. Can you help us?"

"Why do you need me? Just ask him."

"It's not that easy. I've talked to him in passing, and from what Donna says, he is some self-righteous little bastard. He is doing this research as part of a vow to his father. I don't think we can convince him to leave NIH and work for us."

"Then threaten him."

"No, we don't want to be that obvious. We need his talent. We need his research findings."

"That's the solution!" John replied.

"What?" Joe said hesitantly. "I don't get it. What do you mean?"

"Remember what I told Orville? 'The best general is the one who never does battle but is able to outmaneuver his enemy.' Do you need Santiago or his research findings?" John asked.

"His research findings."

"And didn't your old grandma used to say, 'You can catch more flies with honey than you can with vinegar.'?"

"Yeah."

"Well, then, who is the honey?" John asked.

"Of course. I know who you mean," Joe said. "Much obliged."

CHAPTER 28

Fall 1994

G od damn it, Joe!" Orville said. "What the hell's all this
bullshit? Who does the president think he is? He's asked
for a congressional inquiry of all things, and he's subpoenaed
my friend, Stu Brown, and six other CEOs. We have to stop
this. We have to cut off his balls and shut him up." He pounded
his desk.

"What are you saying, that we should remove the president?"

"Shit, I don't see no other way, do you?" Orville replied.

Eloy was making good progress with the Alzheimer's
model. He had the help of several technicians and the
constant collaboration of Don in his laboratory next door.
Eloy was also fortunate that Donna Stone wanted to talk about
transferring from Dr. Atkins' lab to work with him. She had
just called Eloy and wanted to meet with him for lunch in the
Building 10 cafeteria.

The cafeteria was bustling with activity as researchers,

clinicians, patients and staff circulated in and out, and a buzz of conversation thickened the air. Donna spotted Eloy when he entered and motioned to him from where she sat.

"Hello. Sit down. I'm glad you could come and have lunch with me." Donna's face was as beautiful as ever. She removed her sunglasses and her large dark eyes sparkled. The expression on her face revealed the unsubtle pride she felt in her attractiveness. It was impossible not to notice her trim, firm figure even through her lab coat, and she was especially sexy whenever she lifted her long legs to cross them.

"I know you're busy, so I'll tell you straight out. Working with Atkins has become a living nightmare. You know that little Napoleon will do anything to further his own career," she said. "He has withheld critical data from his collaborators in France so he can receive credit for their surgical techniques. He has even falsified data. He will stop at nothing. It's unethical and, more importantly, it can have grave scientific consequences, as you well know," she said, looking up from her salad. "It goes against every scientific principle. In short, I can't work with him anymore. Before I called you, I talked to Zoren at NIA, and he said that if you agreed, he would okay the transfer. What do you think?" she asked, setting down her fork.

Eloy knew that Donna's training was primarily in molecular genetics and recombinant DNA techniques, which fit his research program well. He explained that they were now entering a critical stage in the development of their cellular molecular model: using a viral vector to induce the Alzheimer's condition in their experimental animals.

"Oh, I would love to do that type of research again. I know you've read my research papers. Doesn't that convince you of my abilities?" Donna responded with excitement.

"I've never had any doubts about that. Don has always praised your research talents," Eloy said.

"Knowing Don, I'll bet those weren't the only talents he mentioned," she teased.

"He said you were well rounded," Eloy bantered back. He knew he would be fortunate to have her, but he wondered about her loyalty. Was this a setup so that Roger could get inside information about the progress of his research? He would have to be very careful with her.

"So what's your decision, Eloy? Can I work with you?"

"Sure, I guess," Eloy said. "I'll call Zoren. He can begin the transfer process, and you can start in my lab next week or whenever you want. I'm sorry, but I've got to rush back to my lab. Next Tuesday I'll be giving a presentation on our research in the "Medicine for the Layman" series sponsored by NIH. Maybe you should come. The presentations are held in the Mauser Auditorium from 8 to 9 on Tuesday evenings."

"I'd like that."

"See you later then," Eloy said as he left the table. He hoped he had made the right decision.

Over the next several days, as Eloy prepared for his presentation, he reflected on how little effort he had made to help Don and the others with the research on Huntington's. He felt torn between his promise to Karen to work on the Alzheimer's model and his vow to his father to find a cure for *El Mal*. Even though the Alzheimer's research was related, he couldn't wait to get back to the work on Huntington's, and to do so while he was still young, before time ran out. The ring of the telephone brought him back to reality.

Picking up the receiver, Eloy said, "Hello." It was Zoren.

"Eloy, I hate to disturb you, but I need to reconfirm your place of birth and training. I'm writing an intro for your presentation on Tuesday. It's Lake Maracaibo, Venezuela, right? Santa Rosa de Agua?"

"Right."

"And you're here on what visa?"

Eloy, stricken with panic, didn't know what to say.

"Oh, never mind. This immigration stuff doesn't matter. I can't understand why they even bother asking about it. Okay, I have to go. Thank you," Zoren said, and he hung up the phone.

What was that all about? Eloy wondered.

Tuesday evening arrived, and Eloy entered the auditorium to give his talk. Zoren introduced him.

Eloy began his presentation. "Thank you, Dr. Krekorian and members of the audience. Alzheimer's disease is but one type of senile dementia. It is characterized by a tragic loss of memory. More than 2.5 million Americans suffer from this disease, and it is the fourth-leading cause of death among the elderly, right behind heart disease, cancer and stroke. Alzheimer's claims over 155,000 lives per year.

"Alzheimer's is an incurable degenerative brain disorder that gradually results in loss of memory and brain function. The affected individual begins to forget names, faces and dates. The ability to learn diminishes and the personality changes. As the disease progresses, the patient loses control of body functions and the ability to speak and eventually to walk.

"Neuroscientists such as myself have expended a major effort to discover the causes and possible cures for this disease. Pathologists have determined that many individuals who have died of Alzheimer's show prominent changes in their brains. There are extracellular deposits called amyloid plaques and twisted nerves called neurofibrillary tangles. The amyloid plaques are composed of a substance called beta amyloid protein, and researchers have determined that the production of this protein is governed by a gene located on chromosome 21. This is the same chromosome associated with Down syndrome. Some scientists predict that because of the genetic link, as much as 10 to 30 percent of Alzheimer's may be inherited. Besides the plaques and tangles in microscopic sections, more and more evidence supports the hypothesis that Alzheimer's is a neurodegenerative disease—that is, the specific nerve cells die prematurely. The majority of the effort in our laboratory is to try to determine what causes the death of these nerve cells."

Eloy paused, looked out at the audience, and then continued. "More specifically, in Alzheimer's, certain brain cells that produce the neurotransmitter acetylcholine die in a region of the brain known as the basal forebrain. One of the clues that led us to focus more of our effort on the cause of the destruction of the acetylcholine-producing neurons was the research of Dr. Nestor Rodríguez, Dr. Maria Rodríguez and myself. We found that certain chemicals, such as atropine, can interfere with acetylcholine production and/or block the specific muscarinic receptors required for proper acetylcholine transmission.

"Today we are learning that these acetylcholine nerve cells possess receptors for a protein called nerve growth factor, or NGF. NGFs are a group of proteins known as neurotropins that sustain the development and growth of nerve cells in tissue culture. Without burdening you with too much detail, let me say that NGF seems to promote cell survival because if you withdraw the NGF, the nerve cells die in culture. Therefore, if we want to produce an Alzheimer's-like condition in an animal model to further our understanding of the disease, in theory all we have to do is interfere with NGF production or uptake by nerve cells and we have nerve cell death similar to the nerve cell death in Alzheimer's.

"Again, in theory, if we wanted to reverse or prevent nerve cell death, what we would need to do is to supply neurotropins in the area of nerve cell loss, thereby restoring memory or reversing the memory loss associated with Alzheimer's. We are using neurotropins to stimulate nerve cell growth or neurotropin inhibitors to prevent nerve cell growth to develop our animal model for Alzheimer's. We are devising a method to prevent NGF from stimulating the growth of acetylcholine-producing cells. That is the major research thrust in our laboratory. We are very optimistic that within two or three years we will have the animal or cell culture model for further Alzheimer's research. Any questions?"

"Yes," came a voice from the back of the room. "Dr. Roger Atkins, chief of Alzheimer's research here at the NIH in the National Institute of Aging. How can you say that you are developing an animal model for Alzheimer's when we in our laboratory have been surgically ablating or destroying that portion of the rat brain known as the fimbria fornix, after which the acetylcholine-producing neurons begin to die? We have already developed the model. There is no need for your duplicate research. The public should be informed of your wasteful use of precious tax dollars. We should be using research funds to find cures for pressing health problems like AIDS, smoking-related diseases, cancer and others! How can you take credit for research that we did in our lab?!" he screamed, and stormed out of the auditorium before Eloy could respond. Eloy just shook his head and asked for questions.

"Is Alzheimer's inherited?" one woman asked.

"As I mentioned, more and more evidence supports the

idea that there may be a genetic pattern associated with some forms of Alzheimer's."

Several others asked questions. Zoren then thanked Eloy; the audience applauded. He went backstage and got ready to go back to his laboratory.

Walking across the campus in the cold fall night, he could see the lights on in the windows of his lab and office. He thought that he turned the lights off. Just then he saw the light go out. "That's strange," he thought. "I wonder if the janitor is straightening up in there." Just then, out of the darkness as he entered Building 27, came a voice.

"Howdy, little partner. Remember me? Joe Ray, congressional aide to Senator Orville Reynolds, Republican from Kentucky? Remember I met you at that nerve convention a few years ago at the hotel and then at the Christmas party at Senator Blackman's house?

"Oh, yeah."

"I just heard your presentation there on Alzheimer's. It was mighty interesting. My grandma is senile. It might be Alzheimer's. She's in a rest home in Florida. Poor thing, I love her like a mother. My mother died when I was real young, and my grandma raised me and my brothers. I love that grandma of mine more than you can imagine. Well, I better go. You research guys keep working. I hope you find a cure," he said, patting Eloy on the back.

When he entered Building 27, Donna was leaving the elevator. "Oh, Eloy," she said, trying to hide her surprise. "I heard your presentation on your work with dopamine receptors and thought I would wait for you here to tell you how much I enjoyed it. It was too crowded back there at the auditorium."

Eloy looked at her with curiosity. His presentation had nothing to do with dopamine receptors.

CHAPTER 29

Summer 1995

W hat's that damn Clint Walker going to do next?" Orville asked Joe, running his hand through the coat of his terrier, asleep on his lap. "He lets that blind bastard, his FDA commissioner, call tobacco use a pediatric disease. Then he proposes a plan—not just political bullshit, but a plan—to reduce the number of children who become addicted to nicotine."

He straightened his bow tie and continued, his Adam's apple bobbing. "Shit, last year he had the six major CEOs of the tobacco industry testifying before the House Committee on Health and the Environment.

Joe just stood there, pretending to pay attention to another of Orville's tirades.

"Now those sons of bitches at the American Medical Society have published a series of articles in their journal, exposing hundreds of the tobacco industry's internal memos. God damn it, they have found out what we have known for more than thirty years—that nicotine is addictive and that compounds in smoke cause cancer. Shit. Anyone with an ounce of sense knows that smoking is addictive. Why the hell do you think I smoke? You think I like this shit? Hell no. I'm hooked!" Orville ground out his cigarette in the ashtray and coughed thickly.

"My biggest fear is what this administration is going to do now that they have these internal documents—investigate the tobacco CEOs again for perjury?"

"Walker has already established a commission to take on the tobacco industry," Joe said, licking his mustache.

"Damn it," Orville said. "This is war, and one of the major strategies of war is to take out the general. Get rid of that damn guy."

Spring 1996

Eloy's research was progressing very rapidly. They had repeated their experiment several times and were convinced that, at least in tissue culture, neurotropin-like nerve growth factor could keep acetylcholine-producing neurons alive. In addition, they were able to inject NGF into the ventricles of rat brains and prevent apoptosis, a type of cell death.

Don and his researchers had also helped isolate the gene on chromosome 14 believed to be responsible for the production of NGF protein.

Looking up from the table, Eloy said facetiously, "Donna, if it wasn't for your surgical expertise working with our old friend Dr. Roger Atkins, we would've never developed the delivery system to get NGF into the rat brains and prevent nerve cell death. Now all we need to do is devise a way to do the reverse in order to produce an animal model. We need to prevent the synthesis or binding of NGF to the neurons, or turn off the gene or block its uptake."

The next week, as Eloy and Don were eating in the cafeteria, Eloy discussed the research plans and progress they were making toward inhibiting NGF synthesis or uptake. Don tried to change the subject.

"Come on, *mi amigo*, lighten up. All you do is eat, sleep, and probably shit science. You should be more like me and enjoy life!"

"I do," said Eloy, setting down his hamburger, "but I can't wait to find a solution to this problem. It keeps bugging me."

"All things in time. You have that cute researcher, Donna. Why don't you spend some time with her?"

"You know, speaking of Donna, I sometimes wonder about her. She has been doing some strange things," Eloy said, picking up his cup of coffee.

"What are you saying?"

"Sometimes I think she is just working for me to steal research data."

"Ah, *mi amigo*. You have been at NIH too long. You're thinking like *gringo* scientists," Don said, pointing his thumbs at himself.

"I don't know," Eloy said. He looked out of the window only to see Donna and Roger Atkins walking together toward Building 27. "See what I mean," Eloy said, indicating the pair.

"Nah. You're just paranoid."

A couple of months later Eloy and Don's research team found a way to block the NGF gene. The breakthrough came when Eloy speculated, "Don, you know what I think? I think the mechanism of action of NGF is to bind to the acetylcholine-producing nerve cell receptors. Once the NGF binds to the receptors on the cell membrane, the NGF stimulates them to initiate a series of metabolic reactions resulting in the maintenance of the cell's life. But I think that because the tyrosine kinases are so similar to proteins produced by the cancer-causing *trk* gene, if we isolate or mutate the *trk* gene and insert it into the nerve cells, we will prevent the uptake of NGF, and the nerve cells will either die or give us the Alzheimer's model. And guess what? We did those experiments and prevented cell life. The nerve cells died in culture."

"What? Your cells died?" Don asked.

"Yes, and here's where you come in. If we're going to produce this same condition in an experimental animal model, we can use Donna's technique of trying to deliver the gene into the animal surgically by injecting it into the ventricles of the brain and hope that the gene is taken up by the nerve cells. But then we cannot control which nerve cells are damaged."

"Right. Right."

"All of the nerve cells could die, killing the animal, and what good is that to us? I have another plan. What we could do is use a viral vehicle. That is, take a virus, modify it so that it doesn't produce a viral disease, and splice in the mutated *trk* gene. The virus is then taken into the nerve cell . . ."

"Yes," Don said, "and *voila!* The NGF can't bind to the nerve cell receptors, and the nerve cell dies."

January 1997

 An article in the *Washington Post* trumpeted Eloy's success:

SANTIAGO AND TEAM
DEVELOP ANIMAL MODEL
FOR ALZHEIMER'S RESEARCH

The research team of Eloy Córdova Santiago at the National Institutes of Health, the National Institute of Aging (NIA), has developed the first practical animal model for Alzheimer's disease. They have used techniques from molecular biology and gene splicing to deliver the mutated gene to specific nerve cells that die in Alzheimer's. This gene, the *trk* gene, is spliced into the DNA of a herpes virus that has been rendered harmless. The viruses are placed in cell culture and allowed to multiply, producing millions of viral particles with the *trk* gene. Because the herpes virus has specific proteins on its outer coat, it will only bind with cells that have the specific receptors, like a lock and a key. The herpes virus will only bind with the receptors on the acetylcholine-producing nerve cells. Once the virus enters the cell, the *trk* gene becomes active and prevents the uptake of the nerve growth factor (NGF) that is necessary for nerve cell growth. The cells die, acetylcholine levels drop, and a form of Alzheimer's is produced.

The altered viruses are placed in an aerosol spray and delivered into the brain through the nasal passages. This technique has been used on several primates in Santiago's laboratory to produce Alzheimer's.

Former first lady Judy Winston has hailed this as the major discovery of the century relative to Alzheimer's. Former President Bob Winston was diagnosed with Alzheimer's two years ago.

Dr. Roger Atkins, chief of Alzheimer's Research at the NIA, cautions that upon autopsy, these primate models do not show the characteristic amyloid plaques and neurofibrillary tangles associated with Alzheimer's. However, Dr. Zoren Krekorian of the NIA Alzheimer's Study Group says that the cautions are overstated and simplistic. According to Krekorian, Alzheimer's is not one specific dementia, but rather, a collection of causes that produce the condition known as Alzheimer's.

The animal model produced by Santiago and his research team is, as the former first lady said, a very significant finding and could eventually lead to a cure for many forms of Alzheimer's.

"That son of a bitch. I have been working on this problem my whole life, and that half-breed takes all of the credit," Roger Atkins muttered to himself, putting down the newspaper. "The little shit is probably here illegally, too."

When Eloy accessed his e-mail, he found message after message from people wanting to know if he had found the cure for Alzheimer's. Colleagues wanted him to give presentations at their institutions and at national meetings. Eloy and his team were overwhelmed by the attention.

One e-mail stood out, however. It was from Maria. Eloy had not heard from her in at least two years. She had been very busy as acting surgeon general since Dr. Cooper resigned in 1992. She had been formally appointed surgeon general in 1994. Because of her increased responsibilities, Eloy hardly ever had the opportunity to talk to her. They had no more than a few brief phone calls during that whole time. But he knew that she was fine because he often saw her on TV. Her crusade to help find a cure for AIDS and her campaign to improve children's health care were the topics of many news programs. Eloy was surprised that Maria wanted to see him. She said that it was important that they talk—she had some important news and wanted to meet with him next Thursday at 12:00 in the cafeteria at NIH in Building 1.

Why so secret? Eloy wondered. Was she just being cautious, or was she being cold?

On Monday morning, one of the lead stories on the TV news mentioned that Dr. Maria Rodríguez had received a presidential award for her work in health care. Eloy was very happy for Maria and thought of how their careers had advanced over the past decade. Yet he wondered why she was so vague when they talked. It was almost as if she were paranoid.

When Eloy entered the Building 1 cafeteria at noon the following Thursday, Maria was talking to the director of NIH. Maria asked her if she had been introduced to him.

"Of course I know Eloy. He is one of our shining stars. I think one day we will see him receive the Nobel Prize for his work. You used to work with him in Puerto Rico, didn't you?"

"Yes. Even back then my uncle, who is a researcher in Venezuela, recommended that Eloy leave Venezuela and work with us in our laboratory in Puerto Rico. Eloy and I share many memories."

Eloy thought, yes, many memories.

"Also, before I forget, congratulations on your presidential award. I saw the story on the news a couple days ago," the director said.

"Yes, congratulations," Eloy said as he gave Maria a hug. "I'm so proud of you. You look so regal in your uniform too." But regal wasn't the word Eloy was thinking. She looked more beautiful than ever as he looked at her large green eyes, soft skin and auburn hair. He thought of the time that they spent together on the island of Vieques and the love they shared. So much had happened since then. The director took her leave of them. Just then Eloy noted two men, one white and one black, in dark, three-piece suits rigidly watching him and Maria and surveying the room. They appeared to be on the alert.

"Who are those two?" Eloy asked, nodding toward them.

"Oh, ignore them. They're my bodyguards."

"You need bodyguards?"

"You never know," she whispered. "You can't trust anyone. That's why we're meeting here. Sometimes I think my office is bugged. You can never tell. I don't even trust the Secret Service agents. You remember when Reuben was murdered and the government and media said that it was just a botched assassination attempt? They said that the murderer, Andrew King, who has since died of AIDS, was trying to kill the surgeon general and missed. Believe me, after all of the evidence at the trials, I know that Andrew King would never have been a good enough marksmen to hit any target from the twenty-first floor of the Parklawn building. I think it was a setup, and I have ideas about who is behind it, but that's not why I am here. I think your life is in danger."

"What? Impossible!"

"Yes. I think I should warn you," Maria continued. "My brother Juan was convicted of the murder of those two men in the condominium a few years ago. Juan's AIDS is now expressing itself, and I don't think he will live much longer. He was removed from the prison to a secure wing at the Centro Médico. In prison he had a lot of time to talk to the other prisoners. Well, that's obvious," she digressed. "He talked a lot to Franco—you remember—Raven's bodyguard, El Oso." Tears formed in the corner of her eyes.

"Yes, but don't go there. Please forget La Perla."

Maria regained her composure, straightened her posture, wiped her nose, and whisked away the trail of tears from her cheeks. "Juan told me that Franco is being released from prison in a couple of months and that he has told everyone that his major goal in life is to see you die. He wants to avenge Raven's death. Please be careful. I worry about you."

"About me? You're the one with the bodyguards. I'm worried about you!" Eloy exclaimed.

"We have to get together—I mean socially. I'm so tired of just working. We've forgotten our personal lives. I have almost forgotten to congratulate you for all of your magnificent research," she said. She got up and gave Eloy a warm hug. "I'll call you." She hurried from the cafeteria with the two bodyguards at her side.

CHAPTER 30

June, 1997

My sister is dying of cancer; more specifically T2 N2c squamous cell stage IV carcinoma of the tongue. She has been smoking since she was twelve. Just two years ago, at the age of thirty, she complained of a sharp pain in her neck, the pain persisted, and a year later she found a lesion on the back of her tongue. A biopsy was performed. The diagnosis was squamous cell carcinoma. Physicians concur that squamous cell carcinoma is a textbook case of cancer caused by smoking. The cancer has metastasized to her lungs and her bones. Her prognosis is bleak. My sister will probably die within the year." The president's voice was filled with pain, which quickly turned to anger as he addressed Congress.

"She is dying because of the greed of the tobacco industry. Lack of government action has allowed cigarettes to remain our most deadly consumer product. Did you know they kill more than 425,000 people each year? How can we in the government continue to allow this product to remain unregulated? About 10 million people in the United States have died of causes associated with smoking, including heart disease, emphysema and other respiratory diseases. Women who smoke increase their risk of dying from lung cancer by nearly twelve times. On average, smokers die seven years earlier than non-smokers, and my sister will be one of them. It is estimated that 3,000 people die annually because of exposure to second-hand smoke.

"The critical element in our fight against tobacco use is the finding that nicotine is a drug, and I am going to recommend that because it is a drug, the Food and Drug Administration regulate the sale and distribution of cigarettes and other tobacco products.

"Today we are seeing the beginning of the end of tobacco's insidious hold on the American public. The tobacco industry faces an array of legal challenges, including product liability lawsuits and class-action lawsuits, lawsuits filed by various states to recover Medicaid expenses, and lawsuits by other government agencies. In addition, the attorneys general of forty states recently sued the industry to recover the cost to taxpayers of treating tobacco-related health conditions.

"Just today, representatives of the tobacco industry reached a settlement with more than forty states. The tobacco industry will pay more than $368.5 billion over the next twenty-five years and submit to regulation by the FDA. Because the tobacco industry settled with the government, it will get immunity from future class-action and individual lawsuits, and no more than $5 billion in claims will be paid annually.

"We, ladies and gentlemen of the Congress, need to approve this agreement." The president waved the sixty-eight-page, single-spaced document. "I ask you not only to approve this proposal but to develop other proposals to bring a logical and final end to smoking in this country so that

we can reduce the number of individuals dying of this le-
thal habit and innocent individuals like my sister will not
have to die!" he said, bringing an emotional end to his address.

That's it, Senator Reynolds thought. I am going to get rid
of that bastard, and this time I mean it.

Eloy and Maria gradually rekindled their relationship.
They spent evenings together whenever possible. It was
hard to go out in public because of Maria's high-profile position. The attempted assassination of the former surgeon general required that she have constant protection. Eloy, on the
other hand, had become a well-known personality in his own
right. Because of this, it was difficult for them to take advan-
tage of the culture and entertainments that Washington, D.C.,
had to offer, but they were content simply spending time together in whatever circumstances they could manage.

The important thing was that they were beginning to feel
comfortable with each other again. Eloy knew that he was
free to love Maria because if their romance grew in the direction of marriage, she wouldn't be forced to face the issue of
having children with him. And even though Eloy knew he
could test himself for Huntington's, he never would. There
was really no reason for him to know if he could give it to his
children, especially if he married Maria. Why was he even
thinking like this? he wondered. They were just at the beginning of a renewed relationship, and he didn't want to rush it—
at least not yet.

One summer day, while walking through Rockcreek
Park, Maria said almost out of the blue, "I can't bear the
thought of anything happening to you. I'm so afraid that
anyone I care about will be harmed. I think that I'm cursed.

It's so hard to let my heart love, especially since Reuben's killing. I can't forget that day. Eloy, let me assign you a bodyguard."

"That's not necessary. Nothing will happen." Even though he told Maria that he wasn't concerned, he was. He remembered when he saw the lights go on and off in his laboratory after his presentation at the "Medicine for the Layman" series. He remembered when the antiabortion demonstrators knocked Karen down in that ugly scene at the campus. For a moment his thoughts returned to Lake Maracaibo and the first time he met Karen, the day he rescued her. He thought of the hatred, frustration and anger in Rosa's voice, hitting at him and blaming him for Maria's rape. He remembered El Oso glaring at him and swearing he would kill him one day, and now he had been released from prison. And what about Dr. Roger Atkins? He seemed capable of anything. Except success. Or civility.

Roger had grown increasingly jealous of Eloy's research success and knew that Eloy would probably replace him as the chief of Alzheimer's at the NIA. That position brought Roger more status and identity than anything in his life; no one would ever take it away from him—especially a foreigner without a doctoral degree.

Just who was this upstart? Roger wondered. And then he realized that he could simply walk across campus to get the answer.

"I need to look at Eloy Córdova Santiago's file," Roger demanded of the personnel clerk.

The clerk was a heavyset African-American woman in her late thirties, who clearly stuck to the rules. "You need authorization to see those files. What's the purpose of the request?"

Glaring at the clerk, he arrogantly said, "Do you have any idea who you are talking to? I am Dr. Roger Atkins, Chief of Alzheimer's Research of the NIA."

The woman, not impressed, said, "I don't care who you are. I can only allow you access to these files if I have authorization from your superior."

"I'll be back," Roger said, stomping out of the room. "Damn affirmative action . . . all they do is hire incompetent minorities!"

Eloy remained in the laboratory late that night. With all of his newly found fame, he hardly had time for research. Most of his days were filled with meetings, presentations, media interviews and public relations for the NIH. It was only in the evenings and late into the night that he was able to continue with his first love—science—the quiet endeavor that led to the uncovering of mother nature's secrets, a task he found exciting. Eloy remembered his experiences in the jungle where he truly felt close to nature. Here in Bethesda, Maryland, among all of the objects created by humans, it was easy to forget the connections that humans had with nature. He remembered Domingo's chant and drinking the *honi xuma*.

Phantoms revealing spirit of the vine,
We seek your guidance now,
To translate the past into future,
To understand every detail of our existence,
To improve our life,
To reveal the secrets that we need to find the cure.

He remembered the euphoria and the vision. He could see the past, the future, the white woman, the house.

It was late. Eloy was alone in the lab and had fallen asleep at his desk. He heard a sound at the door and wondered who it could be. Lifting his head from his desk, he saw through half-closed eyes a female form. "Donna, is that you?"

Donna looked surprised to see him there. She quickly regained her composure and said, "Oh, sorry to disturb you. You startled me. I didn't think anyone would be here at this hour. I just . . . just . . . was a little concerned about the viral vectors. I wanted to make sure that the host virus's cells were viable. I would hate to lose them, this new batch of *trk* viral vectors," she mumbled, looking away from Eloy.

"Go right ahead. I just thought I'd spend the night here in the lab. See you tomorrow."

Eloy lay down on the couch. What was that all about? he wondered. Before he drifted off to sleep, he noticed that Donna had already left. Boy, that was fast, he thought. It didn't take her ten minutes to check the cultures.

Eloy finally went to sleep, at peace with himself and his dreams. His dreams took him home to a *tambito* that seemed so far away, his village, a time of innocence. He was playing with his brother, Miguel, fishing with his father and enjoying his mother's wonderful food. When he woke the next morning, he felt more peaceful and rested than he had in a long time.

Swarms of katydids had invaded the Bethesda/Rockville area, and in the morning their sounds filled the air like the hum of a muffled chain saw. The sun rose in the east and shone through the windows behind Eloy's desk. The sunlight reflected off the aluminum-shrouded, automated nucleic-acid-and-protein-sequencing equipment. It was the beginning of a new day. Mornings were Eloy's favorite time of day during the summer in Bethesda. The summers there were beautiful. This day was clear and filled with expectation and promise. The humidity, however, was unbelievable, and as morning turned into afternoon, the blue skies turned gray. Promise turned to gloom.

That afternoon, as Eloy checked his e-mail, he saw a message from Miguel.

"Eloy, it's Mamá. She is near death. Her emphysema has turned to pneumonia. I fear she will die. Come home as soon as you can."

"Oh, no, not Mamá." Eloy's heart filled with sorrow. *"Mi Mamá, mi Mamá,"* he cried. He got a ticket for the first flight to Maracaibo. Eloy e-mailed Miguel with his itinerary and asked him to inform Juan, the old bush pilot, to have his plane ready to bring him home.

He looked around the lab and decided what he should take, went home and packed. Although he remembered his forged immigration papers, he wondered if he would ever be back.

CHAPTER 31

When Eloy arrived home, he knew that he was too late. Mournful wails similar to the four-note call of the jungle partridge reverberated through the evening air. He knew before climbing the bamboo ramp to his *tambito* that his mother had died.

"Eloy, Eloy," Miguel cried. *"Mamá se murió."*

"Sí, I know. I heard the mourning," Eloy said, trying to hold back his tears. But with Miguel's confirmation of what he had sensed, Eloy couldn't contain his sorrow and let loose a deep cry, not only for his mother but for himself. He had let ambition and his mission take him away from his home, and more importantly, his family. He had sacrificed them, and he had missed his home and his mother so much.

He lingered over her body. She looked so old, but her face seemed peaceful. Mamá is happy; she is with Papá, Eloy thought. He hugged her frail body—how thin she had become! He cried for her. But he cried more for himself—for the years

235

spent apart from her and Miguel, and for the curse that shad-owed the past as well as the future.

"Mamá wanted a Catholic burial. Father Garza will per-form the services at the little church here in the village," Miguel said.

The next day was devoted to preparing for the funeral. A steady stream of mourners and friends passed through the house, and Eloy's sadness was eased by the comfort of being back home, among his people.

After the services and burial, Eloy and Miguel had occa-sion to talk. Eloy had never felt so close to his brother as in this time of sorrow. He and Miguel talked into the wee hours of the morning, telling each other the recent details of their lives. Eloy listened intently as Miguel related how he took care of their Mamá in her last days and proudly as he described his work in the university lab. Miguel had heard of Eloy's accomplishments many times, but Eloy had hidden the events of La Perla from him, so rather than talk about work, he de-cided to convey the whole truth about the personal side of his life. He told Miguel about Puerto Rico, La Perla, Raven, El Oso, Don, Karen, and Roger. He also told his brother that Maria had come back into his life. After Reuben's murder, Eloy explained, he and Maria found their way back to one another and realized that despite their years apart they still loved each other, and that love continued to grow.

On the eve of his departure, Eloy took his brother aside. "Miguel, I want to give you something," he said as he removed a bound manuscript from his suitcase. "I've written to you many times about our research and our ability to induce a sudden onset of Alzheimer's in a primate model. I want you to have this copy of my lab notes on the procedures." Miguel accepted the volume and began to leaf through it.

"Why did you write your notes in a mixture of Spanish and Huni Kui?"

"I must tell you that the ways of science in America are very complicated and competitive. Some researchers will stop at nothing to steal or alter research results. My brother, you have no idea how blind ambition drives some scientists. At NIH, Dr. Roger Atkins, who I told you about, has been trying to steal my research data. I let his former post-doc, Donna, work in my lab. That was a big mistake. I think he planted her in my laboratory to spy on me." Miguel set down the notebook and reached into his pocket to get a package of cigarettes. He lit one.

"Just a couple of nights ago I surprised Donna at the lab when she thought I wasn't there—it wasn't the first time. Dr. Atkins is very upset that I have developed a successful Alzheimer's model. He has been trying to develop one throughout his research career with no success. He is very jealous of my achievements. I think he would do anything to get rid of me."

"Are you afraid of this man?"

"Atkins? No, Miguel. He is no real threat to me, just my work. But there is a man I do fear. After Maria was raped in La Perla and I was forced to purify Raven's heroin, I was so consumed with anger . . . I did a terrible thing. I gave Raven my Ranita, *Phylobates terribilis*, whose toxin killed him. Then El Oso, Raven's bodyguard, hit and killed my Ranita, which sent him into convulsions. El Oso swore he would kill me. Now he has been released from prison, and even though Maria has her own bodyguards, Miguel, I still worry about both of us, and I sense that we are in danger. All of my life I have feared death because of the gene that we might carry . . ."

"Yes, I understand. I might carry it too."

"But now I am afraid of being attacked or killed by El Oso."

"Eloy, it's a miracle that you and Maria survived such an ordeal. But it was many years ago. Surely this Oso will not find you in America."

"El Oso is looking for me. I am sure of it. And this fear is distracting me from my work—ironically, just when we're at a critical stage in our research—and that's what I want to talk to you about. *Hermano*, can you take off a couple of months from Dr. Rodríguez's lab?" Eloy asked.

"I guess so," Miguel responded.

"I really need your help in Washington. I'm on the verge of a major discovery—something that will change Alzheimer's forever. But I don't trust anyone except you right now. Here's my plan," Eloy explained as he reached back into his suitcase and handed Miguel a passport.

"How did you get the passport?"

"It was easy. I have friends in Tacoma Park who can get anything from Puerto Rican coffee to . . . well, anything."

"Are you sure it's okay, the passport?"

"*Sí*, I want you to come back and work with me at NIH. There are some very important things that we have to do. If something happens to me for whatever reason, who will continue? I have become like the *Americanos*. I trust no one but you."

"I don't know. I have to call Dr. Rodríguez. I have to tell him," he hesitated.

"I thought," Eloy responded, "you told me that Dr. Rodríguez said you could stay as long as necessary. I talked to Felipe yesterday, and he said he could do your work."

"*Sí*," Miguel said. "When Felipe and I were on the way here to see Mamá he said that he could do my work, and stay as long as it takes."

"Then why stay? We can see Felipe tomorrow. He is staying at the church, *sí*?"

"*Sí*," Miguel said.

"Well, can you come?"

"But I have nothing to wear," he said.

"We're the same size. We even look alike—ugly!" Eloy said.

"Look, there's one other thing. I want Felipe to take this back to Dr. Rodríguez's lab in Caracas," Eloy said, reaching into the suitcase again and removing a container.

"What is it?"

"These are cells that I have infected with a viral vector, and I don't want anything to happen to them. Do you think Felipe could take this to the lab and maintain the culture?"

"*Sí, no hay problema*," Miguel assured him. "But why?"

"I'm not sure, but I'm becoming very afraid . . . cautious."

"My brother, I'm also afraid. Too much has happened. We're the only ones left in our family, but let's not be sad. Let's move together, onward, *los Córdova Santiago*!" Miguel said, raising his fist with a laugh, like they did when they were children.

"*Sí*, I'll go. How about Pablo's Cantina for a beer?"

"*Sí*, too much sorrow. Mamá and Papá would like us to work together."

They left their home and walked through Santa Rosa de Agua. The village was increasingly squalid, and open sewers now contaminated roadside ditches and ponds. Eloy thought how much Santa Rosa had changed, how the level of poverty had grown over the years.

When they reached the cantina, loud salsa music was play-ing. They had to walk through clouds of foul smoke to get to the bar.

"*Pablo, dos Polares!*" Miguel said.

"*Sí*," responded the overweight bartender, popping the tops off of two cold bottles. "I haven't seen you two for a long time," he said with a big grin. The grin soon changed. "I am sorry about your mother." He wiped his hands on his Harvard T-shirt, which was soiled and gray. "The beers are on the house."

Eloy picked up the cold beer and took a couple of quick gulps. He savored the taste of the Venezuelan beer. He missed so many things about home.

"Oh," he said to Miguel. "I forgot to toast. *Salud*," he said, touching bottles with his brother. "To us, to science, to the brothers Córdova Santiago, to the cure for *El Mal*."

After a couple of beers, Eloy and Miguel returned home. The hour was getting late and they were tired.

Eloy and Miguel lay in their hammocks in their old *tambito*, listening to the water lap the stilts, regarding the reflections of the moonlight on the water through cracks in the floor, and breathing the aroma of the lake. These things brought comforting memories to the brothers as they began to drift off to sleep. But Eloy was tormented by concern about his notebook now that Miguel was returning with him. He looked at his mother's hammock. It looked so empty. He went to it and knelt down. He carefully lifted the floor boards below it to uncover his mother's hiding place, the urn where she hid her treasures.

Eloy placed his laboratory notes in the urn, and remembered as he did so the look on his mother's face when she handed him his father's passport to use to enter the United States through Puerto Rico. He ran his fingers around the rim of the urn, trying to feel the remains of his mother's touch. He imagined her reading his father's letters over and over again and reliving her memories of him. Then Eloy smiled, thinking she was sleeping with Papá tonight, and returned to his hammock and fell into a deep, peaceful sleep.

The next morning Eloy and Miguel awoke to the sounds of roosters crowing and a bright sun. Eloy made coffee as

Miguel gathered up the few possessions he had brought from Caracas and packed for Bethesda. Over coffee, they discussed their plans. Tia Isabel would watch the house. Miguel would give Felipe the cultures to take back to maintain in the lab until Miguel returned. Eloy told Miguel that he felt it would be safer if his laboratory journal stayed in Venezuela, and he told Miguel where he had hidden it.

Together they walked to their parents' graves to say their farewells.

"Mamá, Papá, we'll be back," Miguel said. "I will be back."

Eloy, on his knees at the headstone, prayed and again vowed, "Papá, I will find the cure!" They remained at the grave in silence until they heard the sound of an airplane. "*Vamonos*," Eloy said. "I hear Juan."

Juan's old converted war surplus airplane taxied up to the dock. Eloy and Miguel said their goodbyes to their friends and Tia Isabel, who waved as they boarded the plane. The surface of the lake was choppy, so the takeoff was bumpy as the pontoons bounced over the uneven water, but the ride got smoother once the plane began to fly. It only dipped and swayed occasionally as it encountered turbulence. Eloy looked at his brother, who was biting an unlit cigarette in sheer terror. Eloy realized that this was Miguel's first plane ride. "*Mi hermano,* flying in a small plane is rough. Once we get on the jet at the airport in Maracaibo it will be smooth."

Settling in for the short flight to Maracaibo, they talked about scientific research and what they would do in Washington. Miguel had always wanted to visit the Smithsonian Museums for one thing, and Eloy said that they would. Miguel looked at his ticket and asked, "Why are we going to Dallas, Texas? My ticket is wrong. It says Dallas."

"No, no," Eloy said. "That is Dulles, D-U-L-L-E-S, an international airport on the outskirts of Washington, D.C., in Virginia."

"Why are we going there and not to the Washington airport?"

"The customs procedures are easier at Dulles, *comprende?*"

"Oh, *sí,*" Miguel said.

"*Mi amigo* in Tacoma said the Dulles airport is better. Immigration officers are very busy. Most international flights land there, and it will be easier for us," Eloy said.

Their plane landed after a four-hour flight.

"*Mi hermano*, here we are, home. Well not really—this isn't home; it's where I work," Eloy said, as they boarded a shuttle bus that took them to the customs area.

"No, this is not home," Miguel echoed.

The customs inspector asked Eloy and Miguel for their papers.

"Place of birth?" he asked them in a voice laced with total boredom.

"Lake Maracaibo, Venezuela," they responded.

"Citizenship?"

"Resident alien," Eloy said. "To visit," Miguel said.

The inspector peered over his glasses and said, "Oh, for a moment I thought you were twins, but I see you aren't. What is the purpose of your visit?" he asked Miguel.

"To work with me," Eloy responded.

"Wait a minute," the customs agent said, coming to life. "*Mi amigo*, you can't work here. You can only visit."

"Oh, I mean to visit . . . ," Eloy said quickly, " . . . to visit."

The customs inspector motioned Eloy to a secondary inspection area. "We need to ask you some more questions and inspect your baggage more thoroughly." Oh, no, Eloy thought, they know something about . . . will they find out? He looked at Miguel and whispered, "Pretend you don't know English. I'll talk for us."

"Purpose of visit?" the second customs agent asked as he went through their luggage without even looking at the two men.

Eloy said, "I work here as a scientist at NIH, and my brother is coming to my lab to learn some new techniques."

The customs agent looked up at Eloy and said, "Oh, yeah. I've seen you on TV. You're that scientist who found a cure for old timer's disease."

"Yes," Eloy said, "Alzheimer's."

"Go on," she said, waving her hand toward the door. "Good luck with your research."

Eloy and Miguel pushed their way through the gate. There were a lot of people in the terminal.

"I have never seen so many people. It's busier than Caracas. Is it always this crowded?"

"Yes, *mi hermano*. This airport is always busy. Also, it is the fourth of July weekend. Maybe that is why it is so crowded."

"But why are they all so unfriendly?"

Eloy noticed a large man who looked familiar, older but . . . nah, he must be tired, he thought. But he glanced again. The man was walking ahead of him; Eloy stared at his back. He whispered to Miguel, "I think I know that man." The man's gait was more a swagger than a walk. He glared at the pudgy hand and, yes, there it was, the tattoo! El Oso was here! Eloy was terrified and immediately grabbed Miguel and headed in the opposite direction. "We need to hurry!" he whispered. "It's El Oso. Hurry, hurry!"

"Eloy, you must be mistaken. This worry is making you imagine things."

"No, Miguel. I saw the tattoo on his hand. It is El Oso. Please, Miguel, let's get out of here!"

They rushed outside and hailed a taxi. As the cab sped down the Dulles access road, Eloy sat quietly, frowning, and Miguel counted the silhouettes of trees in the moonlight.

"Eloy," Miguel began, "I think you're overreacting."

"I'm worried, Miguel. I tell you about El Oso and we see him in the airport. He's here to kill me. I can't think of any other reason for him to be here," he said, terrified.

"It's just a coincidence. You're probably worried for nothing."

"Oh, no. I'll never forget: he swore to kill me. He's here for me, but I won't let him," Eloy said, his voice breaking with the tone of fear.

"Does El Oso know where you live?"

"I don't know."

"Does he know where you work?"

"I don't know."

"Maybe it's better that we don't go to your apartment tonight."

"Yeah, I can call Don and we can stay with him. But it's the fourth of July and Don probably isn't home. He's probably on a date."

"Maybe we can go to a hotel," Miguel suggested.

"Yeah, that's a good idea. Then tomorrow I can call Maria and tell her what's happening. Driver, *amigo*," Eloy said to the small Mexican cab driver. "We've changed our minds. Please take us to the Hyatt Hotel in Bethesda, the one on Wisconsin."

"*Sí, mis amigos.*"

"We'll check into the hotel for a couple of days until I can figure out what's going on," Eloy said, looking relieved.

CHAPTER 32

July 4, 1997

Eloy and Miguel slept soundly and didn't wake up until late in the morning. Eloy rolled over in bed and looked up, expecting to see a thatched roof, but instead saw the ceiling of their hotel room. He looked at the clock—it was already eleven. He looked at his sleeping brother for a moment and thought about how much he loved Miguel. He shook him. "Miguel, *levantate.*"

"*Sí, sí,*" he said, rubbing his dark, almond-shaped eyes and looking at the hotel room with some bewilderment. "*Donde* . . . where are we?"

"El Oso, the hotel," he reminded him. Eloy got up and went into the bathroom, turned on the TV and then asked Miguel, "Want some coffee?"

"Just a minute. I need to get dressed."

"Oh, no. There is a coffee maker in the room."

"*Gringos*—they think of everything," Miguel responded.

"*Sí.*"

Eloy and Miguel sat on their beds, drinking their coffee.

"As far as El Oso is concerned, I'll call Maria and warn her that we saw him. Then I should go to the lab."

"*Hermano*, don't worry. Just do what you have to do."

Eloy dialed Maria's number. After four rings, the answering machine kicked in, so Eloy left a message.

"Maria, it's Eloy. Please call me when you get in. I need to talk to you. It's important—Miguel and I saw El Oso at the airport, although I don't think he saw us. Call me at the lab or apartment and leave a message if I'm not in. I can't wait to see you. I love you. *Adios*." Eloy hung up the phone and turned to Miguel. "She's not home."

Eloy rubbed his face and tried to forget El Oso. He looked at his brother. Why was he being so selfish, not even thinking of Miguel? "How would you like to go to the Mall, and then maybe the lab, or my apartment?"

"I'd rather go to the lab. I don't want to shop."

"No, no. I mean the Mall downtown. You sound like you've never been to America," he joked. "Where the museums are," he said, rubbing his fist through Miguel's hair like he did when they were kids.

Eloy was about to turn off the TV when the newscaster announced an update to the burgeoning crisis in the Middle East. There was an escalating threat of war between the United States and Iraq because of Iraq's failure to comply with the biological and chemical weapons resolution that the U.N. had just approved.

The newscaster reported: "The agreement bans the development, production, stockpiling and use of weapons of mass destruction. Just recently the Iraqi leader promised U.N. inspectors unfettered access to Iraq. Today, however, he provoked a serious confrontation by forcibly ejecting inspectors after they found evidence that Iraqi scientists are developing new biological weapons that use the Marburg virus and the

Anthrax bacterium, two of the most deadly infectious agents known to man."

The reporter continued, "Of greater concern is Iraq's development of 'bio-regulators,' germ agents capable of controlling human behavior and brain activity like sleep, anger, violence and memory.

"The president has given the discovery of these weapons the utmost priority. They pose a threat not only to national security but to the security of the entire world. The U.N. has called for an emergency meeting in the Netherlands at the end of July to address this issue. The president has announced that the United States favors diplomacy but is prepared to take 'necessary actions.'

"Certain members of Congress, however, favor a more emphatic military response. Senator Reynolds states that he is 'tired of this perpetual game and is ready to convene Congress to declare war on Iraq, not just to degrade Saddam's ability to build weapons of mass destruction but to completely destroy his terrorist regime.' Unidentified sources in the White House suggest that Vice President Daniels favors a more aggressive policy as well."

"Hmmm," said Eloy, turning off the TV. "I hope the president can get Iraq's compliance in the Netherlands."

"Yeah, it would be much better. The vice president and that senator look like they want war regardless of the consequences," Miguel said.

The brothers got dressed and took the elevator down to the Metro station below the hotel. They boarded the Metro to take them to the Smithsonian Museum—to the one that housed the dinosaurs, since that was the one exhibit Miguel wanted to see more than any other—and spent the afternoon looking at all the sights.

"What do you think of Washington, Miguel?"

"It's an impressive city, much more than I thought. But it's very hot," Miguel added, as he wiped the sweat off of his forehead and pulled at his *guavara* where it stuck to his back and his chest.

"*Sí*, Washington is as hot and humid as Lake Maracaibo."

Miguel decided to buy a T-shirt from one of the Mall vendors. "Here, let me buy it for you," Eloy said. He selected a maroon shirt that said "Smithsonian" and had a picture of a mammoth on it. "I need to take off my *guavara*," Miguel said, and went to change his shirt in a nearby restroom.

"It's almost five o'clock," Miguel said when he returned. "I'd like to go back to the hotel, if that's okay with you. I'm also kind of tired. Aren't you?"

"*Sí, un poquito*. Let's go." Miguel and Eloy walked to the station and boarded the next Metro.

"I was thinking," Eloy said. "We should go to the lab to make sure everything is okay—you know, with El Oso on the loose. I don't see how he could get past security, but . . ."

"*Hermano*, why don't you go by yourself? I can go with you tomorrow or another day. I would rather just rest now, okay?"

"Then you need to get off here," Eloy said as they neared the Bethesda stop. "I'll be back in a couple of hours. Have a good rest in the meantime. We can go out to dinner when I return, and maybe stop by my apartment to see what the situation is. *Adios*."

Eloy kept looking at the people on the Metro as it continued to the next stop, the Medical Center at NIH. He was jumpy. As he exited the Metro station, he looked toward the clinical center and turned his head to see the grounds of the Bethesda Naval Hospital across the street. The perimeter of the grounds was lined with soldiers. President Clint Walker climbed slowly into a large helicopter, which soon took off. "The president doesn't travel light," Eloy said to a bystander.

"Yeah," the young black man replied. "Nowadays you can't have enough security." Boy, is he right, Eloy thought.

"Why was the president at the hospital?" Eloy asked.

"Don't know. Maybe he was having a checkup."

"On the fourth of July?"

"Well, you know those politicians. Let's hope he's not really sick with all of the problems in Iraq, that germ warfare stuff. It's scary."

"Yeah," Eloy said, "the last thing we need is the president to be incapacitated and Ted Daniels to become president. He'd let the Senate start a war."

"That's for sure. Well, see you. Have a happy fourth," the man said as he boarded the bus.

As he crossed the campus to his lab, Eloy felt as if someone were following him. He walked into his laboratory and immediately sensed that something was wrong—that someone had been in his office. Papers were out of place, someone had rifled through his desk, and his computer keyboard lay at a different angle than he had left it. It looked like someone had accessed his computer. He immediately checked the viral vectors and cell cultures. They looked okay. Donna had left a note in the culture chamber with an update on their progress, which also said she would be in Tuesday because of the fourth of July holiday. She wrote that she was sorry about his mother.

He was getting ready to leave when the telephone rang. His first impulse was to not answer the phone, but he thought, who would be calling on a holiday? He waited for the answering machine to take the message.

"Hello, Eloy. This is Zoren. When you get back, please

give me a call—it's important. I am sorry about your mother.
I am . . ."

"Hello, Zoren. I'm here," he said as he turned off the answering machine.

"I'm sorry to bother you on the fourth, but it's very important that I talk to you. Can I come over to your lab?"

"Sure. The door will be locked, but knock three times so
I'll know it's you." That way he didn't have to worry about
anyone else. Like El Oso. Damn it, why was he so jumpy? He
should just find El Oso and ask him what the hell he planned
to do.

There was a sound at the door. That couldn't be Zoren so
soon, he thought. He jumped off the couch and hid in the supply closet. The outside door to the lab opened and in walked a
man Eloy had never seen before—a tall, muscular stranger with
a crew cut and steel blue eyes. The stranger looked around the
lab, turned his head toward the hall and said, "Okay, come in."

Eloy thought that his heart would pound out of his chest.
As he closed the door slowly, it screeched. Damn! They would
find him. He peered out the crack between the door and the
frame and saw Donna come in. She went to the culture chamber, picked up some culture vials and left something behind.
It looked like a pack of cigarettes. Should he confront her?
What the hell was she doing here? Who was the man with
her? Eloy's sweaty palms held the door closed. The pair left
quickly. Eloy's heart was racing. He was totally confused. He
knew he shouldn't have ever trusted Donna. He was in no
condition to talk to Zoren. He would have to postpone the
meeting.

He dialed Zoren's phone. It rang three times, then four.
"Please, Zoren, please still be there," he said out loud. "Answer!"

On the fifth ring, Zoren picked up.

"Hello, Zoren," Eloy said, trying to control his rapid breathing. "Can we wait until Tuesday? I just don't feel up to it right now—the trip . . . my mother . . . you know."

"Okay, but Roger has been snooping around, and I'm afraid that this time his complaints have some legal ramifications," Zoren said.

"What do you mean?"

"Well, he looked into your personnel file. I don't know how he got access, but he did. The upshot is he says he has irrefutable evidence that your resident alien papers are falsified and that you are in the United States illegally. What does this all mean?"

"I have no idea," Eloy answered.

"Is Roger full of hot air, or does he really have evidence? We need to get to the bottom of this."

"I assure you, all of my papers are in order. Roger is just trying to make trouble. He has never liked me, and all along he has been jealous of my research and my recognition."

"Yeah, I agree. But this time his allegations are serious."

"I know, but they're without merit. I have to go."

"Before you do, I have to tell you that Roger has arranged for a meeting in my office Tuesday with you, our personnel administrators and an INS representative. Tuesday at noon."

"I'll be there," Eloy responded. "Tuesday at noon."

"Okay, I'll see you in my office," Zoren said.

"See you there. Goodbye," Eloy said. He took one quick look around the lab, started to walk toward the culture chamber, but changed his mind and decided to just leave.

Donna and Mark drove North on Old Georgetown Road, then right onto Tuckerman Lane and into their apartment complex. "Hurry," Donna said, running up the sidewalk to their apartment with a wiggle of her hips. She hiked up her skirt to show Mark that she wasn't wearing any panties. She fanned her brow like a Southern belle. "I'm so hot," she said in an exaggerated drawl, "like Scarlett O'Hara. Oh, Rhett, come and get your hot mama," she said, opening the door to their apartment. Mark pursued her inside, where he found her lying on the couch with her skirt pulled above her waist.

Afterward Donna said, "You are such a stud," caressing his chest. "Oh, my God, I love the way you fuck," she said, nibbling at his ear. "More?" she asked, running her tongue down his neck and chest toward his stomach.

"Stop, stop. Not now. Look, did you get the culture? Did you set the timer?"

"Yes. Will it be okay?"

"No one's in the lab. It's the fourth and Don is out of town. Tomorrow will be a better day," Mark said.

"I still couldn't find the notebook," Donna said.

"Oh, we don't need it. You know the techniques."

"I sure do," she said as she slid her tongue around his navel. "Eloy won't get hurt, right?" Donna asked.

"Of course not. He's in Venezuela."

Just then, Mark's pager beeped. He leaned over the side of the couch and retrieved it from the waistband of his pants, which lay on the floor.

"Ah, shit. It's the White House." Mark walked to the kitchen and made a phone call. He hung up the phone, returned to the living room, and got dressed.

"Where are you going?" asked Donna.

"They need me at the White House. I'll only be gone for a couple of hours."

Mark grabbed his keys and bolted out the door.

When Eloy unlocked the door to their hotel room, he found Miguel asleep and the television tuned to the evening news. A picture of the Naval Hospital filled the screen. The newscaster said: "Speculation is that because President Walker's visit to the Naval Hospital was not routine, it involved a sudden, serious health problem—possibly the complications of a sinus infection the president recently suffered. Congress is becoming concerned about the president's health in light of Iraq's recent refusal to comply with the provisions of the biological weapons agreement and the increasing possibility of war. However, the vice president has assured the public that he is completely informed of the situation and is ready to act if need be.

"On a lighter note, let's turn to the activities at the Mall as Washington prepares for the annual July fourth fireworks show." Eloy turned off the TV and woke Miguel. He told his brother about Donna and the man who entered the lab.

"Did you check to see if everything was okay?" Miguel asked.

"Well, sort of, but when I got the telephone call from Zoren . . ."

"Who's Zoren?"

"He's my boss. I think he knows I'm here illegally."

"What are you going to do?"

"I don't know. I keep asking myself, what was Donna doing with that strange man in my lab? And why is El Oso in Washington? I can't figure out what's going on."

"Calm down, Eloy. We'll get this figured out. One thing at a time. Let's go back to the lab and see if anything was really taken," Miguel said.

"Good idea," Eloy said. "Let's go there first, then we can get my truck from the parking lot at the apartment."

CHAPTER 33

N ot again, Clint Walker thought.

Pain consumed him. His head felt like it was going to explode louder than the fireworks flashing over the Mall and lighting up the Washington Monument. One moment he felt euphoric—stronger and smarter than ever—but then the euphoria vanished, like smoke from a flame, and was replaced by stupor. Thoughts evaporated, feelings bounced around in his mind, memory fled. Who was he?

Sounds called him, but from where? He looked around his office and saw no one, yet the screaming continued in his brain.

He tried to call out, but his voice was empty. His mouth and face were out of control. All he could manage was a twisted grimace, which then collapsed into a lifeless mask. He kept hearing the screaming inside of his head. His eyes searched the room, but no one was there.

He stood up from behind his large oak desk. His gut was alive with fire and contractions. His skin burned, and sweat poured from his face. He began to shiver and staggered toward the bathroom tearing at his clothes, ripping off his suit coat. But where was the bathroom? He couldn't remember. He pulled at his tie and tore his shirt open, stripped off his pants. Fear seized him. He needed air. His breathing was labored. His face was on fire. Stumbling and half falling, he reached for the door—but it was too late. His body shook and his legs buckled as he fell to the floor.

Am I going to die? he wondered. "Help," he tried to scream as he lay on the oval carpet. "Help," he tried again, only to hear a primal animal sound emerge from his throat.

"Clint!" Helen cried as she rushed to his aid. "Mark, come here. It's happening again!" Mark burst into the office.

"It's worse than before!" Helen exclaimed. She cried again, "Clint!" and dropped to the floor beside him to hug and comfort him. "What's happening to you?" she wailed. She held his head in her hands and wiped the sweat from his brow.

"Helen," he murmured. It looked like he was going to say more, but he just grunted. The grunts turned to spasms and his body convulsed, his eyes rolling back into his head.

"Mark, call the helicopter! We have to take him back to the Naval Hospital! Call the paramedics now. Call Dr. Green!"

"Yes, ma'am," Mark responded. "But the ambulance is better. With the crisis in the Middle East and all the media focus, the helicopter would draw too much attention."

The president was barely breathing, and foam had gathered at the corners of his mouth.

All of a sudden he stood up and stared at her. She noticed that his pupils were dilated. What is happening? she thought. Is he going insane?

"Help!" she cried, as he started to swing his arms at her. He had found the source of the voices. He would destroy the demons.

Just as he started to strike his wife, two paramedics arrived. They grappled with him until they stabilized him, then placed him on a gurney, rushing him outside to the waiting ambulance. Helen jumped into the ambulance with them. Mark followed.

"Why is this happening?" she said to Mark. He shook his head. "Where is Dr. Green?" she asked.

"He'll meet us at the hospital!"

She looked at her sedated husband lying quietly as the paramedics worked on him. She closed her eyes and tried to erase the vision of his anguish. But she couldn't erase the thought of him dying.

When the ambulance arrived at the hospital, a Secret Service detail was securing the emergency room entrance. As the paramedics opened the ambulance doors, swarms of doctors, nurses and Secret Service agents surrounded the president and rushed him inside.

Mark helped the first lady out of the ambulance. "Thank you, Mark. I'm so glad you were there . . . I don't know what I would have done. I'm sorry you had to see him like that."

"It's my job to be there for the president, Mrs. Walker, good or bad." Mark clutched Helen's arm and guided her toward the emergency room entrance. "Let's get you settled inside," he said.

The first lady was greeted by a nurse who immediately whisked her away to a private waiting area.

Mark turned and walked outside. One of the other agents had offered to take him back to his apartment on Tuckerman Lane. The smell of smoke was in the air. As he got into the car he saw a laboratory building across the street at the National Institutes of Health engulfed in flames.

Part of Building 27 was consumed, and chemicals exploded like a second fourth of July fireworks display. The mounting flames sucked in air with a roar louder than a blast furnace. The night sky was aglow as the firefighters rushed to the scene. The Bethesda firefighters from the Cedar Avenue station began to pump water onto the flames, but before they could enter the building they had to wait for the NIH firefighters to arrive. They were specially trained to handle Class B chemical fires, which involved not only toxic and caustic substances but other hazards as well.

"Just contain the fire!" Captain Alan Nuanez shouted as he followed the stream of water from his hose up the stairs to the source of the fire. The heat was intense. It was hard to breathe, even though he wore an oxygen mask, and his heavy fire gear only served to trap the sweat from his body. "Just confine the fire to the source," he shouted. In a minute the NIH fire team arrived.

"Is anyone in there?" Alan shouted as he pounded on the door of the room where the fire had originated.

No answer could be heard over the roar of the fire. Thank God it's the fourth, he thought to himself as he chopped at the door to the lab with his ax. He noticed that the health hazard was four and the name plate read: Alzheimer's Research Lab, Eloy Córdova Santiago. He pushed through, and he and the NIH fire team entered the lab. It was no use.

"We can't save this lab. Just confine the fire. Keep it from spreading," he shouted, standing just inside the doorway. Within a few minutes the lab was only smoldering embers.

"This lab is pretty well shot," one of the firefighters said. "At least we saved the rest of the building."

"Thank God no one was here," the fire captain said. "These

chemical fires are almost always fatal if you get trapped inside."

"The worst," the firefighter agreed.

"Okay, let's mop it up, clean up any hot spots, check it
out," the captain ordered. Lifting the battered door to the lab,
firefighters discovered a smoking corpse. The unmistakable
smell of burned human flesh fouled the air. Through the ashes
and smoldering flesh that still clung to it, the skull could be
seen, and a set of perfect white teeth.

"We've got one here," Alan shouted. "Call the coroner,"
he said, then ran outside into the fresh night air and pulled off
his mask.

 "Did you hear the sirens?" Mark asked Donna as he
walked into their apartment.

"It was music to my ears."

"Just as you said, ten o'clock," Mark noted, looking at his
watch. He gave Donna a kiss, picked up his glass of champagne from the coffee table and said, "A toast to us, to the
Alzheimer's project, to Kentucky Green Tobacco, and other
things." Mark touched his champagne glass to hers. "We did
it! With all the data we've got and the cell cultures containing
the virus, we'll be rich."

Donna lifted her glass. "To our little friend Eloy and that
magnificent brain." Then with a sneer she raised her middle
finger. "And to that little prick, Roger. May he vanish from
the face of the earth when I take his position as director of
Alzheimer's research for Kentucky Green. We'll be famous
and rich!"

"I'll drink to that. Turn on the TV. It's time for the news."
Mark looked at his glass. "I still don't understand how you'll
get Eloy to work for Kentucky Green," he said.

"He doesn't know," Donna said. "I'll just offer to set him up in Virginia so he can continue his work until the lab is rebuilt."

When she turned on the TV, the weatherman was giving the next day's forecast.

A deep voice-over announced, "We interrupt this program to bring you breaking news from NIH. Let's go to Faye Adams. Faye, tell us what's happening."

"Jim," the thin blonde said, as the camera panned the scene of the fire and came in for a close-up of the reporter. "At present the NIH lab fire is almost contained. The loss is estimated at more than $3 million. Fortunately, the building was empty and no casualties have been reported. Also, NIH is fortunate that the other labs were not engulfed."

"Whose lab is it?" Jim asked.

"Sources say that the lab was that of Eloy Córdova Santiago, an Alzheimer's researcher. He comes from Venezuela and has a reputation as an outstanding scientist in the field. . . . Just a moment," Faye said, as the fire captain emerged from the building. He was breathing hard. "Captain, Captain, can I talk to you?" the reporter asked.

"Yes, yes, just a moment," he said, trying to catch his breath. "There's a body. We found a burned corpse. I have to call the coroner."

"Folks, you heard it first here on WBAC-TV. A body has been found in the NIH lab fire. Can you identify the body?"

"No, it's burned beyond recognition," the distraught captain said.

"Okay, back to the studio. We'll keep you updated as the identity of the body becomes known."

"I thought you said no one would be there," Donna screamed at Mark. "'No one,' you said. We did it . . . We killed Eloy, you stupid bastard," Donna shrieked. She pounded her fists on Mark's chest, sobbing. "We killed him, we killed him . . ."

"Calm down. You have the notes. You know the techniques."

"No, I don't have the notes. Sure, I know the techniques and have the viral vectors, but don't you understand, you cold-hearted bastard? I just wanted to destroy the competition, not the competitor." Her eyes filled with tears. "Poor Eloy, poor Eloy. What have I done?" she cried, sitting down on the couch. "What are we going to do? What about Roger? What if he knows we set the fire?"

"Now that Eloy is dead, he'll probably try to make you look bad," Mark said.

"You bastard! This is your fault. You forced me into it!"

"What? Me? You're the one who did it. I didn't have to force you."

"Yes, but I didn't want to kill anyone," Donna sobbed, hitting Mark on the chest. "Oh, what did I do?" she cried, sliding to the floor.

CHAPTER 34

Maria sat alone on the sofa in her townhouse sipping a glass of white wine. She had just returned from watching the fireworks on the Mall and was listening to the messages on her answering machine. The message from Eloy at first warmed her heart, but at the mention of El Oso she froze. I'll call Eloy in a couple of minutes, she thought, and she turned on the television for distraction. Reporter Faye Adams had just run over to Captain Alan Nuanez in front of what remained of Building 27. Even with the smoke and the darkness, Maria immediately recognized the building. She grabbed the remote to turn up the volume.

"Captain, Captain," Faye shouted as he took off his helmet and mask, "can I talk to you?"

"Yes," he said, trying to catch his breath. "There's a body. We found a burned corpse. I have to call the coroner."

Maria stared at the television in disbelief and dropped her wine glass on the floor. She fell to her knees on the carpet and began to scream, "Eloy, Eloy, *mi amor.*" Her body convulsed with emotion. Then, wiping her eyes, she went into the bathroom and threw up, hugging the toilet for comfort. How she wished she had told Eloy how much she truly loved him.

The 1965 Chevy pickup's headlights lighted up Old Georgetown Road as it headed south. Salsa music drifted through the open window. The old black truck looked out of place in Rockville. The driver rubbed the dirty windshield with the cuff of his sleeve to see if indeed there was a glow in the sky. There were flames coming from Bethesda. It looked like they were from the campus of NIH. Just then the disc jockey announced in Spanish that there had been a fire at NIH and that a body had been found. Preliminary reports were that the victim was renowned Alzheimer's researcher Eloy Córdova Santiago.

Eloy squeezed the truck's steering wheel and immediately pulled over to the side of the road. He couldn't believe what he had heard. The newscaster said he was dead. He turned up the volume. The fire was believed to have been started accidently by an electrical short in a culture chamber filled with volatile chemicals. Officials said that the fire was confined to the point of origin and that damage to the rest of the building was minimal. More important than the damage, however, was the loss of Santiago, who was reportedly on the verge of finding a cure for Alzheimer's. "More news on the hour at eleven," the announcer said as Latino music returned to the air.

Eloy's mouth was dry, and his heart seemed like it was going to burst. Bile filled his throat. He opened the truck door, fighting nausea until he got to the trees. Oh, Miguel, he thought. I should never have left you in the lab to go check my apartment and get the truck. He cried. "*Mi hermano, mi hermano*! It should have been me!" he wailed, filled with guilt.

He sat for a few minutes by the side of the road with salsa music blaring from the radio, numb with guilt and grief. Much more numb though with fear. He was scared—scared to death. What should he do? Maybe he was safe since everyone thought he was dead. At first he thought he should just leave the country and save his life. Go back to Venezuela. Then he told himself, Of course not. I have to find out who killed Miguel. Aside from El Oso, who would want me dead?

He got back into his truck, turned around and headed up Old Georgetown Road to a gas station with a pay phone. The phone rang several times.

"Pick up," Eloy demanded as the phone continued to ring. The answering machine picked up. At the beep, Eloy said, "Maria, Maria, are you there? Pick up the phone! Are you home? Pick up the phone!" he shouted.

Maria was still in the bathroom. When she heard his voice she thought she must be dreaming. Was someone playing a cruel joke?

"Maria, Maria, pick up the phone. It's Eloy. I'm not dead. Maria, pick up the phone."

"Eloy, is that you? Oh, Eloy," Maria exulted.

"Yes, it's me! *Mi amor*, it's me! Maria, Maria!"

"*Sí, sí,* it's you?"

"Yes," Eloy said again.

"You nearly shocked me to death. What happened . . . whose body did they find?"

"Miguel," he said hesitantly. "I brought him back with me from Venezuela to help with the research."

"Oh, no. Poor Miguel. Let's not talk on the phone any more. Come over."

"No, someone wants to kill me. Someone killed Miguel thinking he was me. I think it was El Oso or maybe Donna. Who knows? Meet me."

"Where?"

"You know, our special place."

"I'll be there in half an hour."

"I'm in my truck," Eloy said. "Half an hour."

He drove the truck onto Old Georgetown Road and almost into the headlights of an oncoming red BMW convertible. Eloy thought it looked like Donna's car. But he shook his head, thinking he was going crazy. Proceeding along the east side of the Naval Hospital and Army Medical Center near Woodmont Road, Eloy turned into one of the side entrances to Rockcreek Park. It was almost eleven thirty. Eloy waited. Finally, he saw headlights approaching in his rear view mirror. It was a black car. He hoped it was Maria. For a moment he wondered if it could be the police. No, there were no lights on the roof. Just then the headlights blinked three times. It was Maria! She got out of the car and rushed to him, throwing her arms around him through the open window of the truck.

"Eloy, Eloy, I love you," Maria said. "No more pretense. *Te quiero!*"

"*Yo también,*" he said, untangling himself from her embrace so he could get out of the truck. They kissed long and passionately. He could taste the salt from her tears as he kissed her cheek. Her breath in his mouth breathed new life into him. When they disengaged from each other, Maria said, "I'm so happy you are alive, *mi amore.*"

"Me too, but *pobre* Miguel?"

"Let's hide your truck somewhere. Or better yet, I can drive it back to your apartment and park it, and then we can go home in my car. You can stay with me."

"Good."

"Follow me in my car."

After dropping off the truck, Eloy said, "We have to stop by the Hyatt. Miguel and I were staying there to hide from El Oso until we could talk to you, and I have to get our things." Eloy gave Maria the key to his room and waited in the back of her car as she retrieved the belongings.

Maria drove, and Eloy lay in her lap, out of sight of passing cars. He caressed her, feeling ever so close. He knew that tonight they would make love again.

The soft classical music on the car radio was interrupted by a news update. The reporter said that the coroner was still in the process of identifying the body found at the lab fire at NIH, but Dr. Zoren Krekorian was interviewed, and he said that he had spoken with Eloy Córdova Santiago in his lab a few hours earlier. The probability was very high that the body was that of the researcher. Maria reached down and stroked Eloy's hair.

The newscaster also mentioned that the White House had confirmed that the president's second visit of the day to the Naval Hospital was not for an annual checkup but rather for a minor allergy and sinus problem. Because of concomitant insomnia and stress, the president was to stay overnight at the hospital for observation.

"In regard to the worsening crisis in Iraq," the newscaster continued, "the government of Saddam Hussein has become increasingly defiant and will not allow arms inspectors to return to Iraq. An Iraqi spokesman has reiterated that continued intrusion by the United States in the business of Iraq is pushing the world to the brink . . ."

"I wonder what's wrong with the president," Maria said. "He was healthy, but now with this Iraq situation . . ."

After parking her car in the garage, Maria entered the house first to make sure everything was okay, and then went down to let Eloy in. Before going to bed, Maria took off her beeper and turned down the ring volume on her answering machine. She didn't want to be disturbed tonight because she and Eloy were no longer just friends. They had become lovers again.

CHAPTER 35

July 5, 1997

Eloy awoke to the aroma of Puerto Rican coffee and the smell of fresh pastries. He looked down at the serving tray that Maria had placed on the bed. When he became aware of his nakedness he pulled the sheets over his body.

"Have some coffee," Maria said, kissing him on the cheek. She had never looked so beautiful. Her white satin negligee accentuated the curves of her body, the green of her eyes and the smoothness of her skin. Eloy returned the kiss. They held each other in silence for a couple of minutes, enjoying the interlude.

Maria went to the night table to her answering machine to retrieve messages. She had several from her administrative assistant, Mike. "Sorry, but I have to call him back," she told Eloy, then dialed his number.

"I'm so sorry about Eloy. I'm so sorry," Mike said.

"Yes, so am I," Maria said.

"You are so strong. You don't sound like, like . . . like you are grieving. . . . You're so courageous."

"Oh, I guess I'm, uh, still in shock," Maria said hesitantly.

"The deputy coroner, Dr. Olga Schultz, needs you to identify the remains. All they have is the skull. Oh, I'm sorry I have to talk about him like that."

"It's all right."

"Well, please give her a call."

Maria wrote down the number. "I have to call the deputy coroner," Maria told Eloy after she hung up the phone. "They want me to identify," she paused, "the remains. Should we let them know that you're alive?"

"Let's think about this." Eloy looked over the top of his coffee mug, shaking his head in bewilderment, and whispered, "I don't know. Maybe I should pretend to be Miguel and go to my funeral services. I could be him," Eloy said. "But no, we have to think of the immediate circumstances."

"Should I identify the body as yours?" Maria asked. "Or should we tell them the truth?"

"Well, if we're going to find out who did this, wouldn't it be better if they thought I was dead?"

"Yes. But you'd have to hide, and then what? What if they found out? It would be dangerous. If they thought you were Miguel, you might learn more. At least for now I'll identify the body as yours," she concluded and gave Eloy a big hug.

"Yes, *mi amor*. That's what we'll do for now," he said, his eyes filling with tears. "*Pobrecito*. He's with Mamá and Papá. I never really got to know him as a man. He was only thirty-six."

Maria called the deputy coroner and arranged to identify the remains. She called her bodyguards, George Wilson and Sidney Smith, and told them she didn't need any security for the weekend—she would just stay home. She didn't want them around, not until she and Eloy could figure out a plan.

"Wait here and don't answer the phone," Maria said as she got ready to leave. "Just screen the calls. I'll be back in a couple of hours. You have my cell phone number, right?"

"Yes."

"Don't use it unless it's an emergency. Speak in fragments of Spanish, and disguise your voice."

"I don't like cellular phones. I told you before, I think . . . . Oh, I'm just paranoid."

"Would you like to read the paper while I'm gone?" Maria asked.

"Sure. Why not?"

Maria kissed Eloy, dressed, and opened the door. Eloy could see that it was another beautiful sunny day. Maria tossed the newspaper inside, blew him another kiss, and closed the door. Eloy poured himself another cup of coffee and sat down at the table to read the *Washington Post*.

PRESIDENT CLINT WALKER
DIAGNOSED WITH ALZHEIMER'S

After an examination yesterday at the Naval Hospital, it was determined that the president's problems with memory, concentration, insomnia and marked personality changes are due to Alzheimer's disease.

Physicians are puzzled by the unusually rapid progression of Alzheimer's in the president. But presidential doctors concur that according to the mental state status test, neurological examination and psychomotor testing, the president has Alzheimer's. These presumptive tests have been further confirmed by the use of a brain scan, which shows cell loss in the basal forebrain. The president will remain temporarily at the Naval Hospital in Bethesda. Plans for his long-term care are being coordinated by the White House.

Because President Walker's prognosis is uncertain, Vice President Ted Daniels will take over as president for the remainder of the term. He assures the nation and the world that he will demand that Iraq comply with the terms of the Biological and Chemical Weapons Convention or he will destroy Saddam's government and end his "increasing threat to the world."

Former first lady Judy Winston sends her condolences to the Walker family. Her husband, the former president, who also has Alzheimer's, continues to battle the disease.

Eloy finished reading the article, turned the page of the paper, and said out loud, "The president has Alzheimer's."

On the following page, he saw pictures of himself and of his lab engulfed in flames. The headline read: "Laboratory of Noted Alzheimer's Researcher Destroyed by Fire." He couldn't help thinking of Miguel. He fought back feelings of sadness for the loss of his brother and fear that someone was still trying to kill him. The article mentioned that positive identification had not yet been made but that the remains included a set of nearly perfect teeth, which investigators believe may confirm that the victim was Eloy Córdova Santiago. Eloy put his head between his hands and cried. His soul overflowed with guilt.

"It should have been me; it should have been me! Oh, *Dios,* why?"

 Dr. Olga Schultz was a large-boned woman who looked more like a no-nonsense security guard than a deputy coroner. She was very matter of fact and had little social grace. As soon as she had introduced herself, she went right to work. She opened a drawer that contained the ashes and skull of the corpse and a piece of maroon cloth.

"Do these look like the teeth of Eloy Santiago?" Dr. Schultz asked as she held the skull up to Maria's face. They're absolutely perfect—there's no evidence of dental work. I personally don't think we can even get a positive I.D. through dental records, although we haven't been able to get them from Venezuela yet."

"Yes, yes. . . . I don't know. . . . I guess so," Maria said, turning her head away.

"Well, then, sign this document to identify the remains. That's good enough for now. We can analyze the DNA later, using cells from the pulp of the teeth, and have the results in a couple of weeks."

"Sure," Maria said reluctantly. She had never felt so weak and nauseated in the face of death. How could Dr. Schultz show no compassion? No wonder she was a coroner, Maria thought.

"Will you contact the family to plan the funeral? If so, it will have to be in a couple of weeks. We'll have to have a positive I.D. before we release the body. How do you want to dispose of the remains after the I.D.?" Dr. Schultz asked.

"Dispose?" Maria fired back. "What do you mean, dispose? He was a respected scientist and a wonderful human being, not some piece of flesh to be disposed of like spoiled meat."

The deputy coroner just stared at Maria, expressionless.

"I'll contact you later, after arranging for a proper funeral, to claim the body," Maria said and stalked out of the coroner's office.

Eloy tried to sleep, but fear, anger, grief, guilt and love swirled in confusing tides through his consciousness. His life was totally out of balance. He smelled the pillow where Maria had lain. The scent of her perfume made his heart feel full, but the thought of his brother's death made his heart feel empty.

The phone rang. The answering machine picked up the call. "Maria, Maria, what happened? I just read about *mi amigo*'s death," Don said. "The fire . . . Eloy . . . I can't believe . . . what the hell happened? Please call me."

Eloy recognized Don's voice and almost, as if by instinct, reached to pick up the receiver but hesitated, remembering Maria's instructions. But this was Don.

"Don, is that you?" Silence on the other end of the line. "Don, is that you?" he repeated. "It's Eloy. I'm not dead."

"*Mi amigo*—you're alive!! You just scared me shitless. I thought I was talking to a ghost. What the hell's going on?"

"Please, I can't talk now, but I need your help. I'm at Maria's. I don't think the fire was an accident. Don't tell anyone. Can you come over?"

"Sure. It will take me an hour or so. I'm in Gaithersburg."

"Do you know how to get here?" Eloy asked.

"Sure."

"Come around the back and knock three times so I know it's you."

"Okay*, mi amigo*. I'll see you soon. I can't believe you're alive, you little shit," Don said before he hung up. For a moment Eloy thought maybe he shouldn't have talked to Don. Maybe he shouldn't trust him. Maybe Don started the fire. Oh, hell, he thought. Who could he trust if he couldn't trust Don?

Eloy heard a noise at the front door, looked at his watch,

and knew that it was too soon for Don to arrive. Besides, Don knew he was supposed to knock three times at the back door. Who could it be? Eloy decided it would be better to be safe, so he rolled off the bed to the floor and under the bed. Just then he heard Maria's voice.

"*Mi amor?*"

Eloy said, "*Aqui*," and crawled out from under the bed, trembling from the rush of fear and adrenaline. He stood up, still shaking. "This is no good. I can't stand this hiding. And one lie will lead to another lie and another lie and another, and I've already lied too much. Did you tell the coroner it was me?"

"Yes, *mi amor.*"

"I know I said to, but that wasn't a good idea. We need to tell the authorities the truth. I can't exist as a fugitive of my own creation. We have to end this charade before it gets worse."

"But someone is trying to kill you."

"I'm not so sure about that. Maybe it was an accident. If someone wanted to kill me, why didn't they just kill me? I have been thinking, and it seems like someone just wanted to burn the lab to destroy my research. I didn't tell you this before, but yesterday evening I went to check on the lab to see if El Oso had been there, and I heard a noise at the door. I hid in the supply closet and saw Donna and a man with a crew cut enter the lab. They went to the culture chamber and took some viral vectors and left something behind. It was small, like a pack of cigarettes, and looked like it was made of plastic. I think Donna is working for Roger and wanted to destroy the lab, not kill me. I think it was just an accident that my brother happened to be there. It was an accident, like what happened to Reuben."

"Let's hope not!" Maria exclaimed.

"What do you mean?"

"Just that I don't think Reuben's death was an accident," she said hesitantly. "Remember what I told you?"

"What?"

"I think it was deliberate. I think Reuben was the target all along. There is no way that Andrew King was a good enough marksman to kill Reuben. Whoever shot him was a professional," she said, moisture collecting in the corners of her eyes. I think there is something more going on here—a conspiracy, if you will.

"That may be, but no matter what," Eloy said, "I can't hide. We can't continue to lie."

A few minutes later, they heard three knocks at the back door.

"Who could that be? Hide, Eloy. Hide back under the bed."

"No, no. It's Don. He knows I'm alive. I asked him to come here."

"What?" Maria exclaimed. She opened the door and Don stood outside, gaping.

"Eloy, *mi amigo*! Shit, it is you," he said, grabbing Eloy in a big bear hug. Tears of joy wet his cheeks. "I thought I would never see you alive again." Eloy gently broke the embrace. "You little shit," Don said, wiping away his tears. "Don't you ever do that again! Boy, I'll bet Zoren and everyone will be glad to know you're alive."

"Zoren," Eloy echoed.

CHAPTER 36

July 5, 1997

Mark Wilson welcomed his brother George into the picnic area behind their apartment. The steaks Mark was grilling on the barbecue smelled wonderful to him. It was dinner time, and George was famished. "Sit down. Have a beer," Mark said.

"Sure, but let's go inside first. I want you to listen to something," George said. "I think you'll find it very interesting."

George and Mark went into the apartment. Mark put the audiotape into his cassette player and took a long swig of beer. "Boy, it's hot," he said, wiping his brow with the beer can as the tape started to play.

"July 4, 11:45 A.M.," the automated answering machine voice announced. "Maria, it's Eloy. Please call me when you get in. I need to talk to you. It's important. Miguel and I saw El Oso at the airport. . . . I can't wait to see you. I love you. *Adios.*"

"What's the big deal?" Mark asked. "So Eloy was in town with some guy named Miguel. Big deal. That's why he's dead. Who's this El Oso?"

"Wait. There's more," George said.

"July 4, 11:05 P.M.," the answering machine voice-over noted.

"Maria. Maria, Maria, are you there? Pick up the phone! Are you home? Pick up the phone!"

"What!? Whose body did they find?!" Mark screeched.

"Someone killed Miguel thinking it was me. . . . I think it was El Oso, or maybe Donna. Who knows?" the taped voice of Eloy said.

Mark's jaw dropped. "Who the hell is Miguel?"

"It's his brother."

"Great. We kill his brother, he's still alive, and he thinks we did it! Son of a bitch, now we really have to kill him. Why didn't you tell me he was in town with his brother before we set the timer?" Mark fumed, glaring at George.

"I couldn't. I didn't know. I was with Maria all day. I couldn't check the tape until just a little while ago. And I have more from our hidden camera," George explained. "You know how thorough Orville is with surveillance. Ever since Cooper was surgeon general, he has wanted to make sure that we have no antismoking bullshit. And if we do, that it's no surprise to us." George slid the videotape into the VCR.

He pushed the play button, and a high-angle shot from a camera hidden in the corner of the recessed lighting in the hallway between the bedroom and living room filled the screen. Eloy and Maria were making love.

"Look at the little fucker," Mark remarked.

George hit the fast forward. "Yeah, I thought you'd like the porno. You'd think you'd be tired of all those porno films that Donna's always making."

"Let's not talk about Donna right now. Let's talk about what you have here. Is this all you have?"

"No, there's more." George pushed the fast forward button, and the images of Maria and Eloy and the room danced on the screen. "Here it is. Look at this."

Eloy was telling Maria that he had been hiding in the storage closet in his lab when he saw Donna and a tall, muscular man with a crew cut enter the lab and take some cell cultures. He saw them leave something that looked like a package of cigarettes in the growth chamber. Maria also talked about Reuben's death and how the shooter couldn't have been Andrew King.

"That little bastard saw us," Mark shouted. "I'll kill him. He could ruin it all. We have to get rid of her too."

"Hell no! I'm paid to protect her," George responded. "You want me to lose my job? We can't kill everyone. Calm down."

As the video continued, Eloy said that he thought that Donna was working for Roger.

"He knows too much. We've got to get rid of him," Mark shouted. "He could blow our whole cover and all of Stu and Orville's involvement."

"Mark, I think I have a plan," George said.

Ten o'clock mass had just ended, and the Cafe Caribe was filled to capacity as many of the churchgoers stopped for breakfast. For such a large crowd, the room was almost silent, not typical of the usually loud, mostly Hispanic clientele. Most of them divided their attention between eating and watching the television that blared from a raised shelf in a corner of the restaurant. It was tuned to the national news. Reports discussed in turn the president's condition, the increasing probability of war with Iraq, and the transfer of executive power to the former vice president, now president,

Ted Daniels. He was a tall, handsome man who looked more
Ivy League than Southern, but his accent indicated Southern
roots. With his loving wife and four daughters standing beside
him as he was sworn in as the president, he seemed the epitome
of the family man.

Toward the end of the newscast there was a brief mention
of the fire in Eloy's lab and the tentative identification of the
remains by Surgeon General Dr. Maria Rodríguez. The sound
of a large fist pounding the table punctuated the end of the
story. Startled, most of the patrons in the restaurant turned to
see the cause: a very heavyset and disagreeable-looking individual sitting by himself.

"Shit. He's dead," he muttered and set down his cup of
coffee. A tall, muscular man with a military-style haircut,
dressed in a gray three-piece suit with a red tie, put his hand
on the large man's shoulder.

"Franco?"

"Yeah, who wants to know?"

"It's not important," Mark said. "Have another cup of
coffee. I'd like talk to you." Mark looked closely at Franco's
hand as he lifted the cup of coffee to his lips. Yes, it was him.
There was a tattoo of a bear and the words *El Oso*.

"What do you want? Who are you?"

"Let me just say that I know all about you. For example,
I know you were just released from prison. I know that you
have vowed to avenge the death of your friend Raven by killing Eloy Córdova Santiago. That's what I want to talk with
you about."

"Okay, talk to me."

"Look, let's go outside. We can't talk in here," Mark said,
looking at the crowd. Mark threw a twenty-dollar bill on the
table and walked outside with El Oso.

"Listen to this," Mark said. He pulled a small cassette tape recorder out of his pocket and pushed the play button. El Oso listened intently as Mark quickly replayed the message from July 4th, 11:05 P.M.

"Eloy is not dead," Mark said, shutting off the tape player.

"That little bastard is alive? Is that what you are trying to tell me? *Como?* How can it be? They just said on TV that he was dead."

"I can assure you, he's alive. And I know where he's hiding."

"Whose body did they find?" El Oso questioned.

"Never mind. Stop asking questions. Do you want to hear what I have to say?"

"Yeah, man. Tell me more."

"Do you still want to kill him?"

"*Sí.* More than anything. I make a promise to Raven, and El Oso, he never break a promise," he said. "But how do I know you're not trying to set me up? Why do you tell me all of this?" he asked, sucking air through his teeth.

"Let's just say that I can give you your wish and also a kilo of cocaine. All you have to do is kill Eloy."

"*Sí, porque no.* I will kill him, the little *puto*," he asserted, wiping his runny nose and rubbing his red eyes. "Let's see the *coca.*"

"I don't have the whole kilo, but here's some of it," Mark said, removing a plastic bag with white powder from his pocket. "Try it."

El Oso dipped a finger into the bag and rubbed it onto his gums. "Good shit. Real good shit," he said. "You have a deal. *Sí,* shake on it," El Oso said, putting his pudgy fingers in Mark's firm hand.

"Okay, here's the plan," Mark said.

July 6, 1997

"It's better talking here at our place," Maria explained as she, Don and Eloy sat outside under the trees but hidden from view of the road. "Look, I haven't told you this, but I know that something is going on. I have felt for a long time that my home is under surveillance. The security cameras look out, away from the house, but I think that some of them are looking in too. I also think my place is bugged."

"Do you think someone knows I'm alive?"

"Probably. That's why I want you to use one of my security guards—either George or Sidney—to watch while we try to figure out what's going on."

"I don't trust those goons you call your security guards," Eloy said. "Hell no. I don't need any protection."

"Okay," Maria said. "It was just an idea. Look, we're all tired. Too much has happened. It's almost four o'clock, and I have to go see President Walker at the Naval Hospital. It's only a couple of miles away. Eloy, you and Don just stay here and take it easy. I'll be back in an hour. The first lady wants me to talk to her, poor thing. His Alzheimer's came on so suddenly. She doesn't know what to make of it. While I'm gone, don't go anywhere. If necessary, page me, but only if absolutely necessary. I don't want to use my cellular. You can always call me on Don's."

"Call us from a pay phone if you want." Don gave Maria his cell phone number.

"Come on, *mi amigo*, don't worry. We'll get to the bottom of this. Let's rest," Don said, lying back on the grass. "It's a great day even though it's so damn hot and sticky."

Maria drove to the Naval Hospital. Security was tight. Audio and video surveillance blanketed the grounds, and SWAT teams were stationed in the tower building. Maria had to pass through several identification checks until she arrived at the door to President Walker's room. A tall, muscular Secret Service agent with a military-style crew cut looked her up and down with steel blue eyes and opened the door for her. He seems familiar, Maria thought.

Maria looked at former president Clint Walker. It was so strange to see him gazing blankly into space. He seemed just a shell of his former self, and he had lost the ability to speak.

"I'm so glad you came," Helen Walker said.

The women looked at Clint.

"Dr. Rodríguez," she asked, "does he feel pain? Does he think? Does he know anything?"

"He still feels pain, but Alzheimer's deadens memory and the ratiocinative processes."

The first lady's face blanched with anguish. "How could this happen so fast?"

"I don't know. It's very uncommon."

"It certainly couldn't have happened at a worse time for the country." She wiped Clint's nose.

The former president still suffered from various allergies. His eyes were constantly puffy, something he had always worried about before his public appearances. Now he just stared blankly out the window.

"This must be very frustrating for you," Maria said.

"Today is our wedding anniversary, and he can't even kiss me," Helen said with tears in her eyes. "How does Judy Winston cope? She must be a very strong woman."

"Don't worry, Helen," Maria said. "The president is receiving the best care possible here at the Naval Hospital; and with all of the research being conducted by Dr. Roger Atkins and Eloy Córdova Santiago and others around the world, a cure may be found."

"But Santiago is dead," Helen said.

"Yes."

"It was so awful—that fire," Helen said.

"Oh, yes, but treatment will improve and hopefully so will the quality of the president's life," Maria continued. "But I must be honest. You should accept that you probably will never have him back."

Helen reached into her purse and retrieved an aerosol nasal spray that she squeezed into her husband's nostrils. "It clears up his sinuses," she said.

When Maria left the Naval Hospital the sun was low. It was five thirty. She arrived at Rockcreek Park, parked, and walked briskly toward Eloy and Don.

"How's the president?" Eloy asked.

"He's not good. The Alzheimer's is getting worse, and his allergies are still bothering him. You should have seen him just staring out the window. He looks absolutely miserable. And Helen is another story."

"Why?" Eloy asked.

"She doesn't know what to do. She's beside herself. It's so sad because she is in denial. She thinks he'll be okay. She even gave him some nasal spray for his allergies."

"Nasal spray?" Eloy asked.

"Yes, why?" Maria wanted to know.

"That's it!" Eloy exclaimed.

"What?" Maria and Don asked simultaneously.

"It just came to me. I introduced the *trk* viral vector into the primates with a nasal aerosol spray."

"Yes," Maria said, "and President Walker is always using nasal spray to clear up his sinuses. Just like today."

"Yeah," Eloy said. "Not only that, but President Walker's Alzheimer's is an extremely rapid version, similar to the Alzheimer's found in my primate models. I was gone from my lab for a week, and Donna Stone had access to the viral vectors. She also knows how to administer the protocol." Eloy's mind was racing. "I just saw her in my lab yesterday before the fire when she and that guy took some cultures and left something—a timer. That's how the fire started!"

"Yes," Maria interrupted, "and here's the clincher. . . . When I went to see the president, I thought I recognized one of the Secret Service guards at the president's door, and then it came to me. It was Mark Wilson, the brother of my Secret Service agent, George. And then I remembered who Mark's girlfriend is."

"Who?" Don asked.

"I'll bet it's Donna Stone," Eloy said.

"Right!" Maria exclaimed.

"Are you suggesting that the president's condition was induced using Eloy's technique and that Donna did it?" Don asked. "Why?"

"Maybe Donna gave the aerosol to Mark or . . . I don't know . . ." Suddenly Eloy felt confused. It sounded far-fetched.

"We don't know who did it, but Miguel was killed—probably by accident. Whoever did it probably didn't intend to kill your brother. He only wanted to destroy the viral vector and prevent you from developing a cure for Alzheimer's," Don said.

"Who would do that?" Eloy questioned.

"Roger," Don answered.

"Yeah, Roger. He wants all the glory," Eloy said.

"If they gave the president Alzheimer's, maybe the president knows who did it and why. But he'll take that to his grave," Maria said.

"No, I don't think so," Eloy said.

"What do you mean?" Don asked. "Alzheimer's is fatal."

"Well, I'm not sure about that."

"What?!" Maria exclaimed.

"Look, I have a plan. We've been here too long. Where can we talk that's secure?"

"How about the convent at NIH?" Maria suggested.

"Let's go. I think you'll find my proposal interesting," Eloy promised.

"Let's not talk in the car because it might be bugged too," Maria said.

They drove to the convent in silence.

CHAPTER 37

July 7, 1997

Ted Daniels made the transition from vice president to president not altogether smoothly. Only two days after the swearing in, he had to address a joint session of Congress in regard to business left unfinished from the Walker administration.

"I felt it was necessary to convene a joint session of Congress because our dialogue with the Iraqi government has come to a standstill and our relations have deteriorated to the level of national emergency. I would like to reiterate my position toward Iraq: Unless Saddam Hussein's government meets with U.N. representatives in the Netherlands at the end of this month, and agrees to comply with the arms treaty we expect to negotiate, we are prepared to take the steps necessary to put an end to this crisis, up to and including military action. I am ready to go to war as the ultimate solution, even if it costs us dearly, because in the final analysis allowing Iraq to continue to develop weapons of mass destruction would entail far greater costs for the entire world." In typical fashion, party loyalists and sympathizers cheered and rose to their feet, while the opposition sat quiet.

President Daniels then segued from the situation in Iraq to other international and domestic issues, highlighting the differences between his positions and those of his predecessor. He spoke for twenty minutes about how he pretty much followed President Walker's policies except where he felt the rights of the individual may not have been adequately protected. He cited instances such as voucher programs in education and health insurance programs for those who weren't covered. The last item Daniels discussed was smoking.

"Finally, I would like you, as lawmakers, to revisit President Walker's position on tobacco use and associated health risks. No one disagrees with the conventional wisdom that the social and economic costs of smoking are enormous. Health statistics from the Centers for Disease Control show that smoking-related diseases cost the American public $50 billion annually. Not only does smoking directly impact health care costs, but government economists estimate that the economy lost $47 billion in the last five years due to smoking-related deaths. In addition, smoking-related illness means time missed from work, which means reduced national productivity. The obvious conclusion is that smoking is unbelievably costly to our national economy.

"However, one of the nation's most prestigious research institutes has suggested that we look at the costs of cigarette smoking from another perspective. Although costs in the short term are astronomical, we need to look at the long-term effects of smoking on our national budget. Yes, smokers do generate higher health and insurance costs. They do drain our economy of revenue because of lower productivity. They do reduce our gross national product, and their lost wages do reduce income tax revenues. But let's look at this another way. Dead people don't need convalescent homes. Dead smokers don't need health care. Dead smokers don't receive pensions."

Congress erupted in loud dissention. "That's absurd!" several members shouted, standing up.

"Order! Order!" the speaker demanded. "The president is speaking."

The president waited until the members took their seats again. He looked out over the audience. "Let me continue," he said. The institute I mentioned earlier estimates that because 425,000 smokers die per year, they save us $30 billion annually. Yes, $30 billion every year. If you calculate those statistics on a per-pack basis, smokers' net cost to American society is 33 cents per pack, which is well below today's average 57 cents per pack excise tax. So the more people smoke, the more revenue we actually receive. Reducing the number of seniors in our society results in savings to our economy, and selling more cigarettes increases our revenue.

"The only conclusion that can be drawn is that smoking saves the country more than it costs. Therefore, I am ordering the secretary of health and human services to direct the head of the office of the FDA and the office of the surgeon general to rethink the war on smoking and to temper our commitment to having a smoke-free society by the year 2000. We must seriously consider the economic effects that such a ban would have." The president made some final remarks, stepped down from the podium, and left the chamber. Stunned lawmakers shook their heads in disbelief.

One congressman remarked, "This is the most ludicrous proposal I have ever heard! Here we are on the verge of war, and he completely reverses the former president's position on smoking and health care? Just a couple of weeks ago President

Walker had the tobacco industry on its knees. Now this guy says that smoking is good because it kills!"

The president's position on smoking and health caught the nation by surprise. The news media and political analysts were aghast.

Clint Walker stared at the television screen, but his eyes were blank and unregistering. Helen wiped his nose. "Oh, Clint, what's going on with Ted? It's just not like him. Look what he's doing to your diplomacy with Iraq and your anti-smoking work. Who would have ever thought something like this would come to pass?" she said, kissing him on the cheek and wiping his nose.

Eloy was dressed in the khaki work clothes that all custodians wore at the Naval Hospital, just one of the many invisible staff. He pushed his mop bucket down the hall and surreptitiously went through a door that opened into the old section of the tower.

The previous night Maria had suggested that they work in the lab of her old friend, Dr. Data Singh, an East Indian who reminded her of Ghandi in both appearance and voice. Data was a molecular virologist, and his laboratory was equipped with everything Eloy, Don and Maria. He was going on vacation to Ocean City for a couple of weeks, so his lab would be available if they needed it. Maria called him from a pay phone and arranged to do so.

Maria took some time off work. She told the secretary of health and human services that she needed to grieve for her friend and to try and contact the family to arrange for funeral services. She also told her bodyguards, George and Sidney, that she no longer wanted them protecting her.

Maria and Don were already in the lab when Eloy pushed

his mop bucket into the room. "Okay, let's get to work," he said, closing the door. "Don, did you get the disk?"

"Yes, *mi amigo*. It was hidden behind the picture of your brother in your apartment just like you said."

"Miguel," Eloy said sadly. He put the disk in the computer.

"Shit," Don said. "It's gibberish. What's wrong?"

"No," Maria said. "It's Spanish and something else."

"What language is that?" Don asked.

"It's a mixture of Spanish and the language of my people, the Huni Kui. It's to keep it confidential. I left the hard copy in Venezuela." Eloy continued to scroll through the pages from his journal, saying, "Look, like I said last night in the convent, I have done more than establish a model for Alzheimer's. Sure we could use the modified *trk* gene to prevent nerve growth factor uptake in acetylcholine-producing brain cells, and of course that's how my model works. But if what we suspect is correct, this may be how President Walker contracted Alzheimer's. In theory it would be very simple to hand the president an aerosol with the viral vector, and two or three puffs in the nostrils would deliver it right to his brain. In just a couple of days the symptoms of rapid-onset Alzheimer's would appear."

"But how could we know for sure that the Alzheimer's is due to your viral vehicle?" Don asked.

"I added a gene segment coding for the production of a bioluminescent molecule that I took from the dinoflagellates. You know," Eloy said, looking at Maria, "the dinoflagellates that make the phosphorescent bay, *La Bahia Fosforescente*, glow. I saw it when I landed in Puerto Rico, near Guánico. I spliced these genes into the viral vector, and the cells containing the viral vector glow in the dark. That's how I knew the modified *trk* gene was present in the cells."

"You are some smart cookie, my little *amigo*," Don said.

"All we have to do," Maria said, "is get a nasal sample from the president and find a bioluminescent cell, and then we'll know. It should be easy for me to get a nasal swab from him."

"But what good is that?" Don asked. "All that will tell us is that Donna or someone else induced the president's Alzheimer's. But why bother—Alzheimer's is incurable."

"I want to tell you something else," Eloy said. "Something I wanted to keep secret until I was certain. Even though I was working at NIH, several of the gene-splicing companies here in the D.C. area wanted me to work with them to produce the cure for Alzheimer's, since they knew there was a high probability that I was on the right track. Can you imagine the profits they would reap if they had a cure for Alzheimer's?"

"Hell, a company would make billions," Don said.

"Yes, but I wanted no part of it because if there were a cure for Alzheimer's, it should be for everyone—not just for profit."

"My little *amigo,* you have always had such a good heart, but boy are you naive. What did you think Donna was doing? She was trying to steal your research."

"Yeah, I know that now, but I have always suspected her, so I did a lot of my research at night."

"You know Donna. Night time is play time!" Don interjected.

Eloy continued. "I tried to engineer skin cells with the appropriate recombinant DNA to make them secrete nerve growth factor and then surgically implant them into the brains of experimental animals. But the rate of acetylcholine production was too low to reverse the Alzheimer's. In the process, I was able to develop a line of herpes viral vectors in which I had inserted a gene for acetylcholine production. When these vehicles were introduced into experimental animals, enough acetylcholine was replaced to reverse the Alzheimer's."

"What?!" Maria exclaimed. "Are you saying that you developed an antidote, a technique to reverse Alzheimer's?"

"Yes. Look at this," Eloy said, pointing to his lab notes on the computer screen. "The reversal usually occurs within two days of the introduction of the viral vectors. Levels of acetylcholine are high enough to reverse the memory loss and other symptoms associated with Alzheimer's. Now, if we wanted to find out who gave the president Alzheimer's, and maybe who started the fire that killed Miguel, all we have to do is have the president tell us."

"Wait," Don said. "Whoa. Where are the cells? How are we going to work this miracle?"

"I have the cells."

"What?" Maria said.

"Where?" Don asked.

"In Venezuela."

"Let's get those suckers, *mi amigo*. Let's get to the bottom of this."

"You know, I think that's why Donna burned down the lab. She thought she had the acetyicholine-producing vectors as well as the ones that induced Alzheimer's, but she didn't. I am beginning to think that's why . . . oh, I don't know," Eloy said.

"Yeah. I bet Roger is somewhere behind this," Don interrupted.

"Look, all I have to do is e-mail Felipe in Dr. Rodríguez's lab in Caracas," Eloy continued. "I gave the vectors to Felipe. He is, I mean, was . . . ," Eloy hesitated, " . . . a friend of Miguel's. They worked in the lab together. I was afraid that something was going to happen to me, so I gave the cell vectors to Felipe to maintain. He can send us some of the cultures."

"E-mail the son of a gun," Don said. Let's help the president."

"Wait. Not so fast. How do we know it's safe?" Maria questioned. "How do we know that it's your cells that caused the Alzheimer's?"

"We don't, but what do we have to lose? In my research," Eloy said, again pointing to the computer screen, "viral reversal of Alzheimer's occurred in 90 percent of the subjects."

"That's good enough for me," Don said.

"Are there any side effects?" Maria asked.

"Not that I have noted in the year that I've been doing this."

"But we haven't done any clinical trials. Are we willing to let the president be our guinea pig?"

"We have no choice."

"I guess you're right," Maria conceded.

"How do we administer the viral vehicle to the president?" Don asked.

"That's easy," Maria stated. "I can do it when I see him."

"Okay. E-mail Felipe."

Eloy transmitted the message to Felipe, and he responded that he would send some of the cultures to Dr. Singh's lab addressed to Dr. Maria Rodríguez tomorrow afternoon via Federal Express.

They continued to work until late in the afternoon getting the lab ready to process the cultures.

"That's it," Maria said, putting away the last of the culture media. "Enough for today." She whispered to Eloy, "*Mi amor*, let's go home. We need to rest," she said suggestively, kissing him on the neck.

"Oh, stop it. You're embarrassing me," Don said.

"Okay, let's call it a day."

"See you tomorrow. I'll be at the NIH. I need to see about the damage to the lab, even though I heard it was minimal. Page me and use a false number—something with a lot of 69s!" he joked. Then he said, "Actually, that's a good idea. Use 6969 as the number, and I will know it's you and call you back."

Eloy pushed the mop bucket down the hall and outside and waited until Maria pulled her black Toyota Camry around. Eloy got in and lay down in the front seat.

The driver of the white Ford Explorer parked about fifty yards from Maria's townhouse. He slouched down in the front seat and pulled his sunglasses over his eyes, trying to rest. He wiped the sweat off of his brow. As he watched, the garage door of Maria's house opened and she drove her car into the garage.

Maria and Eloy entered through the kitchen and Maria said, "Will you please get us some iced tea? I need to use the bathroom."

Eloy opened up the refrigerator. He could have sworn someone had been in it. The wine bottle was gone. He closed the door, set two glasses on the table, and poured the iced tea.

"Eloy. Eloy, run!" Maria shouted.

"Shut up, *puta,*" Eloy heard a voice growl with a heavy Puerto Rican accent.

Eloy dropped the iced tea. Glass shattered on the kitchen floor, and he ran toward the bathroom.

"The night stand!" Maria shouted.

Eloy reached into the night stand and picked up the small revolver hidden in the drawer. Then he saw him—El Oso!

"I wouldn't do that, my little *puto*. I have your darling

pussy right here," he said. In his pudgy hand he held a .38 caliber pistol to Maria's head. Eloy pointed the small-caliber revolver at El Oso.

"Remember me?" El Oso sneered through dirty teeth. "Say your prayers, *cabrón*. I will kill you. Put down the little gun, *puto*, or I will kill your bitch, too." Maria struggled. Her pants were around her ankles and her panties were halfway down her hips. El Oso looked at her body. "We meet again," he said, pulling her hair and forcing her to face him. "Look at me, bitch. This is the *hombre* that's going to kill your little *puto*, then fuck you like I fucked your queer brother in prison."

"You bastard. Leave her alone!" screamed Eloy.

"*Cabrón,* put down that gun," El Oso repeated, his small eyes glaring. His bloated belly growled. Eloy could smell alcohol on his breath.

"How did you find me?" Eloy asked, trying to stall for time so he could figure out how to save Maria.

"None of your fuckin' business."

El Oso dragged Maria to the side of the bed where Eloy stood. Eloy pointed his gun at El Oso.

"*Cabrón*, drop the gun. I'm going to kill you," El Oso shouted as he took his free hand and quickly hit Eloy on the side of his head. For Eloy, light turned to darkness, and the small revolver flew out of his hand and slid across the floor into the bathroom. Eloy fought to maintain his equilibrium but fell to his knees. He shook his head, then stood up and charged directly into El Oso. In size he was no match for El Oso, and the full impact of Eloy's attack barely swayed him. El Oso laughed, his foul breath staining the air. He pushed Eloy aside.

"Don't try that again," he said, "or I *will* shoot this *coño*. That can wait. Right now I'm gonna fuck her like I fucked her queer *puto* brother," he repeated.

"Oh, no!" Maria cried. "Juan died of AIDS!"

"Well, now it's your turn," he said with a leer. "And as for you, Mr. Wizard . . ."

He hit Eloy again on the side of his head with the barrel of his gun. Blood stained Eloy's dark hair, and he lapsed briefly into unconsciousness. El Oso tied Eloy to the bedpost with his socks, while Maria screamed and hit at him.

" . . . You get to watch," he said as Eloy regained consciousness. "I hope you enjoy the show, because when I finish with your *puta*, I'm gonna kill you, and then after I have her again and again, I'm gonna kill her, too." El Oso forced Maria onto the bed, staring at her body as he stripped her.

While El Oso was preoccupied, Eloy managed to free his hands and grabbed a large, silver crucifix off of the night table. Suddenly aware of Eloy's movement, El Oso darted a glance at him. The moment El Oso's small eyes met his, Eloy swung the heavy crucifix with all of his strength and caught him square on the temple. Blood splattered onto the bed, and Maria screamed. Then a split second later a single muffled shot spit more blood from a hole in the back of El Oso's head. His massive body went limp and fell forward, pinning Maria to the bed. She shoved him aside and saw Sidney, her bodyguard, standing in the doorway of the bedroom. Smoke drifted from the silencer on his Smith and Wesson.

"What the hell?!" Eloy yelled, jumping off of the bed and lunging at Sidney. "Maria, run!" Eloy swung at Sydney with the crucifix.

"No! It's my bodyguard. Oh, thank God! Thank you, Sidney . . . but I told you I didn't want protection anymore," she oddly observed, distraught with hysteria. Her body trembled and her heart pounded madly. She held Eloy tightly.

"Calm down," Sidney said. "Sit here. It's okay now. You're safe."

Secret Service agent Sidney Smith was a tall African American. His color was more that of creamed coffee than ebony. Although his facial features were soft and his eyes sparked with intelligence, he had the body of a professional boxer.

Eloy gave Maria a towel. "*Mí amor,* here. Cover yourself," he said and touched her gently.

Sidney looked at him. "You're Eloy, aren't you?"

"Yes."

"I thought so."

Eloy's chest still heaved with excitement, and his head ached badly. He held his hand to the cut on his temple.

"Let me fix that," Maria said, regaining her composure.

Sidney took a chair from the kitchen and climbed on it, reaching into the well around one of the recessed lighting fixtures. "Here it is," he said. He cut the wires and removed a video camera. "Now we have privacy."

"What?!" Maria exclaimed. "You mean my house was bugged?" She threw the camera on the floor. "You bastards. I knew it. You and others have been watching me all along. You have seen everything. Bastards!"

"Hold on, Dr. Rodríguez. It was for your own good."

"Hell if it was," she said. "I want to talk to your boss right now."

"Dr. Rodríguez, wait. Let me explain," Sidney said. "Believe it or not, I'm on your side. Let me tell you what I know."

"How can we trust you?" Eloy asked.

"You can't, but you don't have any other choice."

CHAPTER 38

Maria pulled her Toyota out of the garage, and Sidney drove his sport utility vehicle in. Maria closed the garage door behind him. Sidney dragged the body to the Explorer and pulled it into the cargo area in the back. He wrapped the head in a towel to contain the blood. It looked to Eloy like Sidney had moved bodies before.

"Boy, is he heavy. It's a good thing I'm in shape," Sidney said, sweat dripping off of his nose.

Eloy handed Sidney a black plastic tarp to cover El Oso. Eloy turned his head away. He didn't want to look at or even touch the fat corpse. The memory of La Perla had again become vivid.

"I'll take the body to North 14th Street and dump him in the alley behind a drug house. Don't go anywhere. I'll be back in an hour, around 10:30," Sidney said.

Eloy and Maria went back into the house and lay down on the couch in the living room, holding each other. Eloy asked, "Who can we trust?"

"I don't know."

"Why was Sidney here?"

"I have no idea," Maria said. "I don't know if I trust him." She rested her head on Eloy's chest. "I can't talk about it now. Let's just lie here in peace for a while."

Eloy detached himself. "Just a moment, *mi amor*. Let me close the door to your bedroom. The horror . . ."

Maria started to cry. "I can't live here anymore. I have to move."

After a while, Maria's sobs subsided, and she drifted off to sleep in Eloy's arms.

 An hour later there were three knocks on the front door. Maria awoke and looked at her watch. It was 10:30. She must have dozed off. "Eloy, someone's at the door. It must be Sidney," she whispered. Maria looked through the peephole in the door and confirmed that it was.

Opening the door, she said, "Come in," and looked up and down the street to make sure Sidney was alone.

"Mission accomplished," Sidney said.

"That's good," Maria replied, "but I think you owe us an explanation."

"That's an understatement," Sidney said.

"Well, then," Eloy said, "tell us why you're here."

"Okay, but first, may I have somethng to drink?" Sidney asked. "Taking care of El Oso was a lot of work."

"Of course," Maria said. "How does iced tea sound?"

"Fine, thank you. Let me get to the point. During President Cole's term in 1992, I was assigned to the Presidential Protection Division and worked at the White House in the JOC," he said.

"I thought you said you'd get to the point," Eloy said.

"What the hell is the JOC?" Maria asked.

"The Joint Operations Center. It's located in the White House and functions as the nerve center for the entire eighteen-acre complex. While I was there, I met everyone assigned to presidential security. What I'm getting to, Dr. Rodríguez, is that we know that Andrew King did not kill Dr. Rosario.

"Then who the hell did?" she snapped.

"I'm not at liberty to reveal that, but let's just say that in order to be a Secret Service agent, you must be able to hit a bull's eye at a thousand meters. Mr. Rosario's assassin was a marksman."

"I thought so. Probably one of your guys, and you are trying to cover it up."

"I'm on your side, remember?"

"Right. I'm sorry. So who killed Rueben?"

"Before I tell you *who* I have to tell you *why*. You see, the tobacco industry has always exerted tremendous political pressure on Congress and the president, and in recent years it has focused its lobbying on the health risks associated with tobacco use. Tobacco's most vocal advocate in the Senate has been Orville Reynolds. If you watch the news—the congressional inquiries—you know that he is a good friend of the Kentucky Green CEO, Stu Brown, who is under investigation. Those congressional inquiries are looking into devious and possibly criminal actions by the tobacco industry to addict tobacco users. The lawmakers have uncovered hundreds of internal industry memos that provide evidence the industry has known for decades that nicotine is addictive and has manipulated levels of nicotine to enhance addiction."

"Tell us something we don't know," Eloy said.

"One of those memos—one not made public—ties Orville Reynolds and Stu Brown to a conspiracy to gun down Dr.

Rosario and make it seem like a botched assassination attempt on Dr. Cooper. We think," he said, "that one of our agents betrayed his oath and shot Dr. Rosario."

"I thought so. Who was it? She asked, her eyes filling with rage. "I have never trusted any of those agents, and I barely trust you. Damn it, why in the hell did I even need you or George?"

"Maria, Sidney saved your life," Eloy said, putting his arm around her. "Who's George?"

"He's my other bodyguard. Where is he, anyway?" she asked, looking at Sidney.

"George is in the Netherlands. He's been assigned to plan the security for the presidential limos when they arrive for the president's visit at the end of the month. Okay?"

"Good enough."

"Next, what I tell you is in the strictest confidence."

"Understood."

Sidney continued solemnly. "We have suspected that George is collaborating with his brother Mark, who is assigned to the president. That's why we reassigned George to the Netherlands. Mark is also involved with Donna Stone, who is linked with . . . that's all I am at liberty to say. I have been assigned to protect you, and I am doing my duty."

"How did you know I was still alive?" Eloy asked.

"As soon as we heard about the fire, our agents contacted Customs at Dulles, and the Customs official reported that Eloy and Miguel Córdova Santiago had arrived on July 4th. A Customs agent remembered both of you and recalled how he had recognized you from TV. She had thought at first that you and your brother were twins. We also found fragments of a maroon T-shirt on the . . . deceased that said "Smithsonian," and a T-shirt vendor there recognized a picture of you. He stated that you bought the T-shirt for your brother and that when you left the museum your brother was wearing it, which meant that it probably wasn't you in the lab. I assumed that if you were alive you would contact Maria, so we staked out Maria's house. I saw El Oso enter about a half hour before you arrived."

"Why didn't you kill him then?" Maria asked.

"I wasn't sure why he was in your house, and I didn't know you would be coming home."

"I'm glad you showed up when you did."

"There is something more important I need to tell you."

"What?" Eloy asked.

"The cells glowed," Sidney said.

"What?"

"Yes. Dr. Green ordered a series of tests on the president, including a nasal swab, because of his allergies. The nasal swab was found to be bioluminescent. Even I know that nasal mucus cells don't normally glow. The luminescence had to be a marker to identify the presence of a spliced gene, and our scientists are working around the clock to determine the nature of the gene splicing. It was your vector, wasn't it?"

Maria and Eloy's frustration and anger turned to surprise. "Then we were right," Maria said. "Someone did use your viral vector, and it could only be Donna or someone she knows."

"Does anyone else know about this?" Sidney asked. "Don does, doesn't he?"

"Yes," Eloy said.

"Can we trust him?"

"Yes," Eloy nodded. "So Donna or Roger or someone she knows used the viral vector to give the president Alzheimer's."

"It seems that way," Sidney responded.

"What do you want from us?" Eloy asked.

"We'd like you to help us," Sidney said. "We need to learn more about your protocol."

"Is there anything else we can do?" Maria added.

"It seems like you know it all, but why?" Eloy asked.

"We think somebody linked to the tobacco industry incapacitated the president and set fire to your lab to destroy any evidence or to delay your research protocol. But I don't know the whole story," Sidney said. "We just found out at Federal Express that a package has been sent to Dr. Maria Rodríguez at an address at the Naval Hospital from Felipe in Dr. Paul Rodríguez's lab at the University of Venezuela. What kind of work are you doing there, Maria? And what's in the package?" Sidney asked.

Eloy and Maria looked at each other. "Give us a moment alone," Eloy said as he and Maria left the kitchen table.

"Should we tell him?"

CHAPTER 39

It was almost midnight as Donna drove her red BMW convertible onto the Beltway heading toward her apartment in Rockville. The radio was playing her favorite country and western music, and the warm night air felt comforting on her face. She needed comfort. Nothing went right in the lab in Virginia. She was puzzled. Most importantly, she knew something was wrong with the acetylcholine-inhibiting viral vectors because the cells glowed in the dark. Eloy must have spliced in a luciferin or luciferinase-like gene to serve as a marker for the *trk* gene. Of course the president's lab work-up would show the bioluminescent cells, indicating a recombinant DNA manipulation. It wouldn't take the investigators long to connect her with the president's Alzheimer's and the fire in Eloy's lab.

"Shit," she said. She felt doomed. "I have to get the hell out of here. What's Mark gotten me into?" The radio news update described President Daniels's controversial speech in favor of tabacco use and the outcry it sparked across the country. The newscaster also reported the worsening condition of the former president and noted that the prognosis was grave. Never had the medical community seen such a rapid onset of Alzheimer's, he said. In addition, Ted Daniels went so far as to say that intelligence sources have evidence that may possibly tie the president's condition to "bio-regulator" agents developed by Iraq. Saddam Hussein has stated that such assertions are erroneous and provocative and dangerously escalated the possibility of all-out war.

The apartment on Tuckerman Lane was dark except for the glow of the television screen. Mark sat on the couch in the nude, drinking a beer . He held his erect member in one hand, and with the other he pressed the VCR remote control.

The screen filled with the image of Donna dancing with a tall man in an upscale hotel room. The tall man set down his bottle of whiskey and leaned into Donna, pushing himself into her groin. His hands reached for the zipper of her dress. Donna stepped out of it, naked except for her garter belt and thigh-high black stockings. Donna had full, round breasts with small, upright pink nipples. Her legs were long and shapely. Her rear was round and firm, and white in contrast to her tan line and black stockings. She pulled off her garter belt, and the man dropped his pants. He was erect as he pushed her back toward the bed. The man peeled off his boxer shorts and entered her. Donna rolled over and straddled him, gasping as the man gripped her buttocks. They thrust together.

The man kissed her breasts, and as he did so he looked up toward the ceiling where the camera was hidden. Ted Daniels's face was lit with the throes of sexual pleasure.

"Donna, sweetie, you are some piece of ass," Mark said out loud to himself. "We got him. I will never forget the look on that self-righteous bastard's face when Orville and I showed him the tape. You will do anything we want," he said out loud, stroking himself faster. "Even support us in our war against the antismoking campaign and say that the president's Alzheimer's was caused by Saddam."

"Mark, are you home?" questioned Donna as she opened the door. She went to turn on the light.

"No, leave the light off," Mark said, panting.

"What are you doing? We need to talk," she said, setting down her purse. She could see the television screen and the video of her and Ted Daniels.

"Come here," Mark said, and he stood up and grabbed her roughly by the hands. She saw his hard penis. "Suck this," he said as he roughly thrust himself into her mouth. She tried to push him away, to no avail. He climaxed almost immediately and released her.

"Ugh," she said.

"You are some piece of ass. I don't know if watching you fuck someone else turns me on more than fucking you myself," he said with a sneer. "What the hell's the matter?"

"Oh, nothing," she said, rubbing her wrists, and went to the bathroom to wipe herself off. Shit, she thought, that's all I've ever been, just somebody's pussy. Even to my dad, that bastard. Thank God he's dead.

"Come here. Let's do this right," Mark said. "Let's see the tape again."

"Mark, no. We have a problem. Forget your cock for a minute. Look at this," Donna said, reaching into her purse and bringing out the culture vial. "It glows."

"So? Big deal. Your culture glows."

"Yes, you asshole! That is a big deal. Eloy inserted a phosphorescent gene to mark the *trk* gene. Any scientist worth his salt knows that this is a common technique in genetic engineering. They can trace the cells back to us, you dumb ass."

Mark slapped Donna across the face. "Don't ever call me a dumb ass."

She kicked him square in the groin. Mark fell to the floor with the wind knocked out of him. Donna kicked him in the testicles again and again.

"You damn bitch!" he screamed, catching her foot the fourth time she tried to kick him there. He dragged her down to the floor beside him and put his hands around her throat, squeezing and squeezing and squeezing. Donna went limp. "Dumb bitch," Mark said. Then he thought, I have to get rid of her. She knows too much.

He dragged her into the bedroom, withdrew some of the pantyhose from her lingerie drawer and tied her to the bed. He went into her purse, grabbed the atomizer and filled it from the culture vial. He sprayed the viral vector up Donna's nostrils in five quick puffs, just like he did to the president.

"Sweet dreams. Pleasant memories."

Mark left the apartment ready to initiate his backup plan. He opened his briefcase and looked at the $2 million Orville had given him for taking care of the president. It was so easy. As they were flying back from Albuquerque on Air Force One, all Mark had to do was hand him the aerosol. The president medicated himself all the way back to Washington. Just like that, he'd brought that self-centered bastard to his knees. He had taken a vow as a Secret Service agent assigned to the Presidential Protection Division to keep the president safe from harm, whatever the cost. He had sworn to take a bullet if necessary to protect him. For a paltry $70,000 to $75,000 per year. Not nearly enough.

He remembered the day back in 1981 when President Winston was shot by a crazed kid. He shielded the fallen president with his own body and waited for the cops and the EMTs to arrive. The son of a bitch didn't even thank him—didn't even thank him. He was tired of day after day having presidents treat him like he was invisible, like he was a piece of shit. Now he had brought them to their knees and he was free. Not only free—but rich!

He got into his black Mercedes and started to drive to National Airport. "Amsterdam, here I come!" he shouted. He would meet up with his brother in the Netherlands and then they would disappear off the face of the earth. "Enough of this shit," he said out loud. "Fuck you, assholes! And fuck you, Donna. Enjoy your Alzheimer's."

July 8, 1997

 Maria paged Don early, and he came over to the lab at the Naval Hospital. He looked at Sidney. "Who is he?"

"He's my Secret Service agent, and he knows."

"What?" Don asked.

"Let me explain," Eloy said.

Eloy told Don about the previous night's events and how they knew that the president's Alzheimer's was induced by the viral vector.

"Let's get everything ready," Eloy suggested. "We should have the culture this afternoon."

"Can we get more help? This crap will take forever," Don grumbled.

Maria was about to answer when Sidney stepped between them and said, "No. This is strictly confidential. If the president's memory isn't restored, no one can know what we are doing, not even the first lady."

"Even worse, if the president isn't able to negotiate with Iraq at the end of the month, Ted Daniels will attack, and our intelligence sources fear the Iraqis will retaliate with germ warfare, which will have a global impact. And if we bomb Iraq, it could set off a wave of terrorism around the world."

"Are you saying that Iraq is capable of worldwide destruction?" Don asked.

"Yes," Maria interrupted. "I remember Saddam boasting that he had enough biological agents to kill every living thing six times over, along with his 'bio-regulatory' mood-altering germ agents."

When the cultures arrived, Don, Maria and Eloy took the cells that contained the spliced acetylcholine-producing gene and transferred them to mouse cells, along with the herpes viruses containing the acetylcholine gene, then induced the cells to reproduce, eventually obtaining a large amount of herpes virus containing the spliced acetylcholine gene ready to go into the aerosol.

Eloy, Maria and Don took turns working as Sidney watched. They slept in Dr. Singh's lab, where there was a small couch available. Maria periodically checked on President Walker. Security was tight, but it was easy for her to be admitted to see him. His condition was worsening, and Helen was very worried, as were his physicians. Clint Walker was going to die, and soon, unless they could reverse the Alzheimer's.

July 12, 1997

Eloy checked the print-out that showed the levels of acetylcholine synthesis in the president's brain. The acetylcholine gene was being expressed at adequate levels. He took a pipette and carefully transferred the viral vectors into the vial. Then, just as carefully, he transferred the viral vector into the aerosol nasal spray. His hand trembled ever so slightly. At this stage of development he knew that Alzheimer's could be reversed in primates, but he didn't know if it would work in humans. And not just any human, but the president of the United States.

At last Eloy turned to Sidney, saying, "We're ready. It's time." He handed the nasal spray to Maria. Making the sign of the cross, he said, "*Vaya con Dios.*"

"Well, things can't get any worse," Sidney said matter of factly.

Eloy kissed Maria. She threw on her lab coat, put the nasal spray in her pocket, and headed down the long corridor into the next wing, which housed the president. She knocked on Clint Walker's door. A Secret Service agent checked her ID and motioned for her to enter.

"Maria, Maria. It's happening again. I've never seen it so bad," Helen said, her eyes filled with fright. She ushered Maria into the room toward the president's bed. "Someone call Dr. Green," she screamed to the Secret Service agents.

Maria rushed to his side. She saw his expression go blank. Then his facial muscles spasmed, his arms and legs began to tremble, and his body thrashed. His skull hit the headboard of the hospital bed as his body jerked.

Oh, no, Maria thought. The writhing and the contortions were associated with damage to the base of the brain where the Alzheimer's-producing genes resided. The viral vectors were destroying his brain, and she feared he was dying. She restrained the president as best she could. Then two large male nurses ran into the room and helped her turn the president onto his back. He bit his lip, drawing blood, which trickled down his neck. His back arched severely, and his teeth started clacking like a pair of castanets.

Dr. Green suddenly burst into the room and shoved Maria aside. "What are his vital signs?" he screamed. "Where are the X rays? We need a CAT scan immediately. Stabilize him," he shouted, putting his stethoscope to the president's chest.

One male nurse shouted amid the confusion, "Temperature slightly elevated at 37.7 degrees centigrade."

"It's more than Alzheimer's. It's got to be a tumor, intracranial bleeding or infection," Dr. Green said as he studied the heart monitor. "We need to do a spinal tap," he shouted and reached for the surgical prep. He grabbed a Betadine wipe and snapped on his gloves. "Get the first lady out of here," he ordered, "and her too," he said, looking at Maria.

The Secret Service agents rushed Helen out of the room, but Maria struggled. "No, don't do that," Maria shouted. "Don't do a spinal tap. It will kill him."

"Who the hell do you think you are?" Dr. Green demanded. Then he recognized her.

"Oh, sorry."

"If you do a spinal tap, there could be a catastrophic shift in the intracranial pressure and kill him. I think I know what's happening. It's only a seizure. It should stop."

"Hell, he's going to die."

"No, he won't."

Almost as if on cue the president relaxed. His back stopped arching, and he opened his eyes.

"Just as I thought," Maria said. "Stabilize him and then we'll talk. I need to make a call first."

Dr. Green shook his head and checked the president's vital signs.

Maria called Eloy in Dr. Singh's lab. "Eloy, he had a crisis.

Come here right away. Tell Sidney it's an emergency." Maria turned to Dr. Green. "I know what's going on," she repeated.

"I doubt it," he said sarcastically, looking up from the president's bedside. "He's going to die."

"The cells from the nasal swabs glowed, right?" Maria asked.

"Yeah, but . . ."

"Just a moment. I want you to talk to someone."

CHAPTER 40

Eloy and Sidney rushed into the hospital room. What had been chaos only a few minutes ago was now calm. Maria was standing next to Dr. Green at the president's bedside. The president looked relaxed. He was nearly asleep. The sound of the heart monitor was regular, and the nurse reported, "Rapid sinus over, regular pattern. It looks stable."

Dr. Green stared at Eloy in disbelief, like he had seen a ghost. "But I thought you were . . ."

"No, I'm not."

Sidney put his hand on Dr. Green's shoulder. "Trust me. It's in the best interest of the country and of utmost urgency. Is the president stable?"

"Yes, at least for now," Dr. Green said, taking off his gloves.

"Then we have to talk," Sidney continued, ushering Dr. Green, Maria and Eloy into a room adjoining the president's suite. He closed the door.

"What's this all about?" Dr. Green asked, placing his hands on his hips, "and it better be good. The president needs an immediate spinal tap. We need to confirm. . . . He has all the symptoms of acute sinusitis that has developed into meningitis. He needs antibiotics immediately."

"But remember that I told you the cells glowed. Well, they did so because of the luciferin-like gene spliced into the viral vector that Eloy used."

Dr. Green relaxed and looked at Eloy. "Then it was your viral vector. Am I to believe that the president has Alzheimer's induced by the viral vector that you had been using to produce your primate models?" he asked, shaking his head in disbelief.

"Yes," Eloy said. "And it was . . ."

"No more. That's all you need to know," Sidney interrupted. "Let me just say this. I have been authorized by my superiors to assure the safety of the president, so as of this moment I am placing Dr. Rodríguez and Mr. Santiago in charge. You are not to intervene medically unless you consult with either of them. Do you understand?" he said, pointing his finger directly at Dr. Green. Green nodded.

Sidney continued, "And as the president's physician, you know that you are sworn not to discuss this incident with anyone."

They left the room and returned to the president's bedside. "Okay, Dr. Green. If you would excuse us, we need to confer in private here for a few minutes," Sidney said, escorting the physician out of the room.

"What happened?" Eloy asked.

"He had a seizure, with contortions typical of basal writhing—you know, base-of-brain damage."

"Then we have to administer the antidote immediately. And we'd better give several administrations. His acetylcholine levels or uptake are deteriorating. Give me the aerosol," Eloy demanded.

"I don't know," Maria hesitated. "It's too great a risk."

"No, trust me. I've seen this happen before in my primates. The only solution is immediate administration of the acetylcholine-producing gene in the viral vector."

Sidney walked over and stood between them. "Is it that risky?" he asked Eloy.

"Look, we have no choice. And as you always say, 'you have to trust me,'" Eloy said. "Give me the aerosol, please."

Maria hesitated one more time, then handed Eloy the aerosol.

Eloy looked at the president and stroked his face. "Have faith, Mr. President. I know what I'm doing. Be strong. Get well."

He removed the top from the nasal spray and inserted it into the president's nose. He squeezed the aerosol several times quickly into each nostril. As the viral vector penetrated the president's brain, Eloy imagined the viral vector with its spliced genes entering the acetylcholine-producing nerve cells and coding for the proteins that initiated the series of protein synthetic reactions that would create acetylcholine molecules.

"Don't worry. I've seen this work before," Eloy told Maria and Sidney. "There's a 90 percent chance that within two days the president will improve."

"Let's hope so," Sidney said. "Not only are we concerned about the president's health, but about his meeting in the Netherlands. The tensions with Iraq have to be defused, and this is the only man to do it. So your treatment had better work, my friend, without fail."

Eloy said, "I've done all I can do. I know he'll be okay." He went to Maria, put his arm around her shoulder, and kissed her on the cheek. "Let's go home. All we can do is wait."

"Not so fast," Sidney said. "We have another job for you."

CHAPTER 41

A green Chevy Suburban parked behind the back entrance of the Naval Hospital. Two men dressed in gray three-piece suits got out, opened the back doors, and lifted out a gurney. Lying on the gurney was a body in a black body bag. They wheeled the gurney into the rear entrance and down a long hallway to the laboratory of Dr. Data Singh. Sidney was standing outside the door and motioned to the two men.

"Here. In here. Hurry!" he said, helping the men push the gurney into the lab.

Eloy, Maria and Don quickly unzipped the bag as the door closed. Sidney said, "Agent Eli, Agent Richard—the surgeon general, Eloy Córdova Santiago and Dr. Don Romano."

"The hell with formalities," Don said. "Help me get her out."

Don and Sidney lifted the limp body of a woman out of the bag onto a hospital bed that Dr. Singh had made ready for her.

"She's beautiful," Sidney remarked. "But is she still alive?"

"Oh, Donna," Don said, "what the hell have they done to you?"

Maria quickly examined Donna's pupils and checked her vital signs and said, "She's fine except for the coma. It's the Alzheimer's—viral induced, right?"

"Yes," Sidney answered.

Donna stared blankly at the ceiling, unaware of anything going on around her.

"Maria, give her the other viral vector," Sidney ordered. "It's her only chance."

Eloy handed Maria the aerosol. She quickly turned Donna's face, lifted her head, and wiped away the drool from the corner of her mouth. Maria inserted the tip of the nasal spray into Donna's nose and gave the bottle several quick squeezes.

"Why didn't you tell us it was Donna?" Don questioned.

"I'm not at liberty to say what happened to her besides the obvious. All I know is that paramedics responded to a 911 emergency call to her apartment on Tuesday evening. Neighbors had complained about a smell and banging on the wall. The paramedics found her tied to her bed, lying in her own filth, bewildered and almost dead."

Don touched her cheek. "Poor thing," he said.

"She was rushed to Bethesda Hospital, and she kept mouthing 'viral vector.' The E.R. docs first thought it was a drug overdose, but her symptoms were more like rapid-onset Alzheimer's. Her mental status test, neurological examination and brain scan confirmed it. Dr. Green was called in. He found the fluorescent cells, and we made the connection. Someone gave Eloy's viral vector to Donna.

"Please don't call it mine," Eloy lamented. "My work was not meant to be used this way."

"But who gave it to her?" Sidney asked.

"We don't know, but it could be several people: Mark, Dr. Atkins . . . who knows?" Don replied.

"She does," Eloy responded, "and we should also know in a couple of days."

July 13, 1997

Eloy took a large gulp of coffee and drummed his fingers on top of his desk. Maria was looking out of the window across Rockville Pike toward the NIH.

"What's the matter, *mi amor*?" he asked.

"It's just so frightening. What if it doesn't work? I was thinking about the devastation, biological warfare, Anthrax, Marburg. It gave me goose flesh."

"Don't worry. Here, look at the most recent print-outs of the president's blood tests." Eloy pointed to the computer screen on the corner of his desk. "The curve in the acetylcholine levels is almost exactly what I've seen in my primate experiments."

"Yes, you're right. I'll go check on the president again and draw some more blood." She put down her coffee and got into her lab coat. "I'll be back in a few minutes."

Eloy picked up the Sunday *Washington Post* and scanned the headlines. Taking a sip of his coffee, he read the front-page story on the breakdown of negotiations between Ted Daniels and Iraq and the escalating threat of war. A small article on one of the inner pages about the confusion over the identity of the corpse found in the NIH fire caught his eye. It seemed that the DNA analysis comparing the remains of the deceased and some skin and hair samples from Eloy's apartment were close but not a match. Eloy thought of his brother, feeling sad yet determined to find out who killed him.

He also read several opinions on the editorial page objecting to President Daniels' ludicrous prosmoking position. Eloy looked around the lab that was now a makeshift hospital room. Donna lay quietly and stared, eyes blank. Don kept watch over her.

 Maria hurried back down the long hallway to the lab. *"Mi amor,* it's working."

"Gracias a Dios," Eloy said, crossing himself.

"What?" Don shouted from the bedside.

Sidney came over to Maria and Eloy. "What's this all about?"

"It's working," Maria said, catching her breath. "I just saw the president, and he recognized me. Helen said that he also recognized her. It's going to work," she said, hugging Eloy.

"Sí, mi amigo," Don said, giving Eloy a high five.

"Not so fast. In another day . . . if things work as they did with the primates, acetylcholine should be normal within forty-eight hours, so we will know by tomorrow. Give me the blood sample, *mi amor."*

Maria handed him the sample, and he gave her a kiss. "Don, here, run the levels."

 "Wake up. I need to talk to you," Sidney said, gently shaking Eloy on the sofa.

"Is the president okay?" he asked, rubbing his eyes. "What time is it?"

"11:30. I didn't mean to startle you, but I had to wake you. I need to talk to all of you."

Eloy woke Maria, and Sidney woke Don.

"We just got some important information," Sidney announced.

"What's that?" Eloy asked.

"While going through Donna's apartment, the FBI found a videotape of Ted Daniels and Donna in . . . well, what shall I say . . . in a very compromising position."

"Cut the crap. Donna was getting it on with Ted Daniels, right?" Don exclaimed.

"Yes."

"What?" Eloy and Maria said almost simultaneously.

"Yes. Daniels was involved in a conspiracy instigated by the tobacco industry. He was blackmailed into taking a prosmoking position."

"By who?" Eloy asked, rubbing his forehead.

"Well, again, I'm not at liberty to say," Sidney responded.

"Damn it. It was Senator Reynolds or Stu Brown or their cronies, wasn't it?" Maria said.

"Yes, but let me continue," Sidney said, walking toward Donna's bed.

"When confronted with the tape, Daniels explained how he was introduced to Donna by Secret Service Agent Mark Wilson and how, after a couple of drinks, he had used bad judgment and was seduced by Donna. Wilson and Senator Reynolds used the tape to change his stance regarding tobacco use and to imply that Iraqi terrorists were responsible for the president's condition. Whether or not Clint Walker recovers, Daniels said he would resign the presidency, but with one condition. The videotape has to be destroyed and never mentioned to the nation or his family."

"So what's going to happen?" Eloy asked.

"Ted Daniels will announce his resignation tomorrow afternoon."

"What if Clint is still incapacitated?" Don asked.

"Then, according to the laws of succession, the Speaker of the House will be appointed president."

"That's no help," Maria said. "She's more of a hawk than Daniels. We'll certainly have a war if that's the case."

"I don't think so. The antidote is working. Just a few more hours . . . wait and see," Eloy said optimistically.

July 14, 1997

Clint Walker gave Eloy a big hug and patted him on the back. "How can I thank you? You gave me back my life and my family."

Helen kissed Eloy on the cheek. "You'll never know the gift you gave me. I thought all hope was gone. Sidney just told me what you, Maria and Don have done. I understand the need for security, but Sidney, Dr. Green, why couldn't I have known?"

Sidney looked the other way. Dr. Green was silent.

"Come on, Helen. Leave them alone. They were just doing their jobs," Clint said.

"Sorry," Helen said with a sheepish grin.

"You don't have to thank me," Eloy said. I'm glad that it worked, but I still need to know who gave you the nasal spray."

"It was Mark Wilson," Clint said, shaking his head in disgust. "We were flying back from Albuquerque and my allergies were acting up," he said, rubbing his eyes. "So Mark gave me a nasal decongestant like he usually does, and I used it all the way back. Then I started to feel really strange."

"Yes, honey," Helen said. "That's why I said you should see Dr. Green here at the hospital, but as usual, you insisted that everything was okay. Then that evening—oh, God—I was so frightened," Helen said, hugging Clint, her voice breaking. "I thought you were going to die. Thank God you survived."

"Yes, thank God, but also thank Eloy."

"It was the least I could do, given that it was my discovery that they used to get to the president."

"How did it work? What happened?"

Eloy explained it to the president.

After again thanking Eloy, Maria and Don, Clint Walker excused himself. He had to meet with his advisors regarding the return of the power of the presidency to him. He also had to reestablish more positive negotiations with Iraq to arrive at a peaceful settlement of the arms inspection crisis.

One important question remained unanswered for Eloy. Who started the fire in his lab that killed his brother? Maybe Donna would know. Hopefully tomorrow she could tell him.

July 15, 1997

Coming out of the coma, Donna looked around the room. "Where am I? What's going on? Eloy, is that you? Are you alive? Thank God. I heard that you were dead. Who got killed in the fire? What happened?"

"Not so fast," Sidney interjected. "It is my responsibility to let you know that you are under arrest." He pushed Don aside. "We need to document her statements, and by law I am required to read her her rights."

She said, "I'll answer all of your questions. I want to. I need to sit up." Don placed a pillow behind her back.

"Rest. Don't talk," Don said.

"No, that's all right. I need to talk," Donna responded.

She began, "All I ever wanted was to be respected for my scientific talents, not my sexuality. But no one would take me seriously, not even my dad. Roger promised me that by working for him in the Alzheimer's research project funded by Kentucky Green my reputation as a scientist would grow and I would be on the team that eventually found a cure for Alzheimer's. But the bottom line is that it never happened. Roger proved to be a self-centered petty bureaucrat—jealous of Eloy's progress. He and Orville Reynolds, at Stu Brown's suggestion, had me work with Eloy to steal his data. Working with Eloy was self-serving because I could then use his findings to further my own research at the Kentucky Green Alzheimer's Research Labs in Virginia."

"It was Mark who killed the assistant to the surgeon general. What was his name?" Donna asked.

"Reuben," Maria snapped.

"Orville had Joe Ray contact his buddy, John Barker, the tobacco lobbyist, who hired Mark to kill Reuben so Dr. Cooper would resign. One thing led to another, and before I knew it I was involved more than I wanted to be.

"When Eloy perfected the primate viral vector to induce Alzheimer's, I took it and cultured it in my labs in Virginia. Roger was totally out of it. His knowledge of molecular biology is so limited that he couldn't follow what I was doing.

"May I please have a drink of water?" she asked, pursing her lips. Don gave her some right away. Donna took a sip and continued.

"Then Mark, Orville and Stu came up with a plan to whack the president using the viral vector to give him Alzheimer's so that he would stop his antismoking crusade. They had me prepare the aerosol for the president. They also came up with the idea of blackmailing the vice president, and I was paid to seduce him. But who could have imagined the Middle East would flare up again?"

"Mark put a voice-activated video camera in the hotel room and taped me and Ted, and we blackmailed him. He always portrayed himself as a righteous family man—what a hypocrite. So when he became president, we had him. Mark thought we should destroy all the evidence by setting Eloy's lab on fire, and I agreed because it would also give me the chance to refine the Alzheimer's-inducing model and take credit for it."

Don had a worried look in his eye. "That's enough, Donna. Lay back and rest. You can finish this later."

"No," Donna said. "Let me continue. I have more to say. I set the timer in the lab to go off on the fourth of July because Eloy was out of town at his mother's funeral and I thought no one would get hurt. I was very upset when I heard that Eloy had been killed," she said, looking at Eloy. "I have always admired you. I'm so sorry." She began to cry. "I only wanted to be respected."

It was quiet in the room, then Donna asked, "Whose body was found?"

"*Mi hermano*," Eloy said sadly.

"Oh, my God. I'm so sorry. It was an accident," Donna said.

"Please continue, Ms. Stone," Sidney interjected.

Donna dabbed at her eyes. "Mark was greedy and vindictive. He hated his job. He hated working for self-absorbed politicians. Mark never forgot the day he risked his life when President Winston was shot. He was ready to take a bullet for him, and the president didn't even thank him. Mark was more than willing to whack the president. I don't know if Mark loved the $2 million Orville and Stu Brown paid him, or if it was just revenge, an eye for an eye. He wanted payback for a thankless job. Then Mark tried to kill me. He's the one who gave me the viral vector."

"Are you sure?" Sidney asked.

"Yes." Donna said. "Where is that despicable bastard?"

"I'm not at liberty to say," Sidney responded, "but let me assure you that *you* will be vindicated and receive your eye for an eye in a court of law."

July 18, 1997

Eloy read in the *San Juan Star* that Clint Walker had completely recovered and was reinstated as president. The article stated that an error in the diagnosis had occurred—the president didn't have Alzheimer's but rather a rare form of encephalitis that mimicked many of the symptoms of Alzheimer's. The article also reported that Saddam Hussein had refused to comply with U.N. arms inspections. However, President Clint Walker was taking a more diplomatic position, and constant communication between the leaders promised to defuse the crisis.

Eloy turned the page and read that Ted Daniels had left politics entirely.

Eloy gazed at Maria. She looked so beautiful in her bathing suit as the sun set over the Caribbean. They went together onto the veranda, the same veranda at the same country inn on the island of Vieques they had visited so long ago. This time Maria was not uneasy. They sipped champagne and Eloy gave her a warm hug, looking into her green eyes. They were shining with love.

"*Mi amor,* to us!" he said, touching his champagne flute to hers.

"Yes. To us, to peace, to your new lab, to our future," Maria responded.

"*Sí, mi amor, sí.*"

They kissed.